Natalya
A Victorian Fantasy

The Lullaby Covenant
Book 1

Terry Vernon

𝔏𝔅

Lullaby Books

Copyright

First published by Lullaby Books in 2022.

Copyright © Terry Vernon 2022

The author asserts his moral rights to be identified as the author of this work. All rights are reserved. No part of this publication may be reproduced, stored in a retrieval system or transmitted in any form or any means, without prior permission in writing of the author.

All characters in this book are fictitious, and any resemblance to actual persons alive or dead is purely coincidental.

ISBN: 979-8-7959-6030-2 (paperback)
ISBN: 979-8-7973-7672-9 (hardback)

Cover & Artwork
Cover model: Bryoni-Kate Williams
Model photography by D&A Photography
Cover design and illustration by Terry Vernon

For more information visit
TERRYVERNON.COM

For RB, always.

Free Download Offer

Download WOODEN HEART, the prequel to the Lullaby Covenant, for FREE, by visiting TERRYVERNON.COM

A timid girl.

An All Hallows' Dare.

The Dawn of an Awakening.

CONTENTS

1	*The Sound of Thunder*	Pg 01
2	*The Feeding Dark*	Pg 18
3	*Chocolate and Trains*	Pg 29
4	*A Day in the Park*	Pg 44
5	*Encounter at the Market*	Pg 55
6	*Bubbles and Cinders*	Pg 71
7	*From Riches to Rags*	Pg 88
8	*A Game of Dog and Mouse*	Pg 101
9	*A Royal Gift*	Pg 117
10	*The General's Asylum*	Pg 132
11	*A Taste of Magic*	Pg 144
12	*A Walk in the Wood*	Pg 159
13	*The Monster in the Cage*	Pg 169

14	*A Melting of Pigment*	Pg 181
15	*A Study in Crimson*	Pg 198
16	*Masquerade*	Pg 206
17	*Those Eyes…*	Pg 219
18	*Confrontation*	Pg 229
19	*The Journey Home*	Pg 240
20	*The Girl with White Hair*	Pg 259
21	*A Dogged Tale*	Pg 275
22	*A Drunken Tale*	Pg 286
23	*The Foreshadowing*	Pg 301
24	*The Name of the Cause*	Pg 313
25	*Foxglove and Hiccups*	Pg 330
26	*The Devil's Bridge*	Pg 339
27	*Lullaby*	Pg 349
28	*The Departed*	Pg 362
	Author's note	Pg 368
	Readers Club	Pg 370

*'This world may be shaped
by those with
the talent to do so.'*

Chapter 1
The Sound of Thunder

England - 15th April, 1891

The rainbow faded away before Natalya's eyes, melting into the daylight that followed the springtime rain. The downpour had left the valley renewed, water glistening on its canopy of trees.

Natalya loved it up here on the hill, the drystone wall on which she now sat her favourite chair in the world, and she'd often run up from the village on a morning in the hope of catching the rising sun as it streaked the sky in marmalade orange.

She glanced down at the flowers in her hand, freshly picked from the wood. Their tubular pinkness was a thing of beauty, and yet she could hear her mother even now:

Careful, Natalya, you know how foxglove brings you out in a rash.

But Natalya had always felt drawn to the plant, despite their poisonous nature.

She swung her legs over the wall and leapt down onto the other side. Soft, cool mud oozed its way between her toes, disgusting to some, but soothing to her. So what if it meant that the others called her names; she liked being *different*, and it beat wearing shoes.

She carefully stepped her way between the graves, respecting the dead underfoot. Whole generations were buried here, some dating back to the early 1600's. Someday her parents would be buried here, too, her own grave neatly placed alongside.

She came to a stop, her breath misting in the air. Despite the sun, there was a chill to the day. She gazed down at the grave and gave a sad little smile. She placed the flowers on the greyness of the earth.

'Hello, Granny.'

God bless the old woman. Natalya had only been a child when she'd died. Now fifteen, she was practically a woman. How the years had flown.

She brushed a wisp of brown hair from her eyes, accidentally smearing pollen on her face. It sent her freckles into an itching frenzy; those damnable, blotchy things. They made her look like a thrush's egg, and choose how much she scrubbed, she couldn't get them off.

She crossed herself from right to left, paused, then repeated left to right. Right to left was the *orthodox* way, and her granny had been a *protestant*. It had always been a bone of contention that Natalya had chosen her father's faith.

I'll never know what your mother was thinking. Marrying a foreigner, I tell you. Foreigners pollute the blood, you know, just as yours is polluted now.

It wasn't that she'd disliked Natalya's father, it was just that she'd wished he'd married someone else. And she never took it out on Natalya; she was still her flesh and blood, after all.

Natalya finished reciting her prayer and turned back for the village church. It was sat just shy of the woodland trees that stood like soldiers up the slope of the hill. The little stone building also doubled as the school, which meant that its sacred earth, twice a day, became a children's playground.

A boy came running out of nowhere, tripped and fell at Natalya's feet. A second boy came running after him and slapped him on the back.

'Yer it,' he cried, and ran off again.

Natalya raised her eyes in despair. The first boy scowled, clambered back to his feet, and took off after the lad who'd just tagged him.

Tag: the boys played it all the time, and the Lord help anyone who got in their way. The older boys were even worse than the young, charging around like ruffians.

The girls, meanwhile, preferred to play hopscotch, their chalked-up numbers defacing half the stones that formed the churchyard path. Natalya chose to participate in neither, favouring the solace of her drystone wall.

'Argh! Get it off! Get it off!'

Another intrusion. Natalya rolled her eyes. Wasn't play time over yet? This was supposed to be hallowed ground.

She glanced across at the girl in distress; it was Agatha Price, a girl Natalya's age. She was dancing around like some dangly scarecrow at the end of a puppeteer's strings.

The girl swiped something from her hair and it floated to the ground with umbrella-spoked legs. The girl tried to stomp the *spider* dead. Natalya's eyes widened in horror.

'No,' she cried, racing forward. 'What's the poor thing ever done to you?'

She grabbed the girl by the arm and dragged her back. The girl wrenched herself free.

'Get yer hands off me, *Ovski*. I hate spiders. Hate

them!'

'It's Yavorovskaya.'

The girl shot her a glare, pulled a face and stormed off. Natalya scooped the spider from the ground and set it down on the head of a gravestone.

'There, there, *Spideykins*, you're all safe now.'

A Bible came slamming down onto the headstone.

'There, there, *Spideykins*, yer all dead now.'

The boy turned and bowed to the cheers of his mates. He turned back, full of bravado. Natalya unnerved him with a smile.

'What?' he said.

She opened her hand to reveal the spider sitting safely in her palm. The boy lifted the Bible from the headstone; all he'd flattened was some caterpillar moss.

'But it was right there.'

'Obviously not. Back to your mates, now. Go on. *Boo!*'

The boy swallowed and made a swift retreat, falling over himself in the process. Natalya watched with an amused expression. Was he really scared of just one girl?

'What do ya mean, she saved it?' cried one boy.

'Shh!' said another. 'We don't want 'er to hear.'

'Am telling ya, she had it in 'er hand.'

'I told ya she's a witch. Just look at all them freckles.'

That last comment had come from Archie Bennett, the twelve-year-old leader of the group. He was a watered-down version of his elder brother, Thomas, and neither were people you wanted to cross. To rile Archie was to reap his brother's wrath, and it wouldn't be Natalya's first run-in with the pair. Now sixteen, Thomas worked as a woodsman, but that didn't make him any less a thug.

Archie glared at her. Natalya stared back. He glared even harder; Natalya raised an eyebrow. She never used to be so confrontational, but then her life had changed of late.

The boys' words should have been out of earshot, and yet, somehow, she'd captured every one. And saving that spider... she might have looked smug, but she had no idea how she'd done it.

Something was stirring, and it wasn't adolescence. Those years were behind her, even if her skirt didn't quite touch the floor as a lady's should. No, there was something else awakening, a wildness she felt she could barely control. It rose every time she felt threatened, and it scared her half to death.

The church bell rang, recalling them to class. Archie walked off with a parting scowl. Natalya shuddered. This wasn't over yet. There were going to be repercussions.

She freed the spider back onto the headstone and

watched it scuttle away. She glanced down at her feet and gave a sigh. That mud was never coming off.

***

With school over for yet another day, Natalya set off home along the woodland path. The path curved down the hill like a winding river, first in one direction, and then in the other.

It was a lengthy walk, but Natalya didn't mind; the woodland made her feel at one with nature. The sponginess of fungi; the moss upon the trees. The scent of fern and pine that mesmerised her brain. She traversed the length of a fallen tree and leapt high off its end.

Try doing that in a full-length skirt. She almost tripped and fell. She tutted and gave a mischievous grin. One of these days she was going to land face first.

She abandoned the path for a patch of foxglove, one of many to be found throughout the wood. By summer the flowers would be taller than her, dwarfing her five foot seven. She happened upon a rummaging rabbit; he took one look at her and fled.

'Don't go,' she cried, but he was already gone. She frowned and turned her gaze to the trees. The birds were a master of hiding in the branches, and she loved the challenge of spying them out.

Voices: the boys were catching her up. She quickly

chose her flowers and hurried on her way. Archie would undoubtedly be amongst their number, and she saw no point in tempting fate.

Soon the trees were falling away as the path opened up onto a clearing in the wood. The village was nestled in a crescent to the south, twenty single-room houses, made from clay and stone. They had thicketed roofs and crooked chimneys. For fifteen years she'd called one her home.

She started across the well-trodden ground, a stubbornness of grass persisting through the earth. She stopped at the wishing well and, laying down her flowers, released the handle of the pulley.

The bucket went hurtling down into the darkness; she heard it hit the water with a splash. She gave it time to fill, then hoisted it back up. It should have been a chore, but she pulled it up with ease. She tipped the water out onto her feet.

She gasped. The water was icy cold, just like the million other times she'd tried it. She rubbed her feet together, trying to free the mud. She added more water. As always, it was useless.

The group of boys joined her from the path.

'What's the matter, witch?' cried Archie. 'Can't stand the smell of yer own feet?'

'At least it's only my feet, Archie Bennett. You'd need to jump in the stream entirely.'

He came to a stop and narrowed his eyes. 'Come over 'ere and say that.'

For a twelve-year-old boy, he could be quite intimidating. Natalya tensed, but not because of him. Archie, she could handle, but she felt *it* stir inside.

'Archie Bennett!'

He turned to face his mother. She was a formidable woman, even when calm. Archie's mates scarpered in an instant. So much for having friends.

'Where've ya been, m'lad? Those chores won't do themselves.'

Archie shot Natalya a glare and wandered on his way. Mrs Bennett glared at her, too; Natalya stared straight back. What was wrong with her lately? It was as though she had a wish to be dead.

Mrs Bennett marched off with a grunt. Alone, Natalya gazed down at her feet. They weren't any better. She gave a frown, collected her flowers and set off for home. She entered the house to find her mother boiling up some water by the fireplace.

'Hello, Mama.'

Her mother turned, the warmest of smiles on her face. Natalya quickly held out the flowers, hoping to distract her mother's gaze.

'For me? How thoughtful, Natalya.'

'I was careful to pick an *uneven* number.'

Even numbers were reserved for the dead. Ideal for

her granny, not her mama.

'Well that's your father's superstition. Guess what I found beneath your bed?'

Natalya shrugged, knowing full well. Her mother handed Natalya her shoes.

'Sorry, Mama.'

Her mother said nothing; she was a master of the silent stare. Natalya knew her every look, and at least this one was a mere slap on the wrist.

'Anyway,' added her mother, 'it's not my floor you're muddying up.'

'Oh!' Natalya's eyes widened. She'd forgotten all about... *him*.

The *domovoi*: the spirit of the house, he did like the place neat and tidy. She glanced around in the hope of not seeing him; to do so was an omen of one's own death. She quickly slipped her feet into her shoes and hoped he hadn't noticed.

As her mother attended the boiling kettle, Natalya ducked beneath the dividing curtain. She snatched up a book from her bedside table and quickly returned to the room. She grabbed the water-bucket down from the worktop and hid the book inside.

'I'm just going to fetch some water, Mama.'

'From the village well?'

'I was thinking the stream.'

'And meet your father on his way home, no doubt?'

'I hadn't thought of that.'

Her mother gave her another of those looks.

'So the book in the bucket is in case you get lost?'

Natalya squirmed and looked to the table. It was home to an unfinished game of chess; another battle she was about to lose.

She rushed forward and hugged her mother sincerely.

'Love you, Mama.'

'Love you, too, dear.' She planted a kiss on Natalya's forehead. 'Now don't you go falling into that stream. The afternoon rain will have made it swell.'

Natalya flashed her mother a smile and hurried from the house.

***

Natalya weaved her way through the trees, following a makeshift path she didn't need. She'd trodden this way a hundred times before, and she knew the route like the freckles on her skin.

The calmness of the wood embraced her, broken only by the occasional foraging rodent. The stream was a good ten minute walk from the village, and she made the most of every stride.

Her ears pricked at the sound of running water. She hastened her step to the break in the undergrowth. The *stream*, as they called it, was ten feet wide in places, which made it more of a miniature river. It snaked through the wood eating into the embankment, exposing the twisted roots of the trees.

Like her mother had said, the waters were swollen, their usual flow now a dash between the rocks. Natalya could have filled the bucket right here, but then she could have filled it at the village well.

A spring in her step, she set off downstream. The woodsmen were currently working to the east. With the stream swollen there was only one way back, via the fallen oak that acted as a bridge. By the time she reached it, her shoes were caked in mud. That would teach her mother for not letting her go barefoot.

She gazed upwards through the leaves of the trees. The sun was still high, which meant she'd have a wait. Not that she hadn't come prepared; there was a reason she'd brought along her book. She opened it up at the page with the feather and sat down on the stump of a tree. It was home to a growth of oyster mushrooms; they created a welcome cushion.

She began to read. She was just at the part where the heroine attended the manor ball. The thought of all that dancing and fanciful dresses made her imagination swirl. Maybe, one day, in some other life, she'd get to dance at a ball, herself.

Engrossed in her book, she lost track of time, her mind transported to another world and era. The turn of the century, a *will-they/won't-they* romance. Of course, she knew the ending. The book had been a present for her thirteenth birthday and she must have read it several dozen times. A deepness of voices intruded on her ears, drawing her back to the present.

It was the woodsmen, returning from a hard day's labour, axes in their hands or slung over their shoulders. They crossed the fallen oak tree and marched on past, the occasional *gent* tipping his cap.

Amongst the men was Archie's brother, Thomas. For a sixteen-year-old, he had hands the size of shovels. Those fists could stave in a grown man's skull. He gave her a glare as he walked on by. Mr Morris brought up the rear.

'He's on his way, Miss Natalya,' he said. She liked Mr Morris. He had a kind heart. 'He forgot his cap and had to turn back. You know how he likes to keep his 'ead warm.'

Natalya giggled. 'Thank you, sir.'

He nodded and carried on his way. She bookmarked her page and stood to stretch her legs. The resilient mushrooms sprang back into shape.

Minutes passed; no sign of her father. She fingered at the knotted bracelet on her wrist. Each knot represented a prayer to be spoken, and she should have recited the whole bracelet by now. Instead, she'd been seduced by her gothic romance, and she felt just a teensy bit guilty.

In truth, her *faith* confused her. She should really have chosen the protestant path. But she liked the *uniqueness*, which, all things considered, was probably not the best reason for her choice. She'd often get the two faiths mixed up, creating a third of her own.

Another five minutes. She heard voices, but these were on her side of the stream. She turned to see Thomas Bennett and his brother. She felt *it* stir. Where was papa?

'Young'un 'ere tells me ya've been causing trouble.'

'Nothing to do with me, Thomas Bennett.'

'As if I'd believe the word of a *witch?*'

'Careful then, or I'll turn you into toads.'

'Ya 'ear that, Archie? The witch has confessed.'

'Dunk 'er in the river. See if she drowns.'

Thomas approached in a threatening manner. Natalya stood her ground.

He snatched the book from her grasp.

'Give me it back.'

She thought she heard *it* growl, the *beast* that lurked inside.

'Make me,' said Thomas.

Natalya narrowed her eyes. She could feel the blood surging through her veins.

'Please, Thomas, give me back my book.' She was trying her hardest to keep *it* at bay.

'Want it? Go and get it, then.'

He tossed the book into the stream.

'No,' she cried.

She splashed into the current, but the book was already swirling downstream. Archie laughed. Thomas grinned smugly. The *beast* inside her snarled.

'Aw, look at her face, Tom. She's all upset and teary eyed.'

He was right, there was something wrong with her eyes, but it wasn't tears, tears didn't prick, as though every blood vessel was bursting inside.

'Well go on, *Ovski*. Go get yer book? Not so clever now, are ya?'

The *wildness* within her broke free of its shackles.

'The name is *Yavorovskaya!*'

She lunged forward and grabbed him by the hand; or rather, the *beast* in control of her did. It was like she was an observer in her own body, the enraged monster suppressing all reason.

She squeezed, Tom cried out; he fell to his knees. She could hear his bones crunching in her grasp. She'd said that one day he might stave in someone's skull; he'd be lucky to hold a feather after this.

'Natasha! No!'

Natalya froze, her eyes widening in horror. The *beast* within her quickly withdrew, leaving her to take the blame.

Thomas clambered to his feet and ran, cradling his crushed hand in his other. His brother followed, equally panicked. What she'd just done was completely absurd. She looked to the man who'd shouted her name. She hung her head in shame.

Natasha: he'd called her *Natasha,* her diminutive Russian name. But Natalya had always preferred her given title, reserving *Natasha* for when she'd done wrong.

She heard - vaguely sensed - him navigate the oak, but her gaze was on her hands. They were delicate, weak; those of a lady. Her father cleared his throat.

'Don't worry, Natalya. It's not your fault.'

She looked up sharply. 'Not my fault? But his hand...'

'As if you'd have the strength to do that. Besides, who'd believe a lout like him?'

She couldn't believe he was defending her. It was almost as if he knew something that she didn't. She looked to the stream, her mind in turmoil. What was going on?

'Why am I different, Papa?'

'You just have to find your place in the world.'

'But I have found my place, with you and mama.'

'We won't be around forever, you know.'

The mere thought of it made her feel sick. She couldn't imagine a world without them. She tried to push his words from her mind, which only made them echo.

He came to stand beside her.

'Remember, I, too, was at odds with the world, with Mother Russia a thousand miles behind me. But the moment I saw your mother, I knew. I knew I'd found my place at last.'

He'd spoken that sentence in Russian, but Natalya grasped every word. She was fluent in both her parents' tongues, although English had always taken precedence.

Badum.

Natalya wrinkled her brow.

Badum. Badum.

There it was again.

'Thunder,' she said. 'I can hear thunder.'

Her father looked to the blue sky above the trees. Natalya felt the irritation of her nostrils. Was that a smell of…?

'Burning,' she said. 'Papa, I can smell burning. Papa, something's on fire.'

Chapter 2
The Feeding Dark

Natalya raced through the trees, her pace increasing with every stride. Besides the *thunder* she could now hear screams, the taste of charcoal thick on her tongue.

Was the woodland on fire? What about the village? What if her mother was trapped inside the house? If ever Natalya needed her faith... She had to believe her mother was all right.

She leapt through a final clump of bushes and landed in the village clearing. Her eyes widened, her mouth fell agape, plumes of smoke swirling up into the trees. But it wasn't the flames that froze her with fear; the village was under attack.

Who they were, she did not know. Seven horsemen

garbed in black. They carried burning torches, they wielded tarnished swords, herding down the villagers who fled from them in terror.

She blinked. Please, God, let her be dreaming. But the sting of the smoke in her eyes told her not. She squinted in search of her parents' house, but the clouds of smoke had smothered it out.

Her father joined her from the wood.

'Papa?'

'Natalya, get back into the trees.' There was fear in his voice, and nothing ever scared him.

'I'm coming with you.'

'Do as I say.' He placed a reassuring hand on her shoulder. 'Don't worry, I'll get your mother.'

He ran off into the smoke and mayhem. Natalya loitered, dread in her heart. She finally returned to the trees as instructed, but she felt so useless; she felt like a coward.

More screams. More pounding hooves. She dared to peer out into the carnage. A villager fell amidst a stream of beaded blood. She gasped in horror and clasped at her mouth. It looked like Mr Morris.

No, she couldn't hide here anymore. She leapt from the undergrowth and back into the open. She caught sight of her mother through a thinning in the smoke; she was being dragged along by a dismounted horseman.

'Mama!'

She might as well have whispered, her voice drowned out by the screams and raging flames. Natalya's father appeared out of nowhere and struck the horseman down.

Hand in hand, her parents ran towards her. Natalya urged them on with every stride. It was then she saw *him* ride out of the smoke, a bloodied sword in hand.

'Mama! Papa! Behind you!'

She started forward, trying her best to warn them. Her father must have seen the horror on her face; he turned just as the horseman raised his sword and swung it down. Eviscerated blood sprayed the air with red and her father crumpled to the earth.

'Noooo!'

Natalya fell to her knees.

'Ivan!!' she heard her mother scream. The look on her face she would never forget. The horseman rode back and slew her mother, too.

The world around Natalya seemed to slow. She couldn't believe it. She couldn't comprehend. *Get up,* she cried. And yet, they just laid there, soaked in one another's blood.

Natalya leapt to her feet and ran forward, ignorant to any danger. She skidded down between them, her eyes blurred with tears, grabbing at their bodies, blood upon her hands.

'Mama. Papa. Please don't leave me. Please don't

leave me. Please!'

She tugged at their stillness, still in denial, the smell of blood strong up her nose. She nestled down between them, absorbing their warmth, something she knew she'd never feel again.

Someone grabbed her from behind. She pulled free. A second person grabbed her. Together they dragged her kicking and screaming away from her parents and into the dirt.

'*General Craven,* sir.'

The man who'd butchered her parents dismounted. So that was his name; she'd never forget it. She glared up into his sunken face. A pagan symbol was seared into his forehead. She should have felt scared, but she only felt hate.

A pricking sensation returned to her eyes, the *beast* rising up like some rabid animal. Her fingers pained, her nails bleeding claws. Whatever she was, she was going to make him pay.

'Behold, *Witch Hunters.* Satan's child.'

'Murderer! I'm going to make you bleed.'

'See how it speaks the Devil's tongue.'

She must have spoken in Russian?

Recovering her footing, she launched herself at him, her limbs empowered by the *beast* within. Her speed caught him off guard and they hit the earth as one, her claws already wrapped about his throat. She could feel the hate seething through her veins, urging her to squeeze.

Suddenly, her world blacked out, and when she stirred, her mind was spinning. She felt sick; she felt faint. She touched at the blood that seeped through her hair. Was that grit, or fragments of skull? It fell like someone had smashed in her brains.

Run.

'Mama?'

Or he's going to kill you.

'I'm not that sure I really care.'

No. You have to live... for them. Run, wolfcaine. Run! Now!

Confused, Natalya scrambled to her feet and immediately fell back down. Her strength was gone, absent like the *beast*. She gritted her teeth and tried again. With one last effort she managed to stand and stagger towards the woods.

What followed next was vague at best; there was a blur of green that might have been trees. A brushing of shrubbery against her naked ankles. A sickening stench that might have been fungi.

She fell to her knees and vomited lunch, blood still moist against her temple. Her head felt like there was a thunderstorm inside. She couldn't rule out the fact that she might die.

She stayed there, unmoving, for what seemed

forever, allowing her brain a chance to recoup. She tried to move and groaned with the pain, another spell of dizziness clouding her mind. There was blood on her fingers, but no longer claws. She couldn't tell what was real anymore?

A crunching of twigs, a stampeding of foliage, and Craven came riding his horse through the trees. *No. You have to live... for them.* Natalya leapt to her feet and ran.

She staggered, she stumbled, she ran again, the horse snorting its way ever closer. Without the *beast*, she was a weak, pathetic shell, her breathing hoarse and her legs unsteady. She took a moment to glance behind and the horse ploughed into her shoulder.

With a cry, Natalya fell into the flora, disturbing a bed of foxglove. The pollen of the flowers clouded up the air, choking her throat and sending her freckles into an agitated frenzy. She placed a supporting hand against a tree and felt a strangeness sweep through her body.

At first, she thought it was down to the *beast*, but there weren't any claws or any pricking in her eyes. This was something else. Something different. As though her mind was on another plane.

The bark around her hand began to *grey*, its veil consuming the tree like a plague. The old oak groaned, its trunk becoming twisted, hunching over like a crippled old man.

Alarm and confusion swamped Natalya's mind, then the *grey* gave way to vibrant colour. It basked her face in a soft, warm glow that calmed her anxious nerves.

Craven charged his way back towards her, but now she felt no urge to flee. The roots of the tree broke their way through the ground and brought both horse and rider crashing down. There was a crunching sound as Craven hit the earth. The panicked horse galloped back into the wood.

Natalya stared at Craven's form. Was he dead? She dare not go near. She glanced at the tree; it resembled a man. It was then she realised exactly what it was. She gasped and bowed in *his* presence.

'Thank you, gracious *Spirit of the Trees*.'

The tree appeared to turn and bow. In Russian folklore, he was known as the *Leshy*, the protector of the wood and the wildlife within. Natalya felt honoured to be in his presence, for rarely was he seen.

The *veil of grey* returned to flood the landscape and suddenly the *Leshy* was just a tree once more. The vibrancy of colour faded back to normal, and all Natalya's torment returned to plague her mind.

She looked back at Craven. Again, was he dead? She took a step forward and kicked at his body. She sprang back, expecting him to grab her, but his head merely rolled onto one side.

A thick bile oozed out from his mouth, forming a pool of saliva on the ground. The saliva pigmented, it started to haze, rising like heat on a summer's day.

Natalya drew back, unnerved, but intrigued, as a miniature rainbow formed across his torso. A second rainbow formed beyond the first, their colours bleeding between them into *grey*.

A sudden coldness breathed across her skin, an aura of wretchedness eating up the air. It grabbed at her soul, feeding on her sorrow, turning her grief into irrepressible despair.

Her legs buckled and she fell to her knees, tears streaming down her face. How could she go on, knowing that today was the last time she'd ever see her parents alive? To hug them, kiss them, to feel their warmth, to hear their soothing voices.

Beyond misery, she extended a finger and commanded its nail into a claw. She raised its sharpness to the artery of her throat and pressed it against her skin. Just one ounce of pressure and all her pain was gone; she didn't care that it was wrong to take one's life. She sniffed back the tears, drew herself upright, and...

Her left hand snatched her right hand from her throat.

'No!' she cried. 'I can't go on without them.'

Her left hand dug its claws into her flesh. The pain

snapped her mind back to reality. She stared at *the darkness* devouring Craven's corpse.

Terrified, Natalya scrambled to her feet and ran off into the wood.

***

Natalya came to rest against a tree, the claw marks on her arm still dripping blood. She touched at her neck; there was blood there, too. How close had she come to ending it all?

She found herself thanking the *beast* for its action, had it not intervened, *the darkness* would have claimed her. *The darkness*. What was it? Why did it exist? It felt like no place any consciousness should be. It felt hollow, empty, beyond creation; undreamt by any person alive. Even now she could feel its oppression hovering about her soul.

She shuddered and tried to push it from her mind, but her reality was just as troubled. And whose was the voice that had told her to run? Calling her something that sounded like *wolfling*.

She reluctantly started back towards the village, every step a dreaded chore. All that awaited was the aftermath of chaos, and two dead parents lying in the dirt.

Approaching the edge of the wood she took cover, peering out through a tanglement of bramble. The surviving villagers had been herded together not more than twenty feet from where she hid. They were sobbing, distraught; she saw Agatha Price rocking back and forth. Their captors were pacing around them on guard, no doubt awaiting their General's return.

Witch hunters: that's what *he'd* called them. But there hadn't been a witch hunt in over a century. At least, according to the village priest who deemed himself an authority on the subject. For a man of God, he took great pleasure in telling stories of bloodshed and torture. Of women deemed witches, who were hung, burned or drowned; stories that gave Natalya nightmares as a child.

She forced her gaze across to her parents, still laid where they fell, hand held in hand. Her eyes welled with tears, blurring her vision. She blinked, forcing teardrops down her face.

Her parents were now on a journey to the *afterlife*; a forty day trial of their worthiness to God. There should have been prayers and practiced traditions; the prayers she could do, but all else was lost. And even then she was only one voice. She felt so helpless. Useless.

There was a sudden commotion; they'd found Craven's horse. They'd soon find his body and come looking for her. If she was going to live, she had to leave now. She didn't want to go, but she felt she had no choice.

With one last yearning look to her parents, she crossed herself and took off through the trees. She closely followed the guide of the road, keeping to the undergrowth until it was safe.

For the first time in her life, she found herself alone, her only companions being fear and the unknown. Where would she go? What would she do? The answer was simple; she hadn't a clue.

A rainbow formed a bow across the sky, where no rainbow should be.

Chapter 3
Chocolate and Trains

Falling. She was falling. Down through the emptiness, the air rushing past. She hit the water and ripped apart its stillness, plummeting deep into its depths.

The icy current sent shockwaves through her person, making her gasp, stealing her breath. Bubbles of oxygen went scurrying past her face. Her life was floating away before her eyes.

In desperation, she tried to swim, but her blood had abandoned her arms and her legs. Instead, their deadweight only dragged her deeper, into the swirling tendrils of the weeds.

Her anxiousness turned to panic. She couldn't breathe, her lungs were on fire. She called on the beast, but it didn't respond, and then exhaustion claimed her.

At least she would be with her parents now, for death was nought but a pathway to God. Her faith told her that and she chose to believe it, otherwise what was the point of her life?

A shape swam towards her, out of the algae. For a moment she dared to hope she was saved. But it had a frog's face and a fish-like tail; the malevolent water spirit known as the vodyanoy. The creature embraced her between its webbed paws and squeezed at the air that remained in her lungs.

Suddenly, its face creased with horror, its body convulsing as it clasped at its throat. But it no longer had one, its head floating upwards, an empty blackness bleeding from within.

The darkness. Natalya could feel it swim around her, wrestling her soul from God's arms. If the darkness was death, then there was no afterlife. Her faith was misguided, there wasn't any heaven.

A hollow emptiness invaded her soul. Natalya silently screamed.

***

Natalya sat up sharply, gasping for air, barely able to breathe. Her heart was pounding and her skin was clammy, her limbs tingling, inviting her to faint.

The daylight eased through the trees around her,

creating a second wood from their shadow. The night had passed, but she felt no better for it, the nightmare of yesterday still haunting her mind.

She touched at the *hole* in the back of her skull, now a nest of blood-matted hair. That blow should have killed her, and yet, here she was, suffering no more than a bothersome headache.

She struggled to her feet, her body stiff from a night laid on the earth. Her stomach groaned, hungry for food, making her feel ill.

Suddenly, a shrill whistle. The reason she'd chosen to sleep here. She poked her head through the leaves of the undergrowth and stared at the rail track not twenty feet away.

The line connected London to the coast. Two trains passed this way every day. The coast held fond memories; she'd been there with her parents. But those memories were now too painful to recall. And so she'd decided to journey to London, a place she'd never been.

She watched as the steam train hissed into view, its motion sending vibrations up the track. She tensed, nervous; she held onto her breath. She suddenly found herself doubting her own reason.

Sense decreed she should have boarded at the station. She had no money, but she could have snook onboard. But she'd feared the horsemen would be waiting for her there. She swallowed, shuddering at the thought of being caught. Of being tied to a stake and burned alive. She couldn't think of anything worse.

The train neared. She readied herself, her heart pounding inside her chest. She'd chosen this spot due to the curve in the track, so why was the train not slowing?

The locomotive thundered past, making the ground vibrate beneath her feet. Steam from its pistons spat steam across the earth, vexing her freckles and making them sting.

The first carriage passed, the second carriage passed. She gathered her nerve and ran up onto the ballast. Its thick stone stabbed at the soles of her shoes, culling her speed and making her slide.

The plan had been simple: run parallel to the carriage, open its door, climb up inside. But she couldn't even reach the door handle, and besides, the door opened outwards, not in.

She slipped and fell into the ballast. She'd messed it up; tears brimmed in her eyes. She was nothing better than a *nothing* girl from a *nothing* village in a *never-heard-of* wood. She watched as the wheels of the carriage rolled on by, then felt the *beast* awaken.

Before she knew it she was back on her feet. She backtracked to the trees and took another run-up. She leapt into the air and punched her fist straight through a window, tumbling inside amidst a shower-fall of glass.

Gasps and screams besieged her ears. The *well-to-do* diners quickly fell back. Yellow runny egg soaked into her dress, muddied by the blood dripping from her arm. A shard of glass had slit it open. She rallied to her feet.

'Fetch the guardsman,' someone cried.

Tear his throat out, raged the *beast.*

But she wasn't here to kill innocent people. She made a dash for the far-end door. She encountered a waiter coming through; she almost knocked him over.

'Sorry,' she cried, but the damage was done, a gravy boat adding brown texture to the floor. At least it would delay her being followed. She stepped through into the adjoining carriage.

She now found herself in a kitchen, a smell of roast chicken sweetening the air. A boiler leaked soup, potatoes simmered on a stove, whilst cheese and biscuits filled every shelf. Her stomach groaned to remind her it was hungry. She told it to be thankful that it wasn't still *Lent*.

The chef glared at her with incensed eyes.

'Get out of my kitchen! You're bleeding on my floor!'

But she needed to get to the door behind him. She took a step forward; he grabbed up a saucepan, wielding it like a weapon.

'I'm warning ya, girl.'

She glanced at his legs. He'd widened his stance to steady his balance. The craziest thought entered her mind, and she tried to dive between them.

What followed next must have looked hilarious, with both of them ending up on the floor. Squirming like a worm, Natalya regained her footing; he grabbed at her skirt and ripped off a piece. She left him, lying there, a pan in one hand and a six-inch strip of her skirt in the other.

Her heart racing, she rushed into the goods van, half falling over a sack of potatoes. A dozen of the vegetables went tumbling to the floor, forcing her to dance between them. It was almost as if she was playing hopscotch; if only she'd had more practice.

Sidestepping a similar sack of carrots, she found herself stood in a landscape of crates. They were stacked to the ceiling and precariously balanced, although a few lower down might provide a place to hide. She placed her hand against a wooden panel and found herself having to peel off her palm. She gazed at the bloodied handprint on the grain, which gave her an idea.

Hurrying along to the end of the van, she left her blood on the handle of the door. She then backtracked to hide behind a crate, the gap just large enough to squeeze her slender body. Her legs slipped out and she quickly pulled them back, wrapping her arms around them as a tie. She heard the door from the kitchen open. She nervously held her breath.

'Can't you keep those things in their sacks?'

'You try cooking on a moving train.'

'Then stick to your cooking and leave the girl to me.'

'If that's how ya want it, *Mr Griffiths*.'

She heard the latter leave.

The guardsman - at least, she presumed it was the guardsman – now started his search of the van. The closer he got, the more Natalya tensed, the *beast* still present and ready to strike.

But she didn't want *it* to strike. The man was only doing his job. She tried to stand *it* down, but the *beast* wouldn't listen. It was as if it wanted the guardsman to find them.

The guardsman shifted a nearby crate; she was on the verge of being discovered. Then he suddenly paused and abandoned his search, making his way through the far-end door. Her ploy with the blood must have worked?

Relieved, she allowed herself to breathe, whilst the *beast* slunk away, disappointed. But it also took with it her strength and resolve, and the pain of her wounds began screaming at her brain. It wasn't just the cut to her arm; her hand felt as though she'd crushed every bone.

'All right. All right. You win. I need you.'

The *beast* continued to sulk. She gritted her teeth, wrestling with the pain, her face screwed up in anguish.

'Please,' she begged.

It still ignored her. It was teaching her a lesson. She still couldn't work out exactly what *it* was. Was it actually *her*, or something *else*? How scared of it should she be?

The guardsman returned to the carriage, putting her back on alert. He resumed his search and she swallowed, mortified. There was no avoiding it, she was going to be found.

The door from the kitchen opened.

'There you are, Mr Griffiths.'

'I'm busy.'

'Sir Malcolm would like a word.'

'Ah.'

She heard the guardsman leave the carriage. She couldn't thank Sir Malcolm enough. She suddenly realised her hand wasn't hurting. The *beast* must have taken pity.

'Thank you,' she said.

But without the pain, a different suffering returned to her brain. She closed her eyes, fighting back the tears, memories of her parents haunting her mind.

London was still many hours away, more than enough time to cry.

***

Time passed slowly, tormentingly so, each visit from the kitchen placing her on edge. But it was always to fetch more supplies, nothing more, the guardsman no doubt still busy with Sir Malcolm.

With her eyes bled dry by all the tears, she became distracted by her grumbling stomach. It was loud enough to be heard in the next carriage. And yet, it had a point, she was famished.

Warily, she left her cover, her body stiff from being cramped in one place. She sniffed at the air; there were vegetables aplenty, but she also caught a scent of something *scrumptious*.

She followed her nose to one of the crates. It was marked, *J.S Fry & Sons, Bristol*. She struggled with the lid, the *beast* gave assistance, and soon she was staring at the dozen boxes neatly stacked inside.

She opened one up; it was full of chocolate bars, labelled *Fry's Chocolate Cream*. She picked a bar out and bit into its texture, its coldness crunching between her teeth.

For a moment she thought she was in heaven, the inner fondant sugary on her lips. Her eyes were already seeking out a second when her conscience intervened.

She shouldn't be doing this. Stealing was wrong. She gazed at the half-eaten bar in her hand.

If it's needed to survive, then it doesn't count.

Never had her father spoken truer words.

There was a sudden commotion from the kitchen, and panicking, she grabbed a mailbag from the wall. She stuffed in as many boxes as she could and made her exit through the far-end door.

She found herself stood outside in the cold, a drifting fog eating at her warmth. It may have been spring, but it felt more like winter, and she didn't even have her shawl.

The train suddenly began to slow as they approached a layout of multiple track. Was that a dome she could see in the mist? The end of a railway platform? Were they here? Was this London? Thanks to the fog, she could hardly see a thing.

She took a deep breath; she suddenly felt sick, and it had nothing to do with the chocolate. The unknown awaited; the vastness of London. Now she was here, she wished she was home.

The carriage wheels clunked over a rail-point, and then a couple more. She dropped back in the hope of not being seen as they entered into the station. There was a squeal of brakes, a burst of steam, and the train shuddered to a halt.

Carriage doors opened; people piled out. Natalya quickly joined them on the platform. She tried her best to merge in with the crowd, but it was like being swept into a claustrophobic nightmare. There were bodies everywhere; her mind was in a spin. She found herself looking for the quickest way out. As luck would have it, the station had signs, but not a single one read *Exit*.

'Oi! You! Stop there! Thief!'

She froze, hoping to be swallowed by the earth. A policeman came rushing his way through the crowd. She tried to run, but her legs wouldn't let her.

An adolescent boy came charging out of nowhere and sent her sprawling to the ground. The policeman ran past her in pursuit of the boy. She gave a sigh; he hadn't meant her.

Grabbing up her bag, she found it open. Half a box of chocolate was strewn across the floor. She tried to scoop it up, but to her despair, she found herself staring at a pair of booted feet. She felt the blood drain from her face.

'That's a lot of chocolate ya've got there, Miss. And what's it doing in a mailbag?'

She stared up at the policeman with widened eyes, her tongue frozen in her mouth.

'Is this the girl, *Mr Griffiths*?'

'Yes, Constable. That's the one.'

Judging by his name, it was the guardsman from the train, but he was lying, because he'd never actually seen her. The policeman dragged her to her feet.

'I'll take that.'

He grabbed her bag. Natalya yanked it back. He

grabbed her arm, aggravating her cut. There was a pricking in her eyes and she felt the *beast* rise. Claws began to bleed from her fingers.

'Get off me!' she cried in Russian.

There was a pain in her gums and a wetness on her tongue. It felt like her canine teeth were growing. What was she, some sort of *werewolf*? Her granny had told her tales of such things. Creatures transformed by the rise of the full moon. She noted the look on the policeman's face; one of absolute horror.

'What in God's name…'

She snatched herself free. She turned and ran, the policeman calling after her. She pushed and squeezed her way between the people, her heart racing and her mind in confusion. A gentleman tried to trip her with his cane; she shot him a glare as she leapt it with ease.

She found herself back at the train again, a crowd having gathered around the broken carriage window. On the platform beyond, another train was leaving. She leapt down onto the rail track and gave chase.

She'd always been fast, but now she was faster; her muscles strengthened by the *beast*. She navigated rails and sprang between sleepers, her only thought being one of escape.

In reach of the train, she stumbled and fell, gouging a hole in her dress and her knee. But it wasn't the blood or the pain that concerned her, it was the bars of chocolate now littering the ballast.

'No!'

She glanced behind her. The policeman was in pursuit. She secured what chocolate remained in her bag and took to her heels again.

With gritted teeth she fled after the train, the engine now gaining speed. She eyed the handrail on the rear carriage, gulped down a breath and threw herself at it. She somehow managed to grab a hold and hoist herself up onto the buffers. Not bad for a girl who didn't have the muscle to free an axe from a tree.

Her bag secure beneath her arm, she glanced behind again. The policeman was shrinking in her view by the second, and then they were clear of the station.

With the sleepers blurring fast beneath, she turned her thoughts as to where she might sleep. She'd lost track of time. Was it day or was it night? It was hard to tell through the dirty, London mist.

She shivered. It was getting colder. Back home she'd have had a nice fire for warmth. But she had her chocolate and she had her freedom. At least it was a start.

The train began to slow.

She froze; a dozen thoughts flashed through her mind. She peered around the corner of the carriage. The signal ahead was horizontal, which according to her father meant the train was forced to stop. But stop for what?

Her or something else? She couldn't take the chance.

As they broke to a halt, she leapt from the carriage and began to cross the many lines of track. An incoming express shone her up in its headlamps; she quickened her pace and slid down amongst the coal that was heaped at the side of the rails.

At least the exertion had warmed her, her own breath turning to fog. She looked to see if anyone had followed, but she seemed to be alone.

The train she'd bailed off tooted its whistle and steamed its way forward again. She'd obviously overreacted, but better to be safe than caught.

Picking herself up, she turned her attention to the small wooden shed just twenty feet away. She crossed to its window and tried to peer through, but its glass was caked in hardened soot. She checked the door; it was guarded by a padlock. She curled her fingers around its chain. She called on the *beast* and wrenched it apart. The padlock dropped to the ground with a clunk. She opened the door and stepped inside, pulling it shut behind her.

She now found herself in a tool-shed, with all sorts of implements hung upon the walls. She noticed the broken shard of a mirror on the table and quickly threw her bag on top. Breaking a mirror was bad luck enough, but to see one's reflection within it was worse.

She began to nosey around the shelves. She found

another mirror, this time unbroken. She picked it up, but dare she look in it? Was she ready to see her *heinous* self? She took a deep breath, briefly closed her eyes, and gazed into its glass.

What stared back was nothing but herself, although her eyes were menacingly bloodshot. She re-angled the mirror to look inside her mouth. Her canines were longer, but hardly werewolves' fangs. As for her claws, they were fingernails, again. She allowed herself a sigh of relief.

Taking a seat on the wooden chair, she grabbed up a sooty old blanket from the floor. She wrapped it around her to trap in the warmth. She fingered at her bracelet; time for her to pray.

In the eyes of the Lord, her parents' deaths had been *unclean*; *unnatural* by nature. That made their acceptance into heaven even harder. Every prayer was essential to their journey. She'd just about reached the thirtieth knot when tiredness stole her away.

Chapter 4
A Day in the Park

Natalya awoke to the sound of voices. She sprang from her chair in a panic. Her legs buckled, lacking circulation, and she had to steady herself against the wall.

She allowed a moment for the blood to return; the voices were getting closer. She snatched up her bag, stuffed in the blanket, took a quick breath and burst out the door.

'Oi! You! Stop right there.'

There were four of them; workers on the early morning shift. At least, she assumed it was morning, the glimmer of a sunrise fighting through the mist.

The men quickened their pace towards her. She made

a run for the perimeter wall. It wasn't high, but it was spiked with glass, and she applied her bag so as not to shred her hands. She vaulted over into the unknown.

To her dismay, she found herself falling. The wall was only low on one side. She gave a cry as she plummeted downwards, it was a fifteen foot drop, and then she rolled another ten. She ended up lying face down on a dirt track, her bag still clutched to her chest.

Her body sore and aching, she slowly picked herself up. A well of tears formed in her eyes, and she scolded herself for being such a baby. But the last few days had been the worst of her life, and today had started no better.

The chime of a bell rang out through the mist, announcing the turn of the hour. It confirmed it was day, but the air remained icy, and she pulled out the sooty blanket from her bag. She wrapped it around her and gave a shiver, the fog already clinging to its yarn.

Hobbling, she set off up the track towards the street, back-to-back houses emanating light from a world already busy with life. The glow of the gas lamps soaked through the mist, creating a golden miasma.

Coal sellers, chimney sweeps, merchants with handcarts; everywhere she looked there were tradesmen of some sort. Horses and carriages filled the cobbled streets; she felt like an imposter, intruding on their lives.

She suddenly ran out of pavement. The road before her beckoned. She leapt over the horse dung sitting in the gutter and was nearly trampled by a horse and cart.

Heart in her mouth, she hurried forward. Another horse and cart came charging through the mist. She dug in her heels and nearly overbalanced. The carriage raged past; she ran forward again. She made it to the pavement with her nerves in tatters. And this was only the first road of many.

The back-to-back houses now gave way to buildings up to five stories high. They had ornamented windows and huge, elaborate doorways, their balconies guarded by sculpted balustrades.

She came to a stop at a shop window, her own reflection staring back. It was hard to tell, but her eyes appeared white, no longer bloodshot like the previous night. She licked at her teeth; her fangs felt less sharp. Her bestial traits had faded.

'Why am I different, Papa?'

'You just have to find your place in the world.'

But where was her place? Were there *others* like her? What if she didn't have a place at all?

She carried on in no particular direction, the sun now awake and gracing the sky with an egg-yolk of slithery orange. It ate up the fog, revealing the city in all its architectural glory.

And then, amidst all the mortar and stone, she found

herself stood on a softness of grass. She'd seen parks like this in her trips to the coast, but none had been so vast.

She spent the rest of the day exploring its grounds; a lake curved east beneath a bridge with five arches. There were a series of fountains sprouting water from four basins; a growth of trees that gave the twittering birds a home. The gentry frequented it, the poor inhabited it, young women with dresses both dirty and worn finding slumber beneath the many trees. Natalya observed them with a cautious curiosity. Why would they sleep through the day and not night?

Then, as late afternoon came to pass, the women awoke and went washing in the lake. Natalya watched them from a grass-patch of her own, preferring to keep her distance.

Soon the women were leaving the park, whilst another group of women arrived to take their place. Some gathered in groups, others sat alone. A few glanced her way, but ventured no nearer. She could only assume they were homeless like her. She was suddenly one amongst many.

Her first night beneath the stars was spent restless. Each sound, each movement, put her on alert. The daytime women seemed to sleep with no issue, but even with the *beast*, Natalya felt unsafe. She kept her chocolate hidden beneath her blanket, lest a patrolling policeman should realise it was thieved.

Come morning, she was tired, stiff and irritable. What she wouldn't give for a lovely, soft bed. The daytime women now washed in the lake, before setting out into the city once more. The evening women returned shortly after. It seemed like Natalya had a mystery to solve.

That evening, thanks to her bestial hearing, Natalya listened in on the daytime women's talk. Their attempts to find work, their trials and tribulations; their stories of failure and success. They were girls, just like her, struggling through life. Doing their best to survive.

One mystery solved, she turned her thoughts to the other. She eavesdropped on the talk of night-women, too. But their conversation didn't make too much sense, and so she decided to follow them.

It was the first time she'd left the park since her arrival, braving a city she knew nothing about. She took note of the buildings and signs as she went, relying on her memory to find her way back.

It wasn't long before the women dispersed, some in small groups, others alone. They walked off down alleys, up streets and into taverns. *Maybe they're waitresses,* Natalya thought. Even back home at the village tavern there was want of a waitress or two.

As the sun began to set, she found herself alone on the corner of a street, questioning her decision. The city felt more hostile with each growing shadow, and she came to the conclusion that she ought to head back home. She was already attracting unwanted attention, mainly from the drunks who made lewd comments about her feminine looks.

She started back, chasing the day. In her haste, she must have taken a wrong turn. She didn't recognise a single building. She started to panic; then saw a policeman. Sense dictated she should ask for directions. Instead, she fled down an alley to hide.

She stood there, heart racing, keeping to the shadows, her bag of stolen chocolate tucked beneath her arm. Light from a window flickered out across the cobbles, and she felt herself drawn like a moth to the sun.

She peered in through the window. A young woman was hurriedly straightening a bed. She was twenties, pretty; indiscreetly dressed. She rushed to the door and let in a man. He was a gentleman, judging by his suit. He placed his cane on the bedside table. He stole a kiss; she didn't object, but she was far too poor to be his wife.

Natalya dipped back into shadow. She'd witnessed such goings-on back home. But at least the participants there had been married. This was something more *dirty*.

There was a swishing sound as the curtains drew shut. Natalya decided to return to the street. Another gentleman entered the alley. He stepped in her way; she felt the *beast* stir.

'Good evening, Young Miss.'

She looked at him and swallowed.

'Sir,' was all she could think to reply.

The man manoeuvred her back against the wall. She eyed him, anxious. She felt her claws grow.

'I haven't seen you around here before.'

His perfumed scent irritated her nose. He was a gentleman, yes, but he filled her with dread. A woman stepped out from a doorway down the alley.

'Is that you, Mr M?'

Natalya pushed past him and out onto the street. She dared to look back; the gentleman was gone, the woman following him into the house. It was a lucky escape, for both Natalya and the man. She'd kept her dignity; he'd kept his life.

Someone grabbed her roughly by the arm. She spun, expecting the policeman. Instead, she found herself staring at a woman, early thirties with unpinned hair. Her clothes had a musty fragrance about them; they made Natalya's nose twitch.

'Aint you the new girl I've seen in the park? Keeps 'erself to 'erself?'

Natalya nodded.

'What ya doing down 'ere?'

'Nothing.'

The woman tightened her hold.

'Now don't you be telling me lies, girl. This is my patch. Wear ya hair down somewhere else.'

She shoved Natalya roughly backwards. The *beast* snarled. She was making a mistake.

'Oi, you two. On yer way. We don't want the likes of you down 'ere.'

It was the policeman Natalya had tried to avoid. Her night was getting worse.

'Don't know what ya mean, Constable?' said the woman. 'Me and the girlie 'ere were just 'aving a chat.'

'I know a *Lady of the Night* when I see one. Besides, you have a familiar face.'

'All right. All right. I'm on me way.' She turned to stare Natalya in the eye. 'I see ya down 'ere again, me love, and ya'll wish we never met.'

She turned and sauntered off down the pavement. Natalya turned to walk away, too. The policeman's baton fell against her chest. She looked at him, eyes full of guilt.

'As for you, aint seen you before.'

'I'm lost.'

'Sure. Like all the other *harlots*.'

'No, I'm lost. I swear I am.'

He stared her in the eye. She hoped they'd not turned bloodshot.

'Lost, huh? Where ya heading?'

'The park.'

'Hyde Park? You homeless then?'

She nodded.

'It's that way. Three streets down, then left. Go on, I'll give ya the benefit of the doubt.'

'Thank you.'

She turned and started on her way.

'And Miss…'

She cringed. She slowly turned back.

'Try pinning yer hair up in future. That way no one gets the wrong idea.'

She hurried on her way.

It turned out the homeless weren't just in the park. She passed them in doorways and huddled down alleys. They used newspaper and sacking; anything for warmth, trying to catch some sleep before dawn.

She recognised a sign and hurried back to the park, missing her parents more than ever.

***

Having ventured into the city by night, Natalya decided to enlighten her knowledge by day. Besides, she couldn't live on chocolate forever. She needed to find some other source of food.

She set off east, attempting to follow her path of the previous evening. The streets were busy; overcrowded, frequented by both the rich and the poor. It suffocated her senses; placed her on edge. She felt like an ant in an anthill of stone.

The scale of the buildings continued to surprise her, architecturally lined up in a neatness of rows. The street shops had canopies, as did the theatres, providing shade from the overhead sun. She observed the ladies in their fanciful dresses; it made her feel ashamed of her own. She seemed invisible, which suited her fine. Maybe this was her place in the world?

She'd been walking for an hour, maybe more, when she came upon a bottleneck of people. They were fighting their way down an alley between some houses. Her curiosity piqued, she decided to join them.

It wasn't her wisest decision, especially for someone who didn't like crowds. There was pushing and shoving, shouting; more shoving. She found the whole experience traumatic. She finally emerged into a central market, which to her dismay, was even more congested.

Traders and customers were everywhere, shouting and selling and buying needed goods. There were pig heads on spikes, stinking fish in icy caskets, and women sat in rows shelling walnuts into baskets. The fruit and veg traders were particularly gaudy, offending her ears in their rivalry for trade. The flower girls rarely took *no* for an answer, although they didn't waste their time on someone poor like her.

As she anxiously edged her way through the chaos, she found herself verbally abused by some woman carrying a basket on her head. Something about *get out of me bleeding way,* although her accent made it hard to understand. In fact, there were many of these women, their language as foul as the men's. They transported bought goods between trader and buyer, and each one needed avoiding.

Overwhelmed, Natalya retreated to the church at the far end of the square. It was a tall white building with two central columns, supporting a roof over a walkway to its entrance. The columns had plinths and she chose one as a chair, her nose besieged by a multitude of scents. The sweetness of flowers, the mix of fruit and veg; they all combined to create a blend of strangeness.

Food: she found herself surrounded by it, and yet here she was, practically starving. She hated this place, but couldn't deny that its chaos made it ideal for a thief. A thief who required a bit more bravado than some girl who stole chocolate from an empty railway carriage.

Chapter 5

Encounter at the Market

As Natalya saw it, she had three choices. Thieve for a living, sell herself, or find an honest job. The first felt immoral, the second unthinkable, and so she decided on the latter. Besides, she'd no objection to a hard day's labour, and how hard could it be to find honest employment? She set about following the women from the park, to see where they went to find work.

One week later and she hadn't earned a penny. The whole experience had left her feeling crushed. There was so much competition, so many girls for so few jobs, that she'd failed at every opportunity. It didn't help that she was late to the game. Most of the women had been doing this for years. Maybe if she made the effort to make friends, but then Natalya had never been good at it. Not that time was on her side.

Her supply of chocolate was eaten. She was living off air and the water from the fountain. They'd find her one day, laid under a tree, as nothing but a skeleton inside a sooty blanket. She had no choice; she had to change her tact.

Left with theft or prostitution, she found the answer simple. She had no intention of selling herself and being used by a man like a slab of meat. She, therefore, returned to the market. A thief she would have to be. But the thought of getting caught preyed heavily on her mind, and don't even start her on the moral implications.

The first time she tried it, she was noticed in a second. She never even got near the stall. The second time she thought the trader was distracted, but it turned out he was watching from the corner of his eye. The third time she actually reached the stall itself, but she saw a policeman and ran for her life. It wasn't as though he'd even seen her; her mind was making her paranoid.

Deciding she needed a well-thought-out plan, she spent the next evening thinking one up. But it was no more successful than her other attempts, although this time she actually grabbed hold of an apple. She also brought half the crate toppling down, running off to the cries of *Stop! Thief!*

That night she sobbed herself to sleep; she didn't rise till late the next day. Even then, she found it a struggle to prise herself from her grassy bed.

She sat there, despondent with the world and herself. It made her think of happier days. It was then she remembered the incident with the spider, and how she'd managed to save it without knowing. It suddenly occurred that she'd got it all wrong. This had nothing to do with planning.

Instinct. Pure, reactive instinct. No plan. No set-up. Just spontaneity. She returned to the market with a new sense of purpose, informing the *beast* she would need its speedy skills.

Once more, she mingled with the great unwashed of London, not a single goal or strategy in mind. A *barra* boy pushed by, his cart full of fruit; she spun from his path and walked away with an apple.

It was easy. Unbelievably so. Helped by the unnatural speed of the *beast*. She'd finally found a winning combination. Or had she just been lucky?

It turned out luck had nothing to do with it, and soon her bag was growing full. The future looked brighter, even if it wasn't, and she took to her plinth at the foot of the church. She bit into the flesh of a pear and felt its juices run out of her mouth.

Back home, pears had been a rarity. Usually reserved

as a treat. The last one she'd had was for her fourteenth birthday; or maybe it was Easter?

Birthday? What month was this exactly? She worked it out as May. But her birthday was April. How had she forgotten? Not to mention it had been her *sixteenth*. She was now officially a grown woman, and she hadn't even been aware.

Finishing the fruit, she closed her eyes and started on her prayers. In the background, she could hear the sellers' voices, but nothing distracted her till...

'Wolfcaine.'

Natalya opened her eyes. It was the same voice from when her parents were killed. To her alarm, the market was deserted. Hundreds of people suddenly vanished. She sprang to her feet, feeling anxious.

'What's going on? Who's there?'

She was met by ear-piercing silence. She hated crowds, but this was the opposite. She felt like the only person in the world.

She edged her way forward onto the square, her eyes alert to the slightest of movements. She bit down on her lip to make sure she wasn't dreaming, but if she was, it didn't wake her up.

'Hsss!'

She froze. What on earth was that? It sounded like some monstrous serpent.

'Hsss!'

'Who's there? What do you want?'

It had come from inside the indoor market.

If someone was trying to scare her, it was working. Logic told her to run the other way. Instead, she stepped her way towards the entrance. She must have been out of her mind.

A scent of flowers invaded her nose, but there was also a whiff of something else. Something *stale*; something *unpleasant*. The glow from the indoor gas lamps flickered out. She came to a stop and held her breath; and now she could hear a rustling.

She swallowed, urging her eyes to focus. The unpleasant smell was growing worse. It smelled not unlike rotting vegetation. She told herself she was just being daft.

'Show yourself. You don't scare me.'

'*Hsssss!*'

She half-jumped out of her skin. She spun around in search of the source. It seemed to be coming from…

A frenzy of vines tore up from the flower beds, making her yelp and spring backwards. They vibrated through the air, their thick green stems laced with what looked like poisonous thorns.

Horrified, Natalya turned and ran, the vines lashing at her heels. She gulped down air and choked on its foulness, as more vines sprouted up in pursuit.

She cleared the entrance and dared to look back. The

vines smashed their way through the glass of the roof. She stumbled on the cobbles and fell to the ground. The vines closed in towards her.

'Wolfcaine. Wolfcaine, you have to wake up.'

She looked aside to the girl with white hair. She was thirteen, maybe fourteen years old, her eyes an exuberant pink.

'Do I know you?' said Natalya.

The girl reached out and touched Natalya on the forehead.

***

Noise: it flooded Natalya's ears, the chaos of the market all around. Sellers shouting, horses snorting, young waifs vying for the right to sell their flowers. There wasn't a slither of a vine in sight, and she found herself sat on the plinth once more.

She sprang to her feet and spun around in search of the girl with white hair. Someone barged her out of the way, reminding her why she hated this place. She grabbed up her bag and took to her heels. The sooner she was back in the park the better. The walk should have taken her roughly an hour; she managed to do it in forty-five minutes. She took a seat beneath her favourite tree and gazed back in the direction of the market. To her confusion, she could see a double rainbow, where no rainbow should be.

***

The *dream* at the market haunted her all night. Had it been a *dream*, or was it something else? And who was the mysterious girl with white hair who persisted on calling her *wolf-kane?*

With enough food stolen to last several days, Natalya decided to leave the market be. Instead, she ventured from her own park to the next, which led to a building of distinction.

It was immense, like nowhere she'd ever seen before, which for London was saying something. It was three storey's high, but tall enough for six, and measured at least twenty windows across. They were mainly shuttered, as though no one was at home, but she still felt sorry for the poor *domovoi* who had to take care of it all.

She wandered its grounds for nearly an hour, before being lured away by the chime of that loud *bell*. She followed its echo to a golden, clock-faced tower, its associated buildings adding to its grandeur. It was obviously a place of prominence; status. Did the Queen live here, or at that building in the park?

She pondered the question whilst eating her lunch, observing from the bridge that stretched across the river that divided the city in two. The river was vast and busy with steamboats, transporting day-trippers between the many piers. She came to the conclusion that the Queen lived at neither. Surely she'd prefer somewhere a bit more quiet?

Deafened once more by that bell inside the clock, Natalya vacated to a nearby church. She called it *church*, but the thing was colossal, not that size came as a shock anymore. And why had she not discovered it sooner? It was the perfect place for reciting her prayers.

She stole inside behind a middle-aged couple: a *well-to-do* gent and his *prim and proper* wife. But if she'd thought the exterior was elaborate enough, with its high-rise spires and its intricate walls, then its interior was a sculptured masterwork.

Following the transept layout of the floor, she came to a large rose window. It depicted Christ, surrounded by angels. Sixteen in all. She knew, because she counted. This was a place she would visit again. It made her feel closer to God in every way.

But alas, she eventually returned to the market, if only to replenish her food store. Besides, the *dream* had settled in her mind. At least, it had till she returned there.

She flitted past a stall, dodged a paying customer, and hurried away with an apple in her palm. She returned to her usual chair at the church and devoured the fruit to its core.

Her stomach fed, she closed her eyes and set about her prayers. She occasionally checked to make sure no one had vanished, which was when she saw the boy. He was older than her - maybe eighteen – with clothes that implied the wealthier side of poor. He was sketching away at something in a notebook, and intermittently glancing her way.

She narrowed her eyes in irritation.

'Do you mind?'

'What?'

'Staring. It's rude.'

'Well forgive me fer breathing, young Miss. Where were yer morals when ya stole that apple?'

She guiltily lowered her eyes to the floor.

'I didn't steal it.'

'Course ya didn't. Little bit like I didn't steal this.'

He opened his jacket to reveal a wallet tucked inside his pocket. It was made of leather; a gentleman's wallet. It certainly wasn't his.

'You're a thief?'

'Yeah, and you're freckled.'

'Am not.'

'Look. Freckles.'

He showed her the sketch; it was a portrait of her, and really rather good. She purposely tried to look unimpressed.

'Who's that supposed to be?'

'Well.., you, of course.'

'Oh, I didn't realise.'

He looked deflated, which made her feel better. Her granny would have been proud.

Never let the scoundrels stray you from the path. They have nothing but wickedness on their minds.

The boy studied the portrait for a moment, frowned and shrugged his shoulders.

'Yeah. Yer right. Yer not that clean and ya certainly aint that pretty.'

Her smugness faded like a cloud in the fog. How dare he be so cruel? By slurring her, he slurred her mother. His lips broke into a grin.

'Ha! Called yer bluff, dinta?'

'Who said I was bluffing?'

'Come on, even a blind man can see that portrait is of you.'

He was full of himself, like every other boy. She was determined not to like him.

'Oh, go away, I'm busy,' she said.

'Ah, the bracelet thing.'

'What?'

'I saw ya using it the other day. I guess it has some meaning?'

'None of your business. And what do you mean? You saw me the other day?'

'Come on, we're *working* the same market. Surely ya've weighed up the opposition?'

She'd never even considered it.

'I haven't got time for eyeing up boys.'

'God, yer adorable when yer angry.'

'No one ever called my mother *adorable*.'

'Why? Did she look like an *ogre?*'

That did it. She leapt to her feet in a rage. How dare he call her *beautiful* mother such a thing? She grabbed him by the collar and pulled him close; the *beast* demanding permission to kill him.

'Insult her again and I'll rip out your throat.'

He raised his hands in submission.

'All right. All right. Keep yer freckles on, girlie. Feisty little thing, aintcha. Not that I understood a word, but I think I get the message.'

She frowned. What was he talking about? Her diction was perfectly clear. Unless, of course, she'd spoken in Russian? And why wasn't he afraid? Back home, the boys would be running for the hills. It only made her more frustrated.

'Can I have my collar back now?' he said.

She let him go. He straightened himself. Now was her chance to walk away, so why was she still standing there?

'So what brings ya to London?' he said.

'I live here, silly.'

'No, ya don't. Yer far too clean.'

'It's called *washing.*'

'Hmmm. In the *Serpentine*, I guess.'

'The what?'

'The lake. In Hyde's Park.'

'What makes you think I sleep in the park?'

'I never said ya slept there. But thanks fer the confirmation.'

She glared at him; her sternest glare. He was far too clever for his own good. He remained annoyingly undeterred. What was wrong with this boy?

'So what about yer parents?'

'My parents are... dead.' She could hear the quiver in her own voice. She tried her best to hold back the tears, but already she could feel them brimming in her eyes.

'Yeah. Mine, too. I was six at the time.., or maybe it was seven? Here. Something else I borrowed. You'll find it's finest silk.'

She took the handkerchief from him. Maybe he wasn't that bad, after all. She wiped her eyes and blew her nose. She offered it back; he implied she should keep it.

'I didn't steal that apple, you know.'

'Course ya didn't; just hungry, right?'

'If it's needed to survive, then it doesn't count.'

'Really? Who told ya that load of rubbish?'

'My father. And he never lied!'

The boy turned, as if about to leave. It was then she realised she wanted him to stay. She'd had no one to talk to since leaving the wood, and he certainly knew how to keep her on her toes.

'I'm sorry,' she said.

He turned back with a grin. 'Don't worry. Yer scary, but ya've nothing on *Ella*.'

'*Ella?*'

'Story fer another time.' He reintroduced her to the stolen wallet. 'So what are ya principles on stealing these?'

'Only if it's needed to survive.'

'Well pretend it's an apple.'

'You can't eat a wallet.'

'Ya can with what's inside.'

She hadn't thought of it that way, although she wasn't going to admit it. Her brain raced for an appropriate comeback, when...

'That's it, Constable. That's my wallet.'

'Now look what ya've done.'

'Me?'

The boy took off along the side of the church. Panicking, Natalya followed. It was hardly the action of an innocent woman, but policemen still made her nervous.

Racing into the alley behind, she ploughed her way through the crowd. It earned her a few unrepeatable expletives, and then she was out on the street. She glanced around in search of the boy, her heart audibly pounding.

She couldn't see him anywhere. Then she heard angry shouting. There was fruit and veg all over the road; the boy had collided with a trader from the market. The boy scrambled back to his feet and carried on his way.

Again, Natalya followed after him. He was fast, but fuelled by the *beast,* she was faster. She caught him up and overtook him. He glanced at her in stark surprise. She allowed herself a satisfied smile and diverted down an alley.

'Not down there.'

She chose to ignore him. What did he know, anyway? She came to a halt about halfway down. In front of her was a twelve foot wall. Now guess who was laughing?

Footsteps echoed the cobbles behind her. She closed her eyes and swallowed. She was caught. She should have listened to the boy. They were going to lock her away forever.

'I did warn ya.'

She spun in surprise. It was the boy, looking deservedly smug.

'And yet, you followed?'

'I know. I'm a fool. Hey, what can I say?'

He grinned and she burst out laughing. It was something about the way that he said it. Boys were always so full of themselves, but this one had a trace of humility. The problem was, now they were both trapped. The policeman entered the end of the alley.

'We'll have to scale the wall,' she said.

'What? You from the circus, then?'

'Do I look like I come from the circus? But I do like climbing trees.'

Inhaling a breath, she rocked back on her heels, and took a run at the wall. If she got this wrong, she was going to look stupid, but didn't she look that already?

She summoned the *beast* and it answered her call, strengthening the muscles in her legs. She leapt like a frog, dug her nails into the brick, and swung herself up onto the top of the wall. The boy stared at her in stunned amazement. She felt pretty amazed herself.

'Come on. Quick. I'll grab you,' she said.

He hesitated. What was he doing? He looked at the policeman, then back at her. Had her *bestial* side finally scared him?

'Come on,' she cried. 'Or you're going to get caught.'

He shrugged his shoulders and ran at the wall. He took his best leap; she reached down and grabbed him. She hoisted him up with unnatural ease. He looked at her with raised eyebrows.

'Yer stronger than ya look.'

'It's down to the momentum.'

'Sure.' She could tell he didn't believe her.

They dropped down onto the other side and set off towards the street.

'Well that was close. Ya almost got us caught there.'

'I got you caught? It was **you** who stole the wallet.'

'Well no one told ya to follow me, did they?'

'Who else was going to save you?'

He gave her a look, then burst out laughing. She burst out laughing, too. It was safe to say, she liked him very much. He wasn't like the other boys at all.

'Come on,' he said.

'Why? Where are we going?'

'If I told ya that, it'd spoil the surprise. I'm Nathan, by the way.'

She came to a stop and offered him her hand. 'Natalya Ivanovna Yavorovskaya.'

'Say what?'

'This is how we greet in Russia.'

'Oh.' He took her hand and shook it. 'Maybe I'll just call ya *Freckles*?'

'Call me *Freckles* and you're dead.'

Chapter 6
Bubbles and Cinders

The horse-drawn carriage slowed to a crawl as it neared the end of the street. Without warning, Nathan baled off the rear parcel shelf, taking Natalya by surprise. She was still sat there as the carriage pulled away, forcing her to jump.

'Well here we are,' he said.

'Are we?'

'Wouldn't have said so if we weren't.'

She gazed around at the deserted street and its grim, boarded-up buildings. She couldn't have imagined anywhere worse; even the prostitutes had better living spaces.

'Ya know, I once had a fence who was Russian.

Nice old guy. Retired now. I shoulda known ya weren't fully English; ya speak the language too well.'

'Well I'm only Russian on my father's side.'

'Oh, a bit of a *mongrel,* then?'

'Are you saying I'm a dog?'

'I love the smelly things.'

'Well don't you go thinking I'm your pet, because I'm not.'

He led her across to the building on the corner; it was four-storey's high with a sign above the door that proudly boasted, *'CINDERS'*. She wasn't sure if that was someone's name or just a fancy title.

'Come on then, *puppy dog.*'

She shot him a glare. She followed him in through the entrance, nonetheless. The *beast* urged caution. She told it not to fuss, but she'd never have followed the boys back home.

The hallway beyond was dark and musty, making her nose want to sneeze. She caught her toe in the thread of the carpet and stumbled into a table. She almost knocked the oil lamp over; nothing like setting the place on fire.

'So, *Freck*... I mean, *Natalya,* how come ya've got such a complicated name?'

'It's not complicated.'

'Sure it is. *Natalya I-think-I'm-off-to-Australia.*'

She narrowed her eyes.

'That's not what I said.'

Although it was quite funny. But he'd obviously said it to garner a laugh, so she tried her best not to snigger.

'It's Ivanovna Yavorovskaya.'

'I guess yer parents didn't like ya very much.'

'Of course they did. I'm named after my father.'

'What? Yer father's name was *Natalya?*'

'No, idiot. His name was Ivan. Russian middle names are patronymic. It's quite simple. His name was Ivan, so my middle name is Ivanovna.'

He looked at her and scratched his head. Was he honestly confused or just winding her up? She assumed the latter because intellectually he'd proven quite a challenge.

'Well I'm glad we've got that sorted,' he said. 'Ready for the surprise?'

He led her through a simple wooden door. She couldn't believe what was on the other side.

The lounge beyond was large and stylish, with flocked burgundy wallpaper and plush carpeted floors. VIP boxes curved out from a balcony, overlooking a stage and its red, velour curtains. A wooden bar graced the far-end wall, with snugs built into a series of alcoves. Natalya looked at Nathan, feeling excited, but his own expression was one of concern. Despite the lounge being currently closed, there were staff rushing all over the place.

He stopped a passing waitress.

'What's going on?'

'She's back.'

'Already?'

The waitress hurried on her way.

'Who's back?' said Natalya.

'Just keep yer head down. And if anyone asks, yer *fourteen* years old.'

He led her down into the chaos, heading for the far side of the room. Natalya followed, feeling giddy, and looking everywhere but forward. She bumped straight into the back of him. He must have come to a stop.

'Oops,' she giggled. 'Sorry. I didn't…'

'Shhh!'

'But…'

'Natalya, quiet.'

She followed his gaze across to the bar, and the tall, slim female who now turned to face them. Her silky blonde hair was long enough to sit on, whilst a gold, corseted gown clung to every curve. She was beautiful, on a par with Natalya's mother, with skin untainted by twenty years of life. She approached them with a guileful smile, her dress swishing in movement with her hips.

Natalya was absolutely mesmerised.

'So, Mr Croft, who's the *waif and stray?*'

'A *friend.*'

'And this friend has a name, does she?'

'She'll have to tell ya. I can't pronounce it.'

'Natalya Ivanovna Yavorovskaya.'

Ella looked at her; Natalya squirmed, but she did like the idea that Nathan called her *friend*.

'Well, Natalya. I'm Ella Cinders. The name above the door is mine.'

'You look like a princess.'

'You think so? Wow. I'm liking you already. So tell me, *Sweetheart*, what's your age?'

'Fourteen.'

'Damn those politicians.'

'That's not the reason I brought her here.'

'Oh, Nathaniel, don't be such a prude.'

Natalya didn't understand them. And why did she have to lie about her age? Ella eyed her up and down. Then eyed her once again.

'Well she's certainly got the figure for it. A little bit of makeup, we could pass her off as older.'

'Which would look really good when the Chief Constable is accused of sleeping with an underage girl.'

Natalya gave him a wide-eyed stare. Was he meaning what she thought he meant?

Ella pondered the thought a moment, then gave a frown and sighed.

'Hmm. I guess you're right, Mr Croft. So why have you brought her here?'

'Harold sprained his ankle in yer absence. I thought she could help out backstage fer a while.'

'Well Harold doesn't work here anymore. Oh, don't give me that shocked expression. He's of no use to me if he can't do his job. Very well, Nathaniel, I'll give the girl a try. But why her, Nathan? Why not me? You know it's me you really want. I could *educate* you in so many ways. And we older girls are such more fun.'

As she spoke, she moved behind him, wrapping her arms about his body. She slid her cheek up against his and, hiking her skirt, rubbed her thigh against his leg. Natalya stood there, mouth agape; Nathan simply reddened.

'Slacking a bit, aren't we, Mr Croft?'

Ella returned to centre front. In her hand were a number of wallets she'd lifted from his person.

'Well ya weren't due back till next month, Ella.'

'My travels were... *enlightening*, shall we say.'

She raided the wallets of their notes and hid the money in a pocket under her skirt. She offered the wallets back to Nathan. He took a hold, but she didn't let go.

'Best value you can get for them, Mr Croft. And don't be accepting the first price offered.'

She released the wallets, sniffed at the air, and gazed across at Natalya.

'When you show the *waif and stray* where she's

sleeping, I'd suggest you do so via the wash room. We're all respectable ladies, here, *Sweetheart*. Even if we do end up working on our backs.'

It was Natalya's turn to redden. Did she really smell that bad? Ella gave an illusive smile and sauntered off back towards the bar.

'Sorry about that,' said Nathan.

'She's...'

'Psychotic, I know.'

'No, beautiful, Nathan.'

'Well believe me, the beauty runs only skin-deep. Or would ya prefer to be one of *her girls*?'

'Not if you're saying what I think you're saying.'

'Just stick to being fourteen years old. They recently raised the age of consent. She'll only break the law if she thinks she won't get caught. Come on, I'll show ya where yer sleeping. It aint great, but it's warmer than the park.'

She started to follow, then came to a stop.

'Do I really smell that bad?'

'Ya smell like a girl.'

'Oh, not a dog, then?'

She wasn't sure whether to thank him or not.

***

Natalya's new bed was a musty old mattress, dumped on the floor amongst a few dozen more. It was softer than the ground and definitely warmer, but she dreaded to think what all the stain marks were.

Needless to say, she wasn't alone, sharing the room with another fifteen girls. Aged twelve through twenty, their clothes littered the floor, the sequins from their costumes speckling light across the walls.

'Oi. Have you nicked me 'air brush again?'

'Nah. It's her over there nicked yours.'

It was the third disagreement in the past half hour, which entertained Natalya no end. Back home, it was the boys who taunted the girls. Here, the girls taunted themselves. Natalya just stuck to her mattress and kept quiet; the last two arguments had ended in a catfight.

'Hey, you,' she heard someone call. She looked to the doorway and the dance girl stood in it. 'Yeah, you. I'm talking to you. Was told ya need a bluddy good scrub.'

Natalya eagerly sprang to her feet. A lovely warm bath after all these weeks. Being dirty had become a way of life, and she couldn't wait to smell fresh again.

She edged her way past the squabbling *kittens* and followed after the dance girl. The atmosphere backstage was as fraught as out front, attacking her senses with noise and colour that made her feel quite ill. She was glad when the dance girl came to a stop and nodded at a door.

'In there. An' don't take all night about it. Ya'll need

to scrub it out when yer done.'

She flounced away to accost some guy who was happy to have her tongue down his throat. Natalya pulled a face of disgust; it was like the girl was trying to eat his face. When her parents kissed, it had always seemed so dreamy, but this was much more crude.

She entered into the wash room, which turned out to be just a large, dingy cupboard. The air had a fragrance of perfume and sweat, and something else that she'd rather not imagine. The water in the tub was filthy, and crusted with a coat of floating scum. It was a far cry from the mirror-like water that she used to bathe in back home.

Memories flooded her mind: the sturdy wooden bathtub, crafted by her father; the kettle on the fire hearth, used for heating water. She even recalled the tuneful song of the birds as she relaxed in the depths of the water.

It brought a tear to her eye. She suddenly felt so alone. As for the bath that awaited, she'd rather bathe in London's dirty rain. Maybe if she found some scent to mask her own, she could get away with not bathing at all.

'Nah, I wouldn't fancy it either.'

She spun to see Nathan in the doorway. She sniffed back the tears and straightened her posture. She couldn't describe how good it felt to see him.

'Are you supposed to be in here?' she said. 'This is the girl's room, after all.'

'Nah, the boys bathe in here as well. Pretty disgusting, aint it.'

She looked at the water and felt herself gag.

'I think I'd rather just smell bad.'

'Good job I came along then.'

'Why? Do you have a magic wand?'

'No, but I do have a *cactus*.'

***

Natalya followed Nathan up the stairs. She got the feeling they weren't supposed to be here. He was clearly on edge, peering around each corner in case there was someone else coming down.

'First floor, *entertainment*,' he said.

'Sounds like fun.'

'Of the prostitute kind.'

She quickly followed him up the next flight. *Entertainment* was strictly out.

'And the second?'

'Rooms for the privileged few. Head Barman. Music Conductor. Senior Stage Hand.'

'What about Ella?'

'She lives on the fourth.'

'So what about the third?'

'Yer about to find out.'

He stepped through a doorway and invited her to follow.

She now found herself at the end of a long hallway; she peered through the window immediately right. A drainpipe ran within a foot of its glass, carrying water from the rooftop to the alley.

She still felt a teensy bit giddy, although the *beast* kept reproaching her for being so naive. Had she forgotten what her granny had told her? *They have nothing but wickedness on their minds.*

'Natalya. Come on. Before someone sees us.'

The *beast* within her readied its claws.

He's not like that, she told it sternly.

How can you be sure?

She followed Nathan into the third room down.

There was a bed, a dresser, a side-table and chair. Not a yellow stained mattress or squabbling girl in sight. Her eyes widened on seeing the bath tub. She gazed into its empty cleanness. Sat at the bottom was a spined, fleshy plant, which looked like a fat, green parsnip.

'I told ya I had a cactus,' he said.

She'd never seen one of these in the wood.

'Did ya see that pendant around Ella's neck?'

She shrugged.

'It's pagan. She's a *practicing witch.*'

'A witch! What? Like a *real* witch?'

'A *practicing* witch.'

'There's a difference?'

'Dunno. Do witches even exist? Her potions, though, are something else.'

He unstopped what looked like a scent bottle and poured its content over the plant. The cactus began to soak up the potion, before swelling until it couldn't swell anymore. Its skin split and water gushed everywhere, filling the bath tub in seconds. Natalya looked on in shocked amazement, water slopping to the floor.

'How..? How did you do that?'

'Beats me. I just borrowed the potion.'

'When you say *borrowed?*'

'All right, I stole it. She'll never know. She's got dozens of the things.'

Natalya dipped her finger in the water. 'Argh!'

'What's wrong?'

'It's cold.'

'Oh, I fergot. Ya need to add this.'

He peppered the water with powder from a snuffbox and the water immediately began to effervesce. Soon the whole tub was a simmering oasis of steam and bubbles that frothed down its sides.

'That's... incredible,' she gasped. She could barely curb her smile.

'Time I was gone.' He turned for the door. 'Enjoy

yer soak, and stick the chair behind the door.'

'Why? Is someone likely to come in?'

'I very much doubt it. But ya can never be sure.'

'Whose room is this, anyway?'

'Haven't a clue. Well, actually, it belongs to me.'

He hurried out the door.

His? The room belonged to him? His pickpocketing skills must have earned him Ella's favour. *See,* she told the beast. *He's a perfect gentleman.* It still insisted on the chair behind the door.

Door wedged, she began to undress, bubbles floating around her in the air. She dipped her foot into the water and yelped as something suckered to her toe. It was the wrinkled skin of the cactus.

'Nathan!'

***

Natalya made her way downstairs, taking care not to be seen. She didn't want Nathan getting into trouble, especially after all that he'd done.

How long she'd been, she didn't know, but it felt like the bubbles were still popping on her skin. She'd taken the time to wash her clothes, too, although she'd never thought about getting them dry. Her undergarments were now clung to her skin, although at least they gave her dress a chance to air.

She stepped back into the lounge. The atmosphere

was one of apprehension. Ella was sat, observing rehearsals, and she wasn't afraid of voicing her opinion.

Adjusting her clothes, Natalya moved backstage in the hope of finding Nathan. She was almost knocked over by a man dressed as an onion. It was probably best not to ask.

'Come on, Nathan. Let me 'ave a look.'

It was the squeakiest voice she'd ever heard. She followed its pitch to the corner of the room, where Nathan was rooting through a prop box. The voice belonged to a teenage girl who was vying for his attention. Natalya disliked her at once.

'If yer looking fer *magic*, we could go up to yer room?'

'What?' said Nathan, popping up his head.

'You and me.'

'You and me what?'

'Go up to yer room.'

'Why would we do that?'

Natalya veiled a satisfied smile. Nathan saw her and stood upright.

'There ya are. I was beginning to think ya'd drowned in all them bubbles. They weren't just dirt then?'

'What weren't?'

'Ya know…' He indicated her face. 'The freckles.'

The squeaky-voiced girl pushed her way between

them.

'Bubbles? What bubbles? Come on, Nathan, what about tonight?'

'I can't. I have to teach *her* the rigging.'

'Sez who?'

'Cinders. Take it up with her.'

The girl squealed and stamped her foot, before storming off in a huff. Natalya could mask her smile no longer. Now she had him all to herself.

'Sorry, I think I've upset your friend.'

'She'll get over it. Always does.' He resumed his search through the prop box. 'Hey! Take a look at this.'

He produced a lethal looking dagger.

'Careful, Nathan. That looks sharp.'

'Nah, it's just a magician's....'

He fumbled the dagger, tried to catch it, and fell forwards into her. At first she laughed, but when he stepped back, the blade was jutting from his chest.

'Nathan!'

Panic gripped her heart, any cry for help lodging in her throat. He let go of the hilt and the blade sprang forward, into her trembling hands. She dropped it with a cry.

He grinned and picked the dagger back up, demonstrating its retractable blade.

'You idiot,' she cried, thumping him on the arm.

'Ow! Don't hold back, will ya? Still, it was worth it

fer the look on yer face.'

'Well I didn't find it funny.'

He looked at her, mischief in his eyes. She tried her best not to laugh. A hand suddenly blurred past her face and grabbed him by the throat. The brute attached to it blurred past, too, and pinned Nathan up against the wall.

'Put the prop back in the box, Croft, an' stop showing off to the ladies.'

Nathan obeyed and the six foot behemoth let him down again.

'I'm watching ya, boy. Don't think that I aint. Nicking wallets don't cut it with me. Ya might think yer in with 'er upstairs, but when yer backstage, yer mine.'

He looked at Natalya, gave a scowl, and barged her out of his way. She watched him merge back into the crowd. Nathan rubbed at his throat.

'Are you all right?' she asked.

'It's time that guy took a very long fall from somewhere high.'

'Who is he?'

'The Dogman.'

'He looks after the dogs?'

Nathan laughed, then winced with the pain.

'No, ya fool. That's his name. Gerard Dogman. The Senior Stagehand.'

'Senior Stagehand?'

'Yeah. That piece of work is our boss.'

Chapter 7
From Riches to Rags

Natalya peered through the curtains, excitement and trepidation in her heart. She'd been looking forward to this moment all week; her first involvement in the live shows.

Learning the rigging had been easy, especially with Nathan by her side. Fly spaces, scenery battens: she'd learned about them all, not that Gerard Dogman had been happy with her presence.

'Ya've gotta be kidding me, right?' he'd bellowed. 'No lassie is getting her hands on my rigging.' At that point, the dance girls had burst into laughter, although Natalya wasn't sure why. 'She aint got the strength. Not fer the pull line. Tell ya what, she can work the hoist.

Croft, she's your responsibility, now. She falls to her death, it's on you.'

But Natalya had no intention of falling, even if she was forty feet in the air. Her floor may have been just a few planks of wood, but she'd spent her whole life traversing dead trees.

She observed the gathering audience below, a tide of wealthy, socialite gents. Dressed in their tail suits, they formed a sea of black, the white of their shirts imitating the froth. They sat at round tables and puffed on cigars that clouded the air with a sickly aroma. There was hardly a single female in sight; the men were here for the post-show *entertainment.*

'Excited?'

She almost jumped out of her skin. Nathan's feet were as light as his fingers. She pulled her head out of the curtains and blinked to clear the smoke from her eyes.

'Is it always this busy?'

'And then some. It's the only *Cabaret* show in London. Cinders stole the idea from a Frenchman she met a few years back in Paris. Come on. We've got some last minute checks.'

She followed him along the catwalk, Dogman bellowing at someone below. Shouting seemed to be the stagehand's favourite pastime, and for once it wasn't at Nathan.

'He doesn't like you very much, does he?'

'The Dogman doesn't like himself.'

'What did you do? Steal his wallet?'

'No point really; there's never owt in it. What he doesn't drink, he gambles away. I hear he's got debts all over town.'

'Then why does he hate you?'

'I'm on the third floor, while he's only on the second.'

'That doesn't make sense?'

'Ya have to understand, it's all about status here. Take *Mouse Girl,* for instance…'

'*Mouse Girl?*'

'Yeah, well she squeaks like one, don't she? She follows me around like some lonely shadow, but she was never that keen when I slept downstairs. Then Ella discovered I was handy with these…' He wriggled his fingers in front of her. '..and all of a sudden she's like me third arm. Am telling ya, if ya switch from nicking apples, ya could get a room on the third floor yerself.'

He cranked a hoist, peered over the rail, and observed as a bunch of cardboard stars lowered. He secured the crank back into place, turned to her and smiled.

'Right, I think we're ready.'

The Master of Ceremonies took to the stage, his white-painted face making him look ill. He gave some attention to his villainous moustache before stepping through the velour curtains. The audience cheered, Natalya's heart raced, and she beamed at Nathan with excitement. She caught him eyeing up the dance girls backstage, their costumes exposing more flesh than they covered.

I told you not to trust him, growled the beast. *Never trust a boy. They only want one thing.*

Natalya purposely cleared her throat. He took no notice. She nudged him in the arm.

'Enjoying the scenery?'

'Umm,' he said, then remembered she was there. 'Err, come on, we can get a better view if we watch from the rear catwalk.'

I bet we can, she thought. But what on earth was she saying? She was saving herself for the hero of her novel, not falling for some pickpocket who worked the theatre rigging. She followed him onto the rear catwalk and they sat with their legs dangling over the edge.

The MC finished his five minute turn and the dance girls took centre stage.

What followed was like something out of a comedy, the dancers out of time with each other and the music. One turned left, the others turned right; two collided and caused absolute mayhem. The crowd applauded and cheered them on, and then the girls stripped off their tops.

'What are they doing?' gasped Natalya.

'Welcome to the world of *burlesque*. Hey, they'll be wearing far less than that when they're *entertaining* later.'

'But what is the *prince* going to think when he comes?'

'Prince? Who said owt about a prince?'

'The girls are all saying that when abroad, Ella met an Indian prince.'

A dance girl did something lewd with a boa. Natalya pulled a face.

'Well the last I checked the British ruled India, so if she did, he's no one of importance.'

'No one of importance? A prince is royalty.'

'And Cinders thinks she's a princess. She aint.'

The routine came to an abrupt end and the dance girls bumbled off stage. They were each blaming one another for the turmoil. Nathan gave a chuckle.

'I told ya the view was better back here. They mess it up every night.'

So he wasn't just here for the eyeful of flesh. Natalya felt instantly better.

'Oi! You two. Shift those stars.'

It was Dogman, shouting from below.

'Damn!' said Nathan.

'Don't worry,' said Natalya. She ducked beneath the railing. 'I've got it.'

Without thought of the forty-foot drop below, she leapt across to the other catwalk. She rushed to the winch, turned the crank, and hoisted up the stars. She turned and curtsied to Nathan's applause. She chose to return via the same route. She misjudged the landing, veered backwards, and heard herself give a gasp.

There wasn't a thing she could do. She was about to drop like a sandbag on the pull-line. She tumbled backwards; Nathan lunged forward and managed to grab a hold of her leg. He took her weight and stemmed her fall. It left her dangling with her skirt around her shoulders. She'd nearly just died, but her only thought was, thank the Lord for inventing pantalettes.

Taking the strain, Nathan pulled her upwards. She grabbed hold of the rail and dragged herself through. She collapsed onto the catwalk, her heart racing. *That's what you get for trying to show off.*

'You all right?'

She nodded. He helped her to her feet. She gazed up into his face and the blueness of his eyes. For a moment the world around her didn't matter. He returned her stare; she felt drawn towards his lips.

He turned. 'Oh Lord.'

'What is it?' she exclaimed.

'The comedian's on next.'

'Is he funny?'

'Aint ya been watching rehearsals? Natalya, the

dancers were funny.'

***

The rest of the week just flew by; she barely had time to breathe. And although the acts were the same every night, each performance felt different.

The highlight, however, was always the dance girls. They messed up every time. Natalya and Nathan found it hilarious, although Ella was far less impressed.

The more time Natalya spent with Nathan, the more she felt herself drawn. Of course, he liked her back. She hoped he liked her back. What if he actually didn't? What if he thought she was just another *Mouse Girl*, hanging around for a better, stain-free life? He'd never once mentioned that *moment* on the catwalk, whereas she thought about it all the time.

If she wasn't thinking about Nathan, her point of focus was Ella. She was everything Natalya wanted to be. Beautiful, elegant, respected; although the latter was probably more down to *fear*. As for Ella running a high-class brothel, Natalya chose to ignore that little fact.

'Penny for 'em?'

Natalya spun. He really did need to wear bells on his feet. She'd been collecting the rubbish from the previous night, another one of her daily chores. Nathan followed her gaze across the room to where Ella was charming some noble gent.

'What is it with her?'

'I don't know what you mean?'

'She's hardly a figure of morality. She used to be the *courtesan* here.'

'I know.' She frowned. 'And a *courtesan* is?'

'Come on. I want to show ya something.'

He led her into the Manager's Office. They shouldn't really be here. But if he thought he could sway her mind, she was determined that he wouldn't. Every girl needed someone to aspire to. Why couldn't she have Ella?

'*Ella Cinders* aint her real name, ya know. She changed it when she started working here.' He picked the lock to a drawer in the desk and took out a dishevelled scrapbook. He opened it at a particular page. 'Here. Have a read of that.'

'*...the death is announced of Sir John Charles Henry, a successful ship merchant, in his 45th year. The cause of death was heart disease. He leaves a wife and three daughters. Born in 1840, Sir Henry first married in 1869. They had a daughter, Eleanor Jane Henry...*'

Natalya looked up in excitement. '*Eleanor Jane Henry?* I knew she was a *Lady*.'

Nathan frowned. 'Don't get too enthusiastic?'

'And why is that, may I ask, Mr Croft?'

They looked to Ella in the doorway. Natalya felt a

sudden panic. She preferred to admire the *princess* from afar.

'If you wanted a biopic of my life, *Sweetheart*, all you had to do was ask. But I wouldn't believe what you read in the papers. It wasn't heart disease that got him. It was *syphilis*.'

'Syphilis?'

'You get it from spreading your seed. And my father did plenty of that. The *bastard* passed it onto my mother. She died when I was fourteen.'

'I'm… sorry.'

'Ya hear that, Nathan? She's sorry. I never got that from you. Remember the last time you broke into my office, and what I said I would do?'

She swayed across the room towards him, collecting a paper knife en route. Natalya could see the nervous look in his eye; he really didn't trust her.

'Ya told me ya'd cut off me fingers.'

'Except you couldn't pickpocket, then. Of course, there are other things I could cut off. Did you plan on having children?'

'It's my fault,' said Natalya. 'I asked him to show me in here.'

'Oh? Well I can't very well cut off yours.'

'Leave her alone,' said Nathan.

'What is it with you and this girl?' Ella pressed the knife against his chest. 'Go on, get out. Before I change my mind.'

'Come on, Natalya.'

He headed for the door.

'No. The girl stays here.'

'I'm not leaving her.'

'Get out, Mr Croft!'

He remained where he was. Ella raised the knife.

'It's blunt,' he said.

'Which will make it more painful. Now wait outside or she's out of a job.'

He hesitated, then turned for the door. 'I'll just be waiting out here.'

'Get out!!'

He left. Ella shook her head and smiled.

'Now, then, where did I get to? Ah, yes. My treacherous father. He remarried after that. Poor, silly cow. He gave my stepmother syphilis, too. Shortly after, she gave birth to twins. You should have seen the state of their faces; growths all over the place. The *ugly sisters*, I used to call them. I got out of there the first chance I got.

'I was little older than you are now. Hair no longer than my shoulders. Took my chances on the streets at first, and then I came across here. They called it *BUTTONS PLACE* back then, and Frederick Buttons liked his women young. He wasn't bothered about no politician's law, and it wasn't long before I was his *favourite*. You have to know how to pleasure a man.' She smiled. 'And I was very good at it.'

Natalya listened with a growing apprehension. *She's a princess*, she kept telling herself. But this close up, the image was waning, and she didn't really want to know the truth.

Ella approached and seated herself with one leg propped against the desk. She used the knife to comb Natalya's hair, arranging it on her shoulders.

'I like the hair down. It softens the face. Better a temptress than a talking skull. Not that you couldn't carry it off. How old did you say you were again?'

'Fourteen.'

'Hmm, I bet you are. Who told you to lie? Mr Croft? I think we both know you're older than that. Wouldn't you say so, *Natasha*?'

'It's Natalya.'

'Oh, I'm sorry. I thought in Russia the diminutive took preference?'

'It does, but I prefer Natalya.'

'Oh, a rebel. I like that. You know, one day you could be courtesan, too? You wouldn't believe the money you can make. That's how I bought into this place. Shame about the fire.'

'Fire?'

Ella flicked through the scrapbook, resting on the cutting of a burning building. The headline read, **'Show**

Bar Burned to the Ground'. *BUTTONS PLACE* was mentioned in the text.

'Poor Buttons, he never liked the cold, but he got more than his fingers burned that day. The place came to me, and then with my inheritance, I turned it into CINDERS.'

Natalya gave her a dubious look; she got a feeling that fire didn't start on its own. Ella matched her gaze for a moment, then gave a beguiling smile.

'What green eyes you have, *Natasha*. Do I detect a smidgen of disgust? *Do-gooders* get themselves nowhere in this world. Believe me, I was one of them. Once! No, you have to be a bitch to succeed. Remember I said I came here with short hair. It used to be long; like it is now. But one night my stepmother cut it all off. She hated my looks because her daughters had none. I paid her back with a face full of ashes. Now she looks like her ugly daughters. That's a mistake she'll not make again.'

She stood, using her extra height to dictate her matriarchal status. Natalya gave her a fleeting look, still aware of the wielded knife.

'This place is mine. The rules here are mine. Don't cross me, *Natasha*, or I promise you'll regret it. Fourteen, eh? We'll let it go for now. But one step out of line and you'll be working on yer back along with the rest of the girls. Understand?'

Natalya nodded.

'Good girl. Well go on, *Natasha*. Go join your *friend*.'

Natalya swallowed and left the room. Nathan was waiting outside.

'You all right?'

She nodded. 'But I think I've changed my mind. I don't want to be like her at all.'

Chapter 8
A Game of Dog and Mouse

25th May, 1891

Her encounter with Ella left her feeling stunned; her self-confidence wounded. She could see why Nathan was nervous of the woman. He was right, her beauty ran only skin-deep.

But that wasn't the only thing troubling her mind. The 25th had crept up without warning. It was another reason for reproaching herself. How could she have forgotten?

As the other girls slept, she abandoned her mattress in favour of the bar. She stared at herself through the shelving mirror, tears moistening her cheeks. It was the early hours; almost three in the morning. Some would call it the *witching hour.*

'Never took you for a secret drinker?'

She almost fell off her stool in fright.

'Nathan! What are you doing here?'

She tried to discreetly wipe back the tears.

'Couldn't sleep. Take it you neither?' He took up residence behind the bar. 'Fancy a drink?'

She nodded. He grinned and poured two lemonades. She ran a nervous hand through her hair. He slid her drink across the bar.

'She's some piece of work, aint she? Ella.'

'You did warn me. I feel such a fool.'

'I wouldn't worry. She tricked Frederick Buttons, and he was no one's mug.'

'You knew him, then? The previous owner?'

'Taught me all I know. Caught me trying to steal his wallet. I thought fer sure he'd send me back to the workhouse, but instead he took me under his wing.'

'Workhouse?'

'Yeah. Ya don't wanna go there. Life out 'ere's far easier than there.'

It sounded like he'd had a rough childhood, and here was she feeling sorry for herself. She sniffed back a tear. She saw him notice.

'I'm getting a cold,' she told him.

'And here was me, thinking ya'd been crying.'

Damn him! Damn her weeping eyes. And now she'd

blasphemed, too.

'You still don't mind covering today?'

'Sure. Wouldn't 'ave said so if I didn't.'

'But you've never asked why.'

'None of my business. Figured ya'd tell me if ya wanted me to know.'

She did want him to know. She'd love for him to know. But what if he thought she was *weird?* Back home she didn't care what others thought, but *him...* she couldn't bear losing his respect.

'Today's forty days since my parents died. The day they're meant to pass to the afterlife. It's also the last day I'm meant to mourn them. Beyond that is selfish; it feeds the Devil's will.'

She looked at him, dreading his reaction. Thomas Bennett and his brother would have been in fits of laughter. But no, he just looked earnestly concerned, whether he meant it or not.

'So the forty days is in relation to what?'

'The number of days between Christ's resurrection and his ascension up to heaven.'

'Ah. I see.' He took a sip of drink. 'So what do ya have to do?'

'Pray. There's not much else that I can; although there should be a service, a meal to be had. I'll pay a visit to that church by the river. The one that's near that big-belled clock.'

'Oh, you mean the *Abbey?* I guess ya'll be setting off early then?'

'Just after sunrise.'

'Then ya better get some slumber. We can't have ya oversleeping, can we?'

She rose to leave. 'Aren't you coming?'

'Nah. I've some serious drinking to do.'

'Oh. Good night, then.'

'See ya later.'

She returned to her mattress feeling even more forlorn. Even Nathan didn't want her company, and she dreaded the approaching dawn.

***

Natalya ventured out into the day. The air smelled of soot, not unlike her shawl. There was food in her bag and trepidation in her heart. She touched at her bracelet and its many tightened knots. Another thirty minutes and she'd be inside the *abbey*. She crossed the road and set off down the pavement.

Above, the dawn was putting on a show, sweeping the sky in a spectacle of colour. She missed those days of watching the sunrise from her favourite drystone wall.

Someone came running up behind her and snatched the bag from her shoulder.

'No!'

They ran off around the corner. Natalya took to her heels in chase. This couldn't be happening. Not today. She could feel the fury of the *beast* inside. Whoever they were, they were going to regret it. The *beast* was going to rip out their throat.

She closed the gap in no time. They may have been quick, but she was quicker. The thief turned into a dead-end alley; she tackled them to the ground.

'Give it back.'

She wrenched the bag from them. A sound of laughter filled her ears. She turned the thief onto their back and stared into their face.

'God, yer fast.'

'Nathan? What on earth do you think you're doing?'

He pointed to the shop at the end of the alley. She read the words on its headboard.

'Dymkovo toys – the handicraft of Russia.'

Her eyes teared up and she struggled to her feet. She approached the shop, a lump in her throat. Nathan joined her at the window.

The display was full of small clay figures, carefully crafted and brightly painted. There was a rosy-cheeked woman, a long-bearded man, and animals decorated in wonderful patterns. There was even a woman sat on a duck. Or maybe it was a swan.

'I used to have one of these,' she said. 'A milkmaid. I kept her in the drawer beside my bed.'

'Well *Gusev's* been here as long as I can remember. Maybe this is where yer milkmaid came from?'

'You know the owner?'

'He used to be my fence. Remember, I told ya about him when we met. He's been retired for the past five years, but he does still owe me a favour.'

He entered into the shop, implying she should follow. It smelled of clay and freshly mixed paint. There was an elderly man stood behind the counter.

'You must be Natalya Ivanovna,' he said. 'I am Dimitri Igorevitch.'

'Pleased to meet you, Dimitri Igorevitch.'

She held out her hand; he approached her and shook it, retaining her gaze as a mark of respect.

'Mr Croft, here, has told me all about you. Today is an important day, is it not?'

'It's been forty days…' She glanced at Nathan. 'But I only told you this morning?'

'Yes, sooner would have been better,' said Gusev. 'He came banging on my door at just gone four. But today is about your parents, is it not, and I have *kutia* to eat and *kissel* to drink. We can even set them a place at the table; that way we'll know they've moved on for certain.'

'Then I'll leave ya to it,' said Nathan.

'Wait,' said Natalya. She rushed forward and hugged him. Now she knew why he'd sent her back to bed.

He'd wanted to set all this up. 'Thank you, Nathan. Thank you.'

'Ya'd do the same fer me.'

'We're wasting precious time,' said Gusev.

Nathan duly left the shop.

The old man led her through into the back and up some stairs to the first floor room. On the sideboard was a photo of an old lady, along with an oddly shaped cactus plant. What was it with London and cacti? Did every household have one?

'Do you speak the native tongue?'

She nodded.

'Then we shall say *Panikhida* in Russian.'

'This is really kind of you. I can't thank you enough.'

He smiled. 'Think nothing of it.'

***

'Natalya.'

'Natalya!'

'Natasha! *Wake up!'*

Natalya opened her eyes. She was sat at the table in the old man's home, a half-glass of *kissel* on the tablemat before her. Directly opposite were two empty plates. Plates that should have been full.

Horror flooded her mind. This could only mean one thing. They hadn't passed. They hadn't ascended. They were trapped in some place between Heaven and Hell. Rejected by God and forever condemned to an eternity of torment.

'Mama! Papa!'

Their images appeared, sat across the table. Their faces were twisted, distorted in anguish. Natalya felt a tightening in her chest.

'No!'

She sprang to her feet in a panic. What should she do? How could she help them?

'Natalya...'

'..Natalya...'

'..help us.'

'Natalya. Why did you not give prayer for our souls?'

'But I did, Mama, Papa, I swear. No, this can't be true.'

'Natalya, it's coming.'

'Coming for you. There is no afterlife. Only the darkness.'

A blackness seeped its way through their eyes, tearing down their faces to eat up their skin. Natalya could feel the air drain of life, *the darkness* feasting on their torment and her grief.

'No!' she screamed. 'Someone help them. Someone help them. Please!'

***

'Natalya Ivanovna, wake up. You must wake up. You hear?'

She looked at Gusev, horror in her eyes. She gulped on the air; she couldn't breathe. He slapped her hard across the face. The air came flooding back.

'I'm sorry,' he said. 'You were having a nightmare.'

'I failed them. My parents are trapped there forever.'

'But child, your parents' plates remain untouched.'

She looked across the table. Their plates were full, just as he'd said. Had it really been a dream?

'See. They are in the afterlife now.'

But the image of their torment lingered in her mind.

'I have to go.'

She rushed from the table, her legs almost giving way beneath her. She hurried down the stairs and into the shop. She came to a pause at the door. She heard the old man follow her down. She turned around to face him.

'Thank you,' she said. 'For all you've done. You've been very kind. I'm sorry.'

'Believe me, child, your parents are safe.'

Natalya nodded and rushed out the door.

***

She couldn't get back to CINDERS quick enough. She felt light-headed; consumed by dread. The day was lost and the night was closing in, the accompanying fog nipping at her skin.

With the main entrance closed, she entered via the alley. There was shouting and cheering coming from the stageside. It offended her ears, yet curiosity drew her, and besides, it might take her mind off things.

'He's gunna kill 'im this time for sure.'

She followed everyone's gaze to the catwalk. There was Gerard Dogman, climbing up the frame, wielding a metal bar. And who was that trying to escape him? A pit hollowed out in her stomach. No. No, it couldn't be.

'Am telling ya, boy. Am gunna smash ya skull in.'

Natalya fought her way through the crowd.

'Nathan!' she heard someone squeak. It was *Mouse Girl*. Maybe she did care after all? 'This is so exciting,' she told a friend. There again, maybe not.

Dogman lashed out with the metal bar. Nathan made a desperate leap onto a batten. It swung with his weight and he nearly fell off. He gripped onto its rigging for life.

'Nathan!' cried Natalya. How could she help him?

Dogman glared down at Nathan from the railing. He then turned back along the catwalk. Where was he going? Had he given up? Natalya froze. He was heading for the pin rail.

'Nathan, get off. Nathan, do you hear me? He's going to drop the batten.'

But the pickpocket literally had nowhere to go.

There was blood on his brow and panic on his face.

Natalya ploughed back into the crowd, but they shoved against her, laughing in her face. She dropped to her knees and tried to crawl between them. She heard the sandbags on the pin rail fly out. There was an almighty bang as the batten hit the stage. She felt a sickening dread.

Her breathing on hold, she returned to the stage. He couldn't be dead. He couldn't be. She found him lying there, amongst the shattered pieces. To her relief, she heard him groan. She ran towards him; he cowered back. And then he saw it was her.

'What kept ya?' he managed.

'I was brushing my hair. Nathan, what has he done to you?'

'My ribs... I think he's bust my ribs.'

'And now I'm gunna crush yer skull.'

She turned to block the stagehand's path.

'Leave him be.'

'Get out of my way, girl!'

She eyed the bar in his hand.

'Natalya, get yerself out of here,' gasped Nathan.

'What? And leave you to the likes of him? Like you said, you'd do the same for me.'

There was a pricking in her eyes and a pain in her fingers. The *beast* was rising, and God help Gerard Dogman. He raised the bar; she poised herself to strike.

A gunshot ripped the air.

'Get back to your rooms. All of you!'

It was Ella, wielding a pocket-sized gun. The crowd dispersed in seconds. Ella glared at the Senior Stagehand.

'Problem with your staff, Mr Dogman?'

'A good beating is all they understand.'

'Oh, I agree entirely, but I think I can handle things from here.'

He glared at her, made a scowl, and trudged his way off stage. Natalya and Nathan watched him go. He glared back at them. This wasn't over yet.

Ella approached with a sullen frown.

'Someone needs more sleep. Your eyes, *Natasha* dear, they're bloodshot. As for you, Mr Croft, what kind of man hides behind a girl?'

'He didn't hide. I stood in his way.'

'Oh? It seems I'm going to have to watch you. Your hands, Nathaniel, do they still work?'

'Yeah. I'm just not sure about me legs.'

Natalya felt a sudden panic.

Oh no, she thought. *She's going to throw him out.*

Just like she had with that boy who sprained his ankle.

'I can cover his chores till he's better.'

Ella stared at her, eyes bright blue.

'Why? Good at picking pockets, are you? What

happens when Dogman swings a bar at you?'

'I can handle Mr Dogman.'

'Can you now? You look like a feather would blow you down. Okay, Mr Croft, the girl's bought you a lifeline. But you're on borrowed time; you're losing me money.'

She looked across at a musician in the pits, messing around with some music.

'Hey, you, get yourself up here and give the girl a hand. Mr Croft's room is on the third floor. He dies getting up there, I'm going to blame you.'

***

Natalya anxiously paced the hallway. What was she going to do if he died? The doctor had only been in there five minutes and already she was finding the wait unbearable.

She glanced out the window. Was that a cigarette light? She narrowed her eyes, trying to focus. The moonlight caught the smoker's face. The rage inside her flared.

Dogman! She deemed all life to be sacred, but if anything happened to Nathan... She turned and paced the hallway again. Her anger grew with every stride.

The next she knew she was running down the stairs, her eyes pricking, her fingers bleeding claws. She burst into the alley with her fangs stabbing her tongue.

Dogman looked her way and gave a mocking grin.

'What? Come to tell me he's dead? Best news I've 'ad all year.'

She raged at him, snarling like some *wild-thing*. She lashed out with her claws and his blood spattered the wall.

Startled, Dogman stumbled backwards, his cheek half hanging off his face. She lashed out again and left clawmarks in his chest. He took a swing back. She sank her teeth into his arm.

Salty blood swam into her mouth, spilling over her lips and down her chin. It tasted warm and thick and disgusting and it made her stomach churn. She turned aside and spat blood onto the cobbles. Horrified, Dogman turned and ran.

She should have let him go, but she couldn't. The *beast* urged her on and she gave pursuit. She ripped her fingers through the muscles in his legs. He fell onto his knees with a cry. He tried to crawl. She pulled back his head and curled her claws around his throat.

'No more,' he begged.

'You hurt my friend.'

'Natasha! No!'

It was her father's voice. Or rather, the voice inside her head; the one that was her conscience. She tightened her claws only further.

'Natasha!!'

She let Dogman go. He groaned and slumped to the ground. She nervously gazed at her blood-soaked hands. She turned and fled back inside.

Heart pounding, she rushed to the washroom and tried to scrub the blood from her skin. She quickly returned to the third-floor hallway. The doctor had still to leave Nathan's room.

She dared to gaze out the window. Dogman was still in the alley, hunched over. What had she done? What had she become? She ran a trembling hand back through her hair. She glanced at her dress and saw patches of red. She swallowed. What if she'd actually killed him?

'Looks like **Deadman's** living up to his name.'

She almost jumped out of her skin. Ella was peering over her shoulder. She'd never even heard her approach.

'Did you see what happened, *Sweetheart?*'

Natalya shook her head.

'Good. Let's keep it that way, shall we?'

'I think he might be dead.'

'Oh, I didn't pay enough for them to kill him. Oops! Slip of the tongue, there. Sorry. But I hate it when people get ideas of grandeur and interfere with my earnings?'

What, so she'd arranged for Dogman to be beaten? Said the girl who'd probably just murdered the man.

But if nothing else, it confirmed one thing: Ella was not to be messed with.

'How's Nathan?' She dreaded the answer.

'He'll live, but he'll be out of action for weeks.'

Her heart gave a massive sigh of relief. He was going to be all right. She gave thanks to God.

'I'm holding you to your promise, though, *Sweetheart*. I expect you to cover his chores till he's better. And should the *mutton shunters* come a-knocking…, well, you know nothing about *Deadman*. Understand?'

Natalya nodded; Ella smiled and flounced off through the door and downstairs. Alone, Natalya gazed back through the window. Dogman was now staggering away.

He was alive. Somehow she hadn't killed him. And yet, the guilt hung around her like a chain. Once more, the *beast* had proven itself wild, and it left her terrified.

Chapter 9
A Royal Gift

For the next five weeks, Natalya turned nurse maid, which earned her all sorts of names from the girls. *Harlot. Wagtail. Dollymop.* Was the *evening entertainment* really calling her a *whore?*

Nathan didn't get much love, either. *If that was us, we'd have been out on the streets.* It didn't help that with Dogman gone, the others had to pick up the stagehand's work.

Natalya's life was now one of routine, with barely a moment to herself. She'd rise, check on Nathan, swallow down some breakfast, clean out the rubbish, safety-check the rigging. Work Nathan's chores, attend rehearsals, gulp down some dinner, check on Nathan again. Work the evening show, escort the gentlemen to their harlots, collapse into bed and repeat. At least it made the days fly by, and slowly, Nathan's injuries improved.

Then, one day, as she was going about her duties, she saw a dance girl's dress draped across a chair. She abandoned her rubbish bag, checked to see she was alone, picked up the dress and tried it against her. The fabric swished in movement with her body. She imagined herself as a Lady from her book. Of course, the style was far too salacious, but it was still an improvement on her own threadbare dress.

'Oi, get yer grubby little mitts off me costume.'

The dance girl snatched the dress from her hands. Natalya childishly stuck out her tongue and hurried off outside with the rubbish. Not that she was scared of the girl, she was scared of awakening the *beast inside*. Since Dogman, she'd managed to keep it at bay, and she saw no point in tempting its return.

Dumping the rubbish bag into the alley she looked to the cobbles still stained with Dogman's blood. His fate remained a mystery, even to Ella, and Natalya found herself checking the obituaries in the hope of never seeing his name. It helped to ease her guilty conscience, even if she knew he'd never really be mentioned in the likes of the national papers.

Turning, she noticed someone up the alley, knelt

with their head stuck between the rubbish bags. Curious, she made her way towards them. They looked up sharply, sensing her presence.

'Nathan? Nathan, what are you doing?'

'Me? Nowt. Don't know what ya mean?'

He scrambled to his feet, looking guilty, and trying to hide a grimace of pain. Any quick movement still caused him discomfort. He kept his hands tucked behind his back.

'What are you hiding?'

'Nothing. See.'

He held out his hands; they were empty. Unconvinced, she peered down between the rubbish. Sat, looking back, was a big furry rat.

'Nathan, how on earth could you? What's the poor rat ever done to you?'

'Nowt,' he said. 'I always feed the rats.'

'Well that's just cruel.' She looked at him, confused. 'Feed them? You mean… you're not trying to kill it?'

'Course not. Who do ya think I am? Cinders? She still blames 'em for the *Great Plague of London*. Ya'd have thought she might have forgiven 'em by now.'

He retrieved the apple he'd stuffed down his pants and, biting off a piece, threw it to the rat. The rat scurried forward and snatched it up, its teeth slicing through the juicy flesh. Nathan sat down against the opposite wall and retrieved something from his jacket pocket.

'Here. Fer you? Don't worry, I bought it.'

'With some of the money you stole, no doubt.'

'I never did get yer principles on stealing.'

'If it's needed to survive, then it doesn't count.'

She held out her hand and he dropped *the something* in it. Her eyes widened; she almost squealed.

'Oh, Nathan. Nathan. It's a chocolate cream bar. How on earth did you know?'

'How did I know? Ya mention the things every time yer stomach groans.'

She sat down beside him, her face beaming. She bit off a piece, enjoying its crunch. The chocolate melted onto her tongue. She felt like she was in heaven.

'A dunt spze ud luk a peeze?'

'Ya might as well have said that in Russian.'

She laughed and swallowed the chocolate down. Lord, how she'd missed her cream bars.

'I don't suppose you'd like a piece?'

'Nah, I'll stick with me apple.'

He took a bite and tossed the rest to the rat. It snatched it up and scurried away.

'And he didn't even say goodbye.'

Natalya gobbled down another piece of chocolate.

'The boys back home used to think I was a *witch*.'

'Is that why I saw a broomstick by yer bed.'

'Ha! Maybe I should loan it to Ella?'

'Nah, she has a collection of her own.'

She laughed, spitting chocolate down herself. She tried to wipe it off. She thought for a moment, then skewed her mouth. There was a question she'd been meaning to ask him for weeks.

'Do you ever wonder why I can do certain... *things?*'

'None of my business, really. Do you know why ya can do certain things?'

She shook her head.

'Good job I didn't ask then.'

'But doesn't it scare you?'

'Should it? Question is, does it scare you?'

She nodded. 'I sometimes feel out of control.'

'Good job Dogman took off when he did then, or he might have come to regret it.'

There was sudden activity out on the street, and a distinguished carriage passed the end of the alley.

'The prince!' cried Natalya.

'There aint no prince.' He pondered a moment. 'Let's go and see.'

They leapt to their feet – well, she did anyway; he clambered up at a slower pace. Soon she was at the corner wall, Nathan catching her up minutes later. They peered out onto the cobbled road. The carriage had stopped outside CINDERS.

'I told you there was a prince,' said Natalya.

'We haven't seen who's in it yet.'

A footman opened the carriage door and a distinguished gentleman stepped down from inside. He was wearing what might be Indian attire, his tunic embroidered with golden thread.

'Didn't I say?' said Natalya. 'Come on, let's go inside.'

'Blimey,' gasped Nathan. 'I've only just got here.'

She giggled and took off back down the alley.

By the time they reached the lounge interior, an audience had gathered around its main entrance. Any attempt to push through proved futile, so they dropped to their knees and started to crawl. She heard Nathan groan as somebody kicked him in the ribs, but he soldiered on nonetheless. They finally managed to make it to the front and they sat cross-legged like children. Natalya felt so excited.

'I told you,' she beamed.

'All right. Don't rub it in.'

Ella was stood centre-stage. She was wearing a bustled, white-ribbed gown that was fit for any fairy-tale princess. If no one else was expecting the prince, Ella certainly was.

A footman entered the doorway.

'Ladies and Gentlemen, His Royal Highness, the *Prince Shah Ming.*'

The prince entered the room, followed by several

more footmen. He appeared late twenties, with short-trimmed hair and a carefully shaped moustache. Even for royalty, he was immaculately groomed and definitely handsome.

Ella placed her palms together and gave a dignified bow.

'Welcome to CINDERS, *Your Royal Highness.*'

'Believe me, the pleasure is all mine. It is far too long since I've set eyes on your beauty. I trust you are well, *Lady Eleanor Jane Henry?*'

The use of her real name set whispers flowing, but Natalya was more intrigued by the prince. His English was perfect, almost without accent. It caught her as rather odd. Her father had lived in England for eighteen years, and still sounded Russian till the day that he died.

The prince clapped his hands and a footman stepped forward, carrying a draped, domed case. Ella's bosom heaved in anticipation. Natalya had never seen her so tense.

Shah Ming slid off the cover.

Beneath was an orchid of pure beauty, its petals so pure, so translucent, that they were hardly visible at all. The slightest of movement reflected light off their surface, like quicksilver traversing a mirror's glass. There was a hue of pastoral pink amongst their weave, contrasted against a stalk of green. Ella looked totally mesmerised, as did everyone else.

'They call it a *Glass Slipper* orchid,' said Shah Ming. 'To see it, they say, is to touch life itself.'

'It's the most beautiful thing I've even seen.'

'Which is also what she says when she looks in the mirror.'

Natalya elbowed Nathan in the arm and tried her best not to giggle.

HSSSS!!!!!

She froze. What was that? It reminded her of the *dream* from the market. She glanced about; no one else seemed to hear it, including Nathan beside her.

HSSSSSSSSSSS!!!!!!

This time there was no denying it, even her freckles were starting to burn. She felt herself tense, her fear heightening. She scanned the room again.

The *veil of grey* from when Craven was killed started to smother the room. It oozed through the wallpaper, it swam across the carpet, stealing the colour of everything it touched. The cogs of Natalya's heart turned faster, and still no one seemed aware. The *grey* enveloped the Glass Slipper orchid and revealed it as *something else*.

The translucent petals were gone now, as were the delicate hues of pink. In their place was a cluster of vines that were tipped with thorns of bloated red. They emanated from a putrid core that breathed amongst a weave of nested roots. It had no visible eyes or face, and yet, Natalya could sense its glare. She leapt to her feet in horror.

'Run. Nathan. Everyone. Run!'

The vines lashed out and ripped their thorns through her arm. She gasped, blood dripping from her skin to the floor. Everyone looked at her as if she was insane. Ella's glare was especially volcanic, whilst Shah Ming merely seemed to smile. The only one who seemed concerned was Nathan. The vines lashed out again.

Natalya turned and ploughed into the crowd. They pushed her back, sneering at her panic.

'Natalya!'

It was Nathan, but she had to get away. She somehow managed to force her way through.

The shadow of the vines overtook her, hunting her down like a pit of venomous snakes. She made it to the stageside doors and burst through. She crumpled to her knees.

Her skin, it felt on fire. The cut to her arm was deep. And imbedded in its flesh was the remnant of a thorn, a thick pus oozing from its shell.

Gritting her teeth, she took a deep breath and pushed her fingers into the wound. She tried to grab the thorn, but it suddenly sprouted tendrils that dug into her flesh.

Someone burst through the stage door after her.

'Natalya, what is it? What's wrong?'

'Nathan? Oh, Nathan. Look what it's done.'

But instead of seeing horror on his face, all she saw was confusion.

'Natalya, I can't see anything.'

She grabbed him by the collar and drew him close.

'Then you're not looking hard enough. Look again. Don't tell me that I'm lying.'

'I'm not. I just can't see anything, is all.'

She turned and ran towards the alley door.

'Wait. I didn't say I didn't believe you.'

'No, go away. Just leave me alone.'

She burst outside, confused and panicked, unsure of what to do. With a chill down her spine, she fled towards the street, her only thought being one of escape.

***

Natalya staggered along the pavement, a fevered sweat beading her brow. She felt like the world was a far-off land, the street just herself and the pavement she walked on.

The cut to her arm felt inflamed; a gangrenous green eating up her skin. It stank of foulness and made her want to vomit. She could feel its poison seeping through her veins.

Where was the *beast* when she needed it most? And yet, it was her who'd wished it away. Her energy waning, she slumped against a wall, sliding down its brick onto the pavement. Blurred visions stepped over her person; no one cared if she lived or died.

She fingered at the knots of her bracelet, but neither prayer nor God could help her now.

***

Footsteps. She could hear footsteps. She was in someone's arms, being carried. Their breathing was short, heavy, laboured, their heart pounding fast against their chest.

'Not far now,' she heard him say.

Nathan. Why was she not surprised?

'Where are we going?'

'Home.'

'The wood?'

'No. Back home. To CINDERS.'

Horror surged its way through her body. She fought her way out of his arms. She glanced around, but it was already too late. They were back in the alley outside CINDERS.

'No. Why have you brought me here? What in the world were you thinking?'

'It's the only place in London there's a doctor every night. Natalya, ya have a fever.'

'No, don't you see? A doctor can't cure me. I was cursed before I came and I'm twice as cursed now.'

She turned to run; he grabbed her arm. She turned on

him savagely, a wildness in her eyes.

'Let me go.'

'I'll not give up on ya.'

'Only an idiot wouldn't.'

'Well I think we've both established that I am.'

'Nathan, you have to let me… Argh!'

She crumpled to her knees, clutching at her arm. It was black. Swollen. Weeping pus. The veins across her chest were now painted purple, and she could feel the infection pulsing up her throat.

The *beast,* long absent, raged forth from its lair, confronting the contagion like some monster of damnation. Her stomach heaved, sick choking up her throat, her body becoming the battlefield for war. Her eyes pricked and her nails became claws, her canine's elongating into fangs. And with the *beast's* traits came its wildness and aggression, wrestling away her self-control.

'Go,' she cried. 'I can't hold it back.'

To Nathan's credit, he stood his ground.

'Ya think I'm scared?'

She curled her lip and snarled.

'Yeah, okay. Maybe just a little.'

'I was a fool to think we could ever be friends.'

'Yer a fool if ya think that we can't be.'

The stageside door burst open, and out stormed Ella, anger on her face. Maybe she'd seen them from the third-floor window? Perhaps she'd turned into a psychic, now? She strode towards them, eyes ablaze, and ignorant to Natalya's transformation.

'How dare you mess up my Royal Engagement?'

'Ella...'

'Shut up! It's between me and *her*.'

She grabbed Natalya's arm and twisted it backwards. Natalya lashed out blindly, slicing her claws through Ella's face.

'Argh!'

Ella fell aside, clutching at her cheek. Blood seeped its way between her fingers. She gazed at it in horror.

'My face. What have you done to my face? What have you done to my beautiful face?'

Nathan grabbed Natalya's hand.

'Come on! We have to go. Now!'

He dragged her after him up the alley and out onto the street. She could hear him gasping, drawing breath through gritted teeth. He paused a moment to capture his breath.

She wasn't sure why, but she looked to the entrance, where a man in black had just dismounted from his horse. He looked towards them and narrowed his eyes. Panic overwhelmed her.

It was *him! Craven! The Witchfinder General.* The man who'd slaughtered her parents. But she'd seen him die. How could he be here? She'd seen the *darkness* eat away his body.

'No!' she screamed. 'I killed you.'

'What?' said Nathan, glancing back.

The world spun about her, voices and images flashing through her mind.

A hand grasped her arm. Hysteria kicked in. She grabbed her attacker and hurled them across the street. They slammed into the wheel of a parked carriage and dropped to the cobbles, unmoving. This time she'd do what she should have done then. Tear out his windpipe and sever his head.

'Wolfcaine.'

The name stopped her in her tracks, but this time it wasn't the voice of *the girl*. She looked to the witch hunter striding towards her. But if that was Craven, who...? Horror flooded her eyes.

'Nathan? No. What have I done? Oh, my Lord, what have I done?'

She took a step forward, paused, took another. She paused again; she dare go no further. He was lying in the road, his body broken. Still. Motionless. Dead!

'NOOoooooo!'

She took to her heels and ran, no sense of place or direction in her mind. All she knew was she had to get away. She'd just killed her only friend in the world.

People, horses, carriages flashed her by, reality tripping on the edge of her subconscious. Sweat oozed from her skin, tears streamed down her face, their saltiness wetting her lips.

Her lungs screaming out, she slowed to a halt, crouching over, gasping for breath. She could hear gulls. The gentle swish of water. She blinked, trying to clear her streaming tears. She resorted to wiping them on her sleeve, and still her vision blurred.

Exhausted, she slowly edged forward, the battle within between the *beast* and the infection stealing what little remained of her strength. The cobbles beneath her feet turned to wood. For the split of a second her vision cleared.

She was stood on some platform overlooking the Thames. The tide was out, marooning boats in its silt. She fingered her bracelet, praying for a miracle, hoping she'd soon wake up in bed. But nothing changed. This wasn't some nightmare. This was the world as it stood.

Badum. Badum.

The sound of thunder. No, not thunder; horse hooves. She turned to see the blur of a stallion and the black-garbed rider sitting on its back.

'*Wolfcaine.*'

Natalya took a step backwards, lost her footing and fell.

Chapter 10
The General's Asylum

10th August, 1891
Six weeks later…
Natalya opened her eyes, the ceiling and walls about her grey. Her nose twitched, the air stagnant, and poisoned further by a familiar smell.

She turned her head, following her nose to the flowers that soaked up the water in the vase. Their tubular pinkness was a thing of beauty, and unmistakably *foxglove*.

The last thing she remembered she was falling, trying to escape from… she couldn't think who? She strained her brain, searching its library. Panic gripped her mind. *Craven!*

She tried to sit, but couldn't. She was strapped to a bed in what looked like a cell. She called on the *beast*; it was slow to respond, but once awake, it was frenzied.

Her muscles tightening, she strained against her bonds. There was a ripping sound as their stitches tore apart. She rolled from the bed and fell against the wall. It was as though she hadn't used her legs in weeks. She crossed to the small window in the door and curled her fingers around its bars. She peered through but could see little; it only made her panic grow.

She tugged, she strained, her breaths became grunts, her biceps stretching her skin. There was a groaning of metal, a sound of popping rivets, and the door ripped away in her hands. She flung it aside like some flimsy piece of wood.

Beyond the cell was an open space that led to more doors and more cells. Staff in white uniforms observed her with horror. A glass walled office was sat at one end. She felt like a rat trapped in a sewer. Her eyes fell on the only wooden door.

'Someone, fetch Doctor Schneider.'

Natalya fled towards the wooden door. To her surprise and relief it wasn't locked. She hurried through into a carpeted hallway.

She now found herself in some sort of large house, the hallway just one of a labyrinth of hallways. Each turn led to nowhere. Her anxiousness grew. She felt like she was running through a maze with no exit.

At last, she happened upon a foyer. Her eyes focused on the large, oak door. She made a run towards it, hoping for freedom. She was half way there when…

'Natalya?'

The voice came out of nowhere. She turned and clumsily tripped over her own feet. She fell against the sideboard and landed in a heap, ornaments raining around her.

'Natalya? Good Lord, it is you.'

Natalya looked to the woman on the staircase. Despite a foreign accent, her English was perfect. She looked early forties with tied-up hair. She might have stepped out of Natalya's novel. She seemed more surprised than scared.

Reminding herself she was trying to escape, Natalya scrambled back to her feet. She ran to the door and grappled with its doorknob. It finally turned and she fled outside.

She was *free*. No more hallways. No more cells. Just fresh air. The stones of the courtyard punched at her bare feet. She felt compelled to gaze back at her prison. It took her breath away.

The building resembled a stately manor, its castellated rooftop silhouetted by the moon. Its battlements were guarded by demonic-looking gargoyles, their claws tightly gripped around its ledges of stone. A wall-crawling plant decorated the brickwork, blending both storeys of the building into one.

'Natalya. Wait.'

It was the woman again, now accompanied by a man in a suit. He looked older than the woman; it could have been the beard. He drew a gun which he pointed Natalya's way. Natalya tensed, the *beast* rising up. The woman stepped between Natalya and the man.

'Sister....'

'Obadiah would not approve.'

'That thing comes near, I shoot.'

He meant it; Natalya could tell from his voice, and the *beast* demanded that she rip out his throat. But Natalya wasn't sure what she should do. The woman took a step nearer.

'Natalya, please, we mean you no harm.'

So that's why they had her locked up in a cell. She touched at her face, her freckles burning, her eyes drawn to the manor's walls. The *veil of grey* had returned to consume it, turning the gargoyles into creatures of flesh. They stretched their wings and took to the skies, hovering about her like vultures.

Natalya felt her consciousness slip and she crumpled to the ground.

***

Natalya fidgeted, restless in bed, perspiration seeping through her brow. She was asleep, and yet, her mind was awake, tormenting her soul with the past.

'Mama! Papa! Behind you!'

But they couldn't hear her above all the noise. Craven came riding his steed through the smoke. No. She had to save them.

She raged forward, speed on her side. But as she ran, her skirt grew longer. It tripped her up and she fell into the dirt. She tried to stand, but she was smothered by her clothes. She knelt there, helpless, the size of a child, as Craven rode forward and cut her parents down.

'NOOOoooooooooo!!!'

Natalya fought with the bedclothes. She rolled sideways and fell out of bed. She lay there, stunned and confused for a moment, struggling to separate reality from dream. She slowly sat up, the dust on her eyeballs forming patterns on the wall.

She appeared to be in a lady's bedroom, an army of scent bottles perched atop a dresser. There was a long-tilt mirror, a wardrobe, a washbowl. She struggled to her feet and splashed water on her face.

She still wasn't sure if she was dreaming or not. She crossed to the window and gazed out into the day. There was a landscape of grass, trees and a courtyard. She gasped. It all came flooding back. The cell. The woman. The man with the gun. She caught a glimpse of herself in the mirror. At least she looked the way she remembered. Another figure joined her in the glass.

'Natalya. You're awake.'

Natalya spun. It was the woman from last night.

'Stay away from me.'

'Hush now, child. You've nothing to fear, I promise.'

'Who are you?'

'My name is Gretl Schneider. My brother and I have been caring for you.'

'Caring for me? Why? Where is this?'

'An institute for the mentally ailed.'

'You think I'm insane?'

'No. Not at all.'

'Then why did you have me locked up in a cell?

The woman responded with a sympathetic smile. 'My brother can be… overcautious, sometimes.'

'Ah, I thought I heard voices.'

The brother in question now entered the room. His accent was thicker than his sister's, and his flow of speech more rigid.

'Keep away from me.'

He remained unperturbed.

'Fräulein, you owe me a sample of blood.'

He took a small box from inside his jacket pocket and removed a needle and syringe. Natalya eyed it with horror. The *beast* within her snarled.

'You tried to shoot me last night,' she said.

'I think you'll find I was protecting my sister.'

'Come near and I swear I'll tear you apart.'

'And now you know why I carry a gun.'

'Hush, brother, you're scaring the girl. Natalya, why would we harm you now? It's been six weeks since we pulled you from the Thames. The infection that ailed you..., we thought that you might die.'

Six weeks? Infection? Natalya's brain felt overwhelmed. She found herself suddenly clutching at her arm. Panicking, she made a dash for the door. To her surprise, no one tried to stop her.

Now on the landing, she headed for the stairs, following their descent into the foyer. For the second time she hurried towards the front door. It opened from the other side.

Through its frame stepped a man garbed in black, a large-brimmed hat shadowing his face. He looked at her with narrowed eyes. It was him. Craven! The Witchfinder General.

'No!' she cried.

'So, it's true,' he said. 'The *wolfcaine* has returned.'

The *beast* within her leapt from its lair, pricking her eyes, lengthening her claws. She hated this man, but she also feared him. He went for his sword; she went for his throat. He blocked her attack and pushed her back. He raised a foot and kicked her in the chest. She fell, her ribs screaming with pain, her lungs gulping down air.

'Pathetic,' he snarled.

He sounded disappointed, glowering down from his square-jawed face. She surrendered her full control to the *beast*, something she'd sworn she'd never do again.

Her feeble limbs felt suddenly strong. She sprang at her opponent; sank her teeth into his arm. His face gnarled up, absorbing the pain. Blood moistened her tongue, choking up her throat. She still had her teeth dug into his flesh when he punched her in the face.

Natalya fell, her nose sprouting blood, her eyes smarting with pain. The *beast* commanded her back onto her feet. The hilt of a sword struck her hard across the jaw.

More blood, this time from her mouth. The *beast* was strong, but her mind was running scared. Her chest was burning, her nose felt crushed, and her jaw felt like it had been broken into pieces.

'Come on,' he goaded. 'Is that all you've got?'

Get up, urged the *beast*. But the world was spinning. Her vision was blurred and her legs were shaking. She threw all she had into one last assault. She struck out blindly; felt his skin beneath her nails, and heard him fall to the ground.

The nuzzle of a gun pressed up against her temple.

'I think that's far enough, Fräulein.'

'Please do as my brother says.'

Natalya looked at Gretl in confusion. She'd seemed so nice. What was she saying?

'You're on his side? He's a witch hunter. Evil.'

'Obadiah is my husband.'

'Your husband?'

Those blows must have damaged her ears. She looked to the open door and fled.

The freshness of the day embraced her, but still her mind felt confused. She felt sick, dizzy; her stomach churned and she threw up against the wall of the house. She wiped a drool of vomit from her lips and gazed at her arm and its perfect skin.

More memories came flooding back. The gangrenous infection that ate up her flesh. The cut to her arm. The Glass Slipper orchid. She gasped, her mind about to implode.

She glanced behind, expecting to be followed. To her relief, there was no one there. She touched at her face and flinched with the pain, her nose tender and her lips swollen up.

The snorting of a horse drew her attention and she followed her ears to the stables. The straw on the floor stuck to her bare feet, the horses casually glancing her way.

Here was her opportunity to escape, but she'd never ridden a horse before. Still, could it really be that hard?

The *beast* within gave an uninvited growl.

The horses suddenly looked on edge. The nearest rose up, kicking out with its hooves. She tried to calm it, to work her way around, but it kicked out again, threatening to smash in her skull.

'Your lack of self-control betrays you. It senses the *beast* within.'

She spun to face the Witchfinder General. Her primal traits returned.

Without hesitation, she raged forward. She grabbed him by the throat and pinned him back against the wall. To her surprise, he put up no resistance. He simply glared back with those black, beady eyes.

'Yes. Look at me. Look at me,' he growled. 'Use your eyes, not the image in your mind.'

He had stubble, black hair, and well-fed cheeks, his forehead clear of any pagan symbol. This wasn't *him*. This wasn't *Craven*. She'd been running from a phantom. She'd been fooled by her own mind.

'Not easy to kill in cold blood, is it?' His voice was unsettlingly calm.

'You forget, I nearly just killed you back there.'

'You should have killed me ten times by then. My attack was open. Purposely clumsy. If the fight had been real, you would have been dead.'

'You were testing me?'

'Yes. And you failed.'

'I don't understand. You're a witch hunter; like them.'

He neared his face to hers.

'Open your mind, girl. Those witch hunters weren't real. And despite what you think, I'm not of their kind.'

'Weren't real? Those men... they murdered my parents.'

'Yes, they did. They were there to kill you.'

'Me? Why?'

'Because of what you are.'

She eased her grip, letting him down. *Don't*, yelled the *beast*, but she got the impression he could break free any time he wanted.

'But your clothes... You look like them.'

'And you look like a girl.'

'I am.'

'Are you? Or are you something else?'

She turned away; perhaps unwisely. But there was so much going on in her head. She needed to escape. She needed time to think. It didn't help that her brain was pounding.

'What do you want from me?'

'The *beast* within.'

'So there is a monster inside me?'

The barn door creaked and they looked to see Gretl. Had she been listening, or had she just arrived?

'Obadiah, I think she's had enough. Let her eat,

settle in, and then you can talk.'

He glanced at Natalya, then back at his wife. He grimaced and gave a stiff, reluctant nod.

'Very well. She going nowhere. I have business in London. We'll speak on my return.'

He trudged from the barn; now Natalya could escape. She glanced at the horse. It raised its hoof in warning.

Maybe, for now, she should just play along. There was so much she needed to learn; understand. Maybe this place could offer some answers. Gretl placed a shawl around her shoulders.

'Come on, my dear. You'll feel much better once you've had something to eat.'

'I'm not hungry.'

'You ought to be. Were it not for the *beast*, you'd have wasted away.'

'Gretl, why are you married to a *witch hunter?*'

'He's not a *witch hunter*, dear. Obadiah Bleddin is many things, but the man you think he is, isn't one of them.

Chapter 11
A Taste of Magic

Natalya stared at the plate of food, her stomach begging her to eat it. The smell of bacon hypnotised her senses, its leanness laid between an egg and fried bread. But she trusted no one: lady or cook. She glanced at them whispering near the pantry door.

The kitchen was bigger than any she'd known; it was even bigger than her parents' home. The table alone could seat up to twelve, whilst pots and pans adorned every shelf. The stove was huge, its blackened carcass offset by a series of silver, dangling ladles.

She honed her ears in on their voices, expecting to hear some heinous plan. But instead, she was enlightened with the menu for dinner. Her stomach gave a grumble.

Gretl joined her at the table.

'Come on, Natalya. Eat up now. You don't want it getting cold.'

'Aren't you having any?'

'I ate earlier. Come on. Cook made that especially.'

Natalya sliced up the rasher of bacon. She raised a piece to her mouth. She paused, eyeing it with suspicion. Gretl took the fork from her and ate the meat down. She handed back the fork.

'There. Now we can both die together.'

Natalya grinned and tucked into the food. She caught her swollen lip; it made her wince. But nothing was going to stop her feeding her stomach. The flavours on her tongue were indescribable, and she cleared the plate in minutes. She felt just a teensy bit ill.

'Thank you,' she said. 'That was delicious.'

'You're welcome, me dear,' said the cook.

'Right,' said Gretl, 'let's get you upstairs; washed, dressed, and then down to see Hansel. He can take a look at that nose.'

Natalya stood, feeling bloated. It drew all the energy away from her feet. She followed Gretl out of the kitchen. Oh Lord, she had to mount a flight of stairs.

They met a man coming down; sixties, wearing a tail suit.

'Soames, I'd like you to meet Natalya. She'll be

staying with us for a while. Natalya, this is our butler, Soames. He's been a member of the family for years.'

'Pleased to meet you, Mr Soames.'

Natalya held out her hand. He hesitated, then awkwardly shook it. He glanced aside at Gretl.

'She's new,' said Gretl. 'She doesn't know the rules.'

Rules? Natalya should have known better. You never shook the servants' hands. At least, that's how it read in her novel.

'Sorry, Mr Soames.'

'Don't worry, Miss. If you need anything, just give me a call.'

He carried on his way to the kitchen. They resumed their walk up the stairs.

'Have you ever worn a corset, Natalya?'

'No. Just this.' She plucked at her stay.

'Oh, of course. Silly me. I think you're in for a treat.'

***

A treat? Who was she trying to fool? No one would willingly wear one of these? The bone in the fabric was like a second ribcage, squeezing the life from Natalya's lungs. And unlike her stay, it tied at the back. How was she supposed to get the thing off?

'How does it feel?' said Gretl.

'Tight.'

'I'm sure you'll be fine once your breakfast has settled.'

Well her breakfast might settle, but her bosom certainly wouldn't, her breasts pushed inwards and upwards in a way Natalya never thought possible. Add knee-high stockings, a camisole and petticoats, and she wasn't sure the dress would ever fit.

It was a body-hugging number, bronze with gold thread, which changed its appearance depending on the light. At last, Natalya felt like a lady, although the high-rise collar irritated her throat.

The look was completed with a pair of low-heeled boots. They made her wobble; she felt like she was drunk. What she wouldn't give for her old shoes back, or even no shoes at all.

Clinging onto the banister for life, she followed Gretl downstairs. It wasn't just the boots that proved an issue; it was her first time in a dress that touched the floor. As they reached the foyer, she tripped over the hem. Gretl grabbed her arm.

'Don't worry, you'll be running before you know it.'

'I'll be lying face down in the dirt, you mean.'

'You look lovely.'

'Even with the nose?'

'The swelling adds a little colour to your cheeks.'

Yes, she liked Gretl a lot; except that she was

married to *him*.

A door opened further down the hall and Hansel Schneider stepped out.

'Ah, Fräulein. Excellent timing. You owe me a sample of blood, do you not?'

'Her nose needs looking at, too,' said Gretl.

He gave it a quick inspection.

'Hmm. It isn't broken. I'm so glad your husband didn't mean her any harm.' There was more than a little sarcasm in his voice, sprinkled with resent. 'Don't worry, Fräulein, the swelling will ease. Walk with me, if you please.'

He set off down the hallway. Natalya looked to Gretl.

'Aren't you coming?'

'Don't worry, you'll be fine. My brother's a doctor, you know.'

Yes, a doctor who carried a gun. She felt her apprehension grow. She swallowed and followed after him, occasionally touching at the walls for balance. They came to a familiar brown wooden door. She felt a pang of dread.

'Come along.'

He had an air about him that demanded unquestioned obedience. He was also the type who'd probably refuse to dance with any girl at a ball.

Warily, she entered after him, the *beast* on alert

should she need a quick escape. The medical staff eyed her with suspicion, the doorframe of her cell still hanging from the wall. The whole place sent a shiver down her spine, and she couldn't wait to be out.

'It's like being back home in the village,' she said. 'No one trusted me there, either.'

'Trust must be earned, dear Fräulein.'

'Is that why you had me locked up in a cell?'

He raised an eyebrow and smiled thinly. 'This way, if you'd be so kind.'

She followed him towards the office, passing by a wall pinned with scribblings and sketches. Some were incomprehensible, others showed promise; pictures of monsters and demons and men. She stopped to take a closer look. Hansel backtracked beside her.

'We encourage the patients to draw what they fear. The demons that haunt their minds. We find it helps build familiarity, and through association, thus weakens the dread.'

'I'm sorry, but isn't that you?'

She struggled to hold a giggle. On the wall was a caricatured sketch of a man with a scalpel and googly eyes. He was drooling from a lopsided mouth and sporting a pointed beard.

'Hmm. Gretl finds it amusing, too.'

'If it's monsters you're after, you ought to add me.'

'There are far worse monsters than those with claws.

Now then, shall we proceed?'

She watched as he walked away. What did he mean by that? She followed after him and was soon standing inside the office doorway.

It was a spacious room – if you took out the workbench – its shelving stocked with medical equipment and labelled, coloured bottles. Strange-looking jackets were hung against the wall, their sleeve-ends bound with thick, brown straps. They looked like some sort of torture device. Natalya gave a shiver.

'Close the door and take a seat. This won't take very long.'

She did the first but not the second; she was still wary of everyone. Hansel turned to her with a screw mechanism and a threaded, hanging strap.

'What's that?' she said.

'A *tourniquet*. It will stem the flow of blood through your arm.'

'You want to stem the flow of my blood?'

'It's not as though it's around your neck.'

Was that an attempt at humour? She still didn't move an inch. He sighed.

'We need to make sure the infection is gone, and only your blood can tell us that. Now, will you please take a seat on the chair? It will only take a few minutes.'

A flash of light blinked through the skylight,

followed by a crash of thunder. It disturbed the patients; they started to scream. Natalya covered her ears with her hands.

'Argh!' she cried. 'I can hear their torment.'

'It's the storm they fear; they can't comprehend it.'

'My head. It feels like they're here in the room.'

'You must learn to control your auditory perception.'

She wasn't sure exactly what that meant, but then his voice was starting to merge with the many. Her enhanced hearing had its uses, but now it felt like an unwelcome guest.

'Their screams… it's like they're being tortured.'

'Control it, girl. Shut them out.'

A nurse came rushing into the office. Hansel frowned and threw the tourniquet aside.

'Doctor Schneider….'

'I know. I'm needed.'

'It hurts,' cried Natalya.

'I told you, control it.'

'I can't.'

'Then get out. Go fetch my sister. You're of no use to me here.'

Natalya fled the office.

***

Natalya hurried down the hallway, glad to be back

inside the manor. The screams were fading, but their torment remained, gnawing at her mind. She turned a corner and bumped into the butler, almost knocking him over.

'Oh, Mr Soames, I'm sorry.'

'It's quite all right, Miss Natalya.'

'I need to find Gretl.'

'You'll find the mistress in her bedroom.'

'Thank you.'

'And don't forget to knock first.'

More lightning. More thunder. Natalya's heart was pounding as she reached Gretl's room. She paused to take a breath, gathered herself, and knocked against the door. No reply. She knocked again. She turned the knob and entered. She found Gretl sat at the dresser, a faint, charcoaled smell in the air.

'Gretl, your brother needs you downstairs.'

She caught a glimpse of Gretl's face in the mirror. Her beauty was gone, replaced instead by a patchwork quilt of scars. Natalya gasped; Gretl looked horrified. Natalya turned away.

'Didn't I say to always knock?'

'I did,' said Natalya.

The thunder crashed again.

'Damnable storm.'

Natalya looked back. She blinked to check her vision. Gretl's face was pure perfection. All those screams must have screwed up her mind. Rain coursed its way down the window as the storm became torrential.

'What was that about my brother?'

'He needs your help downstairs.'

'Then I must go.'

She grabbed up her shawl and hurried for the door. Natalya swallowed, feeling guilty. She felt like a naughty child. Gretl place a hand on the doorknob, paused, sighed, and slowly turned.

'Not easy, being different, is it? Being scared of yourself and the world about you. But Obadiah will help you through it, just as he helped me.'

Natalya gave her a sceptical look.

'Oh, I don't blame you not trusting him. He looks like one of *them*, doesn't he? But you have to see past the clothes he wears. Over there, in that drawer. Bring me the matches.'

Natalya crossed to fetch the box of matches whilst Gretl took a seat on the bed. As Natalya returned, the box flew out of her hand; she tried to grab it but it shot out of reach. She stared at it as it hovered in the air; she felt intrigued, excited and confused.

'Can you smell it?' said Gretl. 'You'd do well to take note. Magic emits a certain odour, don't you think?'

'You're a…?'

She hesitated.

'Go on. You can say it.'

'Witch? I mean, a *real* witch?'

'Well there are all kinds of witches, Natalya. I'm not sure how you'd define a *real* one? There are those who tell fortunes, those who mix potions, those who wield Nature, and those who cast spells. Potions are powerful, but need time to be nurtured, whilst spontaneous enchantments require skill and control. Beware the *white witch* who finds herself lured to the dark by a failure to master her craft.'

'Lured?'

'Magic isn't something you own. It's a gift. An offer. An invitation. Acceptance is entirely at a person's own risk, but never gorge on its nectar for long; there comes a point where it won't let you go.'

'I always thought having magic would be fun?'

'You just have to know when it's time to pull back. Drawing magic is easy, but resisting its temptation..? Now that is something else.'

Natalya thought a moment.

'Does *he* know you're a witch?'

'Who? Obadiah? Yes, of course he does, dear.'

'And a witch hunter would never marry a witch?'

'Take a seat. Let me tell you a tale.'

Natalya knelt before the floating matchbox.

'Now when my brother and I were young, we were

abandoned to fend for ourselves in the forest. We found our way here, to this little cottage, where a kind old lady took us in.'

The lid of the matchbox slid itself open and the matches flew up from inside. They swirled in a vortex, then formed a cottage, the matchbox acting as the chimneystack. Natalya observed with a childlike wonder, feeling a tingle of magic in the air.

'Now that lady was a good witch - a *white witch* - and before she died, she passed her magic on to me. It is a gift I have always cherished, but just like yours, one that's also been a curse.

'I was alone that day the *horsemen* came. Men like those who attacked your village. They charged me with witchcraft and condemned me to death. They tied me a stake and set fire to its woodpile.'

The matchstick house now broke apart, reforming as a stake and wooden surround. The stockpile ignited and it all went up in flame, its embers floating to the carpet.

'I wouldn't be here now if not for Obadiah. He literally dragged me from the flames. We'd met six months earlier. We'd fallen in love. He was half way to Dresden when a *dream* called him back.

'Of course, I survived, but I was horribly scarred. And yet, a year later, we were married. I wear this *masking* spell not at his request, but because of the comfort it brings to myself. Now, I must be off to my brother. He'll be wondering where I am.'

She made for the door again.

'Gretl.'

'Yes?'

'Thank you.'

'You're welcome.'

'What happened to the horsemen who attacked you?'

'They disappeared off the face of the earth. Just like the horsemen that attacked your village.'

'Disappeared?'

'Never to return. We don't know where they came from, who they were, or who had sent them.'

'Don't you find that strange?'

'What are you suggesting?'

'It just seems odd that we were both attacked by men who don't exist in this day and age.'

'Life is full of things that don't make sense. Sometimes you just have to learn to accept it.'

She left.

Alone, Natalya crossed to the window, rain still worming down its glass. Gretl's tale had touched her heart; it couldn't have been easy sharing such a thing. It even improved Bleddin's character, but she still couldn't understand his clothing. Why would someone who looked in their fifties dress like someone from a hundred years past?

She gazed around the bedroom, observing a photo of

Gretl and her brother sat upon the dresser. The drawer beneath was slightly open, and she couldn't resist a peek inside.

The contents were nothing special: a shawl, some gloves, a much fingered Bible. But protruding from the Bible was a piece of paper. It was probably private, but she felt inclined to look.

Her heart came to a momentary stop, her eyes narrowing with confusion. Drawn on the paper was a portrait of a young woman. Or to be more precise, a portrait of herself.

Once more she searched the library of her brain. She'd seen this before, but where? She sniffed at the paper, drawing up its smell of pencil. Why couldn't she remember?

She'd been at *the market*. Someone had *drawn her*. She could see them, and yet, she couldn't. She'd spoken to them. They'd spoken to her. But what had they said? Her mind was a mess.

She ran a frustrated hand through her hair, a taste of charcoal drying out her lips. Gretl had said that magic had a fragrance; maybe it had a taste, as well.

She could remember *the park*. She could remember CINDERS. The arrival of *the prince*. Being attacked by the *Glass Slipper*. But something was missing. *Someone* was missing. Like a shadow that lingered just out of sight.

She gasped. She rushed a hand to her mouth, images bombarding her brain with the past. Images of the boy she'd met at the market. The pickpocket she'd come to know as...

'Nathan!'

Tears blurred their way across her vision. She couldn't believe she'd forgotten. She traced the pencil-strokes with her fingers, reliving their friendship for a second time. She remembered it now. She remembered it all. Right down to the moment she *killed him*.

She froze, a chasm welling in her heart. They should have left her to die in the Thames. She'd killed her best friend. The boy she... *loved*. Lord, how she wished she hadn't remembered.

Hugging the sketch close to her heart, she hurried from the room.

Chapter 12
A Walk in the Wood

The storm saw out the afternoon, and it was early evening before Natalya stepped outside. The gargoyles watched her from their perches on the parapets, their eyes dripping rain like illusionary tears.

Once more, *Death* had become her personal stalker. Was the loss of her parents not enough? But this time she'd only herself to blame; was she not the one who'd killed him? Grabbed him; thrown him into that carriage. Who'd run away without trying to save him.

She gazed out across the manor grounds, the river below like a jewelled snake, glistening with a bellyful of current. The grass either side was full of feasting birds, the pounding of the rain having lured out all the worms.

The landscape was beautiful, and yet she felt nothing. All she felt was dead inside. Instead, she felt drawn to the darkness of the wood that sat to the east on the same hill as the house. She followed the shadow of a kestrel on the earth and made her way towards it.

Her feet sank into the muddy earth, water adding weight to the hem of her dress. As the wood grew in height, the sun slid from view, its presence restricted to a soft focal light that drew out the shadows from the trees. A million midges attacked her naked skin, every one wanting to nourish on her blood.

She stepped into the undergrowth, droplets of water still dripping from the trees. The twisted branches pointed out directions: this way into shadow, that way into light. She chose a path between the two, fungal slime adding to the pattern of her skirt.

For a slither of a second, she found herself distracted by the wonder of this unexplored *jungle*. But each pathway only led back to the haunting of her mind, and soon the tears were flowing afresh. Her butterflies vowed to never fly again. Everything she touched, she loved, she *killed.*

A rabbit came hopping out of the foliage, foraging for food beneath the many flowers. Drying her eyes, Natalya held a sniffle. The rabbit sensed her still, and swiftly hopped away.

'You need to learn to stand downwind.'

Natalya spun. It sounded like Bleddin. But she couldn't see him, and wasn't he in London? She spun again. Her mind was playing tricks.

He suddenly came charging out of the trees, sword drawn and ready to strike. Panicking, Natalya tripped over a tree root and ended up sat in the dirt. The tip of his blade came to rest against her throat. She stared at him, her breathing heavy.

'Pathetic. Call yourself a *wolfcaine*?'

'I don't even know what a *wolfcaine* is?'

'You're the heir to the *bloodline*.'

'The *bloodline* of what?'

'A bloodline I've sworn to protect with my life.'

He withdrew the sword and sheathed it.

More questions, more riddles. Couldn't anyone speak straight English, anymore? He scared her, and yet, had he chosen to kill her, she'd probably have thanked him for it.

'Never relinquish your guard,' he growled.

'You're supposed to be in London.'

'I thought you said you didn't trust me?'

'I don't.'

'Then why believe what I said?'

He had a point. He turned from her. She scrambled to her feet. She tidied herself the best she could. She took a deep breath and exhaled.

'Why did you say those *witch hunters* weren't real? The ones who attacked my village?'

'It's not important.'

'Not important? That monster – *Craven* - killed my parents.'

He spun sharply, making her jump.

'What did you say?'

'That monster killed my parents.'

'Not that. His name?'

'His men called him *Craven*.'

He glared at her with haunted eyes.

'Describe him. What did he look like?'

'Your height. Rounded jaw. He had a sunken face. And some sort of symbol burnt into his forehead. It looked like a star. A mark of the Devil.'

He slowly turned away.

'You know who he was?'

'I *knew* who he was. But Thomas Craven has been dead two hundred years. Someone's playing games with us, *wolfcaine*. Want to know what you are? Follow me.'

He set off through the trees. She felt like she had no choice but to follow. Everything was silent; everything was still. It was as though the wildlife had fled for pastures new. Bleddin paused at a ridge of trees where the ground broke swiftly away.

She watched him descend into the undergrowth,

using the exposed roots for support. She took a breath, gathered her nerve, and followed after him through the vegetation. She could feel the *beast* loiter inside, telling her not to trust him.

Twenty feet down and she found herself stood on a rocky plinth that jutted out from a cliff. It stretched across the valley like a giant tongue, salivating water from its moistened stone. Her every footstep echoed off its surface, just like the cobbles back in London. She glanced behind and found herself gaping into the mammoth mouth of a cave. She pulled a face at the fishy-type smell.

'The cave is not your concern,' said Bleddin.

She frowned and crossed to the edge of the plinth. Below was an oasis of woodland green, and what looked like patches of *foxglove?*

'It looks like the village back home,' she said, a sentimental murmur in her voice.

'I didn't bring you here to reminisce.'

'Then what did you bring me here for?'

Above, the sky was starting to pink as the sun began its daily retreat. Bleddin sat down on the ledge and crossed his legs; he reminded her of a meditating guru. For someone so big, it made him look awkward, and she tried her best not to giggle.

'The moths, they come for the foxglove,' he said. 'And *they*, in turn, for the moths.'

'They? You mean the *wolfcaines*?'

'No. You are the last of their kind. Sit, and I'll explain.'

She sat opposite and crossed her legs, too, expecting some tale of monsters and myth. But instead, he just sat there, as though waiting for something. She could feel her impatience grow.

Like a scraping of nails on a blackboard, a screeching noise suddenly rose in her ears. She winced, the screeching getting louder, closer, threatening to trip out her brain.

A cloud of blackness erupted from the cave, blocking out the sun as it screeched towards the moon. But the noise wasn't one voice, it was many, many thousands, and every single one was vying for attention.

Bats. The cave had been full of bats. And now they were embarking on their evening flight. Their cries were worse than the sanatorium's patients. Her head felt like it was going to explode.

She looked to Bleddin. His mouth was moving. He was actually telling his tale. She tried to listen; to lip-read, even, but she never picked up a word.

***

It was dark as they returned to the manor through the trees; even the bats had gone home to bed. Natalya followed at a moderate distance, avoiding any lecture, but not wanting to get lost.

'What did you hear when I spoke?' he'd asked.
'Bats.'
'Don't get clever with me, girl.'
'Nothing.'
'What? Not a single word?'
'I told you, all I heard was bats.'

Even now, her brain was pounding. She felt so drained, and she longed for her bed. At least the bats had occupied her mind, but now they were gone, her thoughts were back on Nathan.

As the woodland thinned, the lights from the manor broke their way through the trees. Soon they were treading across the stately lawn. Natalya quickened her pace, eager for home.

'We try again tomorrow,' he said. 'You must learn to focus your brain. My voice is but one. You must isolate the sound. Ignore what's unimportant.'

'I can't,' she said. 'What you're asking... is *hopeless*.'

'Is that what you said when your parents were killed?'

She came to a stop, the *beast* in an outrage. It demanded she spill his blood.

'How dare you bring my parents into this? I tried to warn them. I did everything I could.'

'And yet, it wasn't good enough, was it? Was that a

hopeless situation, too?'

There was a pricking in her eyes and a lengthening of her nails; she raged at him like some wild banshee. He turned in response to her bestial snarl. He went for his sword; she tore her claws through his chest.

She heard him groan, absorbing the pain. She lashed out again, ripping cloth and shredding skin. She was nothing but a girl, but the *beast* added ballast, and she body-rammed her six-foot opponent to the ground.

She threw herself on top of him; her hands engaged his throat. She'd make him regret his irresponsible words. She felt the hilt of his dagger uppercut her jaw and the world spun left as her body fell right. She tried to get up. He kicked her in the gut. She curled up on the grass, gasping for air.

He came to stand above her.

'The *beast* serves you well, but the talent is raw. It lacks direction; focus. You must channel your anger. Watch your opponent. Determine their point of weakness.'

Not for the first time, he'd played her for a fool. She spat blood from her mouth.

'Obadiah? Natalya? What on earth is going on?'

It was Gretl, come running from the house.

'Oh, my goodness. Obadiah, you're hurt.'

'It's nothing but a flesh wound. *Wolfcaine*, your training resumes tomorrow. There's much you have to learn.'

She watched him march off back towards the manor. Training? Was that what he called it? She managed to sit, her lungs on fire. Gretl gave a sombre smile.

'I know his methods can be cruel,' she said, 'but he only has your best interests at heart.'

'You're wrong. He just wants the *beast* inside me.'

'There is no *beast*, Natalya, only you.'

The witch knelt down beside her on the grass. Natalya wiped the tiredness from her eyes.

'What you call the *beast* is your strength, your courage; your determination to survive. But you are its conscience; its wisdom. Its reason for being alive.'

'No, you're wrong. There's a monster inside me.'

'No, Natalya, the *beast* is you.'

Natalya buried her head in her hands and sniffed back a rising of tears.

'What is it, Natalya? What are you afraid of?'

'The *beast* can't be me... otherwise I killed *him*.'

'Killed him? Who are you talking about?'

'And all he tried to do was help. I threw him. I thought he was Craven. I...'

'Believe me, Natalya, you haven't killed no one.'

'But I have.'

Gretl shook her head. The witch knew who she was talking about.

'Gretl, what aren't you telling me? Please, I have to

know.'

'I shouldn't really be telling you this, but... Nathan Croft is alive and well and works at CINDERS, still.'

Her words were slow to dawn and fuzzy, not unlike a dream. And yet, could Natalya even dare to hope? Could what she'd heard be right?

'He's not dead? How? I saw him lying there.'

'You only knocked him out.'

'He's alive? You mean, he's actually alive!'

She hugged Gretl for all she was worth.

'Now don't go getting ideas, Natalya.'

'I have to see him. Tell him I'm sorry.'

'You can't, Natalya. It's out of the question. I shouldn't even have told you this.'

'But I have to see him.'

'Not until you're ready. And even then I can't promise.'

'Gretl...'

'Yes.'

'I don't care what it takes. I am going to see him again.'

Chapter 13
The Monster in the Cage

Suddenly, Natalya's life had new purpose. With Nathan alive, her world felt worth living. Bleddin, however, seemed determined to break her, his training so harsh that she felt like a rag doll ripped apart by two fighting dogs.

'Watch your opponent... Use your peripheral vision... Never rely on chance. Stabilise your balance... channel your anger. Control it, for goodness sake. You kick like a girl.'

He had her on the last one. She was pretty sure she was. Having said that, he pummelled her face so much that had to wonder if she still looked human. It was a miracle she'd any freckles left, although that wouldn't be such a bad thing.

Thankfully, her body was quick to heal, with her injuries usually curing themselves in only several hours. Hansel cherished each wound like a gift. It was the only time she ever saw him excited. Unfortunately, being beaten up was not her only problem.

The bats. Those darned, screeching bats. She found them impossible to ignore. And Bleddin refused to even speak of the wolfcaines unless she was sat on that plinth at sun-fall.

Frustrated, she took herself to the manor's library, where she spent several hours wading through its books. But there wasn't a mention of a *wolfcaine,* anywhere? Not a single word.

'Not every myth is written in text.' She looked to Bleddin in the doorway. 'You're wasting your time. Come. It's nearly sunset.'

She turned an open page towards him.

'That was the symbol I saw on Craven's forehead.' He gave the image a glance. 'It says it's meant to ward off evil spirits.'

'I'm quite aware of what a *Pentacle* is.'

'But if Craven was the Devil's disciple, why would he want to ward off evil things?'

He hesitated; he was hiding something.

'All in good time. You must first learn to hear.'

And that was it. As much as he would tell her. She

had to find a way around those bats. But it wasn't until a conversation with Hansel that she finally made some ground.

'The bats are not your problem,' he said, one evening, slurping on his soup. 'Human beings have the natural ability to hear one voice amongst many? But the *beast* enhances your auditory perception; you need to tame its input. Reacquaint yourself with your human hearing. In short, the problem is *you*.'

'The bats aren't the problem?'

He shook his head, smiled thinly and slurped another spoonful.

At first, she found it a struggle. That many bats were hard to ignore. But she found that by praying, by concentrating on her bracelet, that she could keep the *beast's* intrusion at bay. And once she began to hear Bleddin's words, they came like an overwhelming flood.

'I encountered them in the Russian Taiga, their leader an exhibit in some abhorrent freak show. Magnificent, he was, but severely malnourished, his grey fur knotted and balding where the shackles had worn against his skin. They had him in a cage a third of his height, intended to curb his strength. To this day, I can see his large green eyes, full of sadness, but determined.

'I set him free. He fled into the forests. I never

thought to see him again. Then ten months later, my men and I were ambushed by Cossacks at the foot of the Urals.

'We were vastly outnumbered, despite our skill. That's when the *wolfcaines* came to our aid. Their leader was *the Grey* I had freed from the cage. Convalesced, he was a wonder to behold. His fellows called him *Grendel*.

'The skirmish won, we returned to their village back in the Ural Mountains. They had women; children. They were intelligent creatures. Persecuted only because they were different. They fed us; embraced us. We became their allies. We swore to help them hunt down their oppressors.

'We fought alongside them in many a scuffle. They had honour; dignity. I was proud to call them *friend*. Then, one day, we happened upon a cottage, where the woman within was on the verge of giving birth.

'The wolfcaines helped to deliver the child, but the following day the bairn was found dead. The woman lost her mind – or *witch*, as we found out. She focused her grief entirely on the wolfcaines. She cursed them that day, swearing never to rest until every wolfcaine was dead.

'Returning to the village we found every wolfcaine slaughtered. Women. Children. The old. The newborn. Their bodies left to rot and be fed on by the birds. We buried what remained, and then *she* came for the men.

'One by one, she hunted them down. We tried to fight back; we set her a trap. But by the time she was slain, it was already too late. Every wolfcaine was dead.

'Left in their wake was a single child. Its father, a wolfcaine; its mother, a human. But whilst the wolfcaine gene lived on in its blood, neither the child nor its offspring ever evolved.

'For nine generations I have watched your family line, waiting for a sign that the wolfcaine might return. It never did. Until you, that is. You had *his* eyes. I knew you were the one. You are their past, their present and their future. The heir to the wolfcaine throne.'

The first time she heard it, she was lost for words. Bleddin assumed she just hadn't heard. The second time, she struggled with its burden. The *beast* was real, but *the heir* to some species that no one had ever heard of? The third time it brought a tear to her eye. There was a sadness to the tale and the way that Bleddin told it. Life was a treasure, and to think of all those women and children just wiped from the earth. In some ways, their deaths mirrored that of her parents; brutal, pointless, and through no fault of their own.

But each hearing of the tale only prompted new questions. *For nine generations....* Just how old was Bleddin? No wonder his attire was from another time. It made him at least two hundred years old. And yet, she'd never heard him talk with such passion. Normally, he would hardly have spoken a word.

Having heard the tale enough times to recite it, she confessed to Bleddin that she'd actually heard. His response was a grunt, which she translated as *good,* although maybe *at last* was more fitting. Or maybe he was simply disgruntled by the fact that he couldn't express his devotion anymore.

'Have you really been watching me all these years?' she asked as they headed back through the trees.

'I had your father to keep me informed.'

Natalya came to a halt.

'My father? You mean you knew papa?'

'I met him during his travels from Russia.'

'Met?' He made it sound like coincidence. She highly doubted that.

'I told him the same tale I've told you now. But I had no proof. He didn't believe me. He then met your mother and they gave birth to you, and still he resisted the truth. It wasn't until you started to change that he started to believe. He contacted me three days before his death. I didn't get there in time.'

She thought back. She remembered that day. Her father had set out earlier than usual. Where he'd been, he never said, but all manned railway stations carried a telegraph.

'How did you find me in London?'

'You left a trail. I only had to follow. A broken train window. A drunk in a pub who spoke of a werewolf attack.'

Dogman. That had to be Dogman.

'I bet he didn't say I was a sixteen-year-old girl?'

'I know a yarn when I'm spun one. I also knew it was you.'

An owl hooted high above them, its eyes reflecting the moon. Somewhere in the foliage she could hear a foraging mouse. *Go home,* she urged it. *Or else you might get eaten.*'

The bats conquered, her thoughts turned to London, or more specifically, Nathan. But if she thought there was light at the end of the tunnel, then Bleddin's tunnel was longer than hers.

Instead, he pressed on with honing her skills to the point where she felt she was losing her mind. Despite her improvement, he found fault at every turn, his criticism unrelenting.

He lunged forward. She sidestepped his blade, spun around and countered. The wind blustered her hair across her face and she stepped straight off the roof.

She fell, the ground thirty feet below, the stone gargoyles laughing at her plight. Just like at CINDERS, a hand caught her leg, only this time it wasn't Nathan's. Bleddin dragged her back onto the roof. She fell into a heap.

'Thank you.'

'How many times have I told you? You must use your peripheral vision. If I was the enemy…'

'I know, I'd be dead.'

'Don't be frivolous, child!'

She looked at him and wanted to cry, but she doubted tears would please him either.

'A *true* wolfcaine…'

'But I'm not a *true* wolfcaine. I don't even know what a *true* wolfcaine is. I'm a distant descendant of some mythical creature that has never been heard of by anyone but you. I know you want your wolfcaines back, but I'm really not the one you're after.'

He glared at her. She felt six years old. He sent that usual shiver down her spine.

'Get up,' he growled. 'If that's what you think. Dr Schneider's office. Now!'

***

Natalya fidgeted on the chair, her sleeve rolled up and her arm aching from the pressure of the strap with the screw-down thing. A *tourniquet,* Hansel had called it, meant to stem the flow of her blood. She watched as he pushed the needle of the syringe into her skin and draw up its red.

She was back in the sanatorium; she just couldn't get away from the place. But what were the cries of a few dozen patients compared to a swarm of bats?

Behind her, she could feel the burn of Bleddin's eyes; she daren't even look around. But the atmosphere wasn't just down to her, the two men had hardly said a passing word. It wasn't the first time she'd noticed. It was the same every night over dinner or in the lounge. They were quite happy to converse with Gretl, but rarely to each other.

Hansel withdrew the needle from her arm and crossed with the sample of blood to the workbench. He returned moments later to remove the tourniquet, much to Natalya's relief. Her arm felt numb, then started to tingle. She flexed her hand to encourage its blood-flow.

'The microscope on the bench,' said Hansel. 'Take a look, if you please.'

Natalya warily crossed to the workbench and peered down through the microscope's lens. The image below was like a river of frogspawn; hardly the most exciting thing in the world.

'Note the blood's composition,' said Hansel. 'It's human. Now compare it to this.'

He switched the slide out for another. Natalya peered down again.

This time the cells were a hive of activity; almost frenzied in their movement. They bore no resemblance to the first slide whatsoever. Natalya furrowed her brow.

'Whose blood is this?

'That came from a *wolfcaine*.'

'What, you mean it's mine?'

He swapped the slide out for a third.

'And this is what I've just taken from you.'

Nervous, Natalya observed again. What if she wasn't a wolfcaine, at all? What if she proved to be something else? The composition was a hybrid of the two. It came as both a relief and concern.

'But this only proves what I said on the roof. I'm not a *true* wolfcaine. I'm half human, too.'

Bleddin leant forward across the table. 'All three samples are yours.'

'Mine? All three? But how can that be?'

'Your blood's in continual flux, my dear.'

She gave the doctor a sceptical look. He leant back against the table.

'When they first brought you here, your body was at war; your immune system fighting a deadly infection. But as the infection eased, your blood's composition changed, returning to something more human. It seems you can change your state at will, and in the mere turn of a second.'

'Now do you believe me?' said Bleddin.

She didn't know what to believe.

'But how do you know that blood is a wolfcaine's? I could be a *werewolf*, or maybe something worse.'

'True, but a werewolf is enslaved by the moon, whereas you can change when you please. Not to mention it is born of infection. Your blood is pure; hereditary; of birth.'

It was almost too much to take in.

'Now can we get back to your training,' said Bleddin.

'And what exactly am I training for?'

'All in good time. You haven't been *there*, yet.'

She looked at him; another conundrum.

'Haven't been where?'

'You'll know when you see it.'

'Will you please stop talking in riddles?'

'Patience is a virtue.'

'But ignorance isn't.'

He glared at her; she glared at him back. It was like a game of who could glare most. She turned to leave. He grabbed her by the arm. She grabbed him by the throat.

'Even now, you allow the *beast* control when you should be showing constraint.'

'I know very well what my hand is doing.'

'But not so much your brain.'

She let him go. He reciprocated. They stood there, staring at each other.

'Whatever you're training me for, *I'm ready.*'

'No. You're not even close.'

'Argh!' she cried.

She stamped her foot on the floor and stormed out of the room.

Chapter 14
A Melting of Pigment

Natalya burst into the bedroom and slammed the door shut behind her. She could feel the anger burning through her freckles, the blood puffing out her cheeks.

She dropped onto the bed and grabbed at the pillow, flinging it at the door. She screwed up her nose, stressing with rage. She gripped the bedcovers for all she was worth.

Let's get back to work, wolfcaine. Stop your pitiful whining, wolfcaine. Wolfcaine, use your peripheral vision. Wolfcaine, ignore those million shrieking bats.

She gave a scream, took a deep breath, held it, and slowly exhaled. Okay, time to settle down, but at this rate she'd never see Nathan again. And where was it she hadn't been?

She finally settled back into her training, but only because she felt she had no choice. Then, as they sat down for dinner three days later, Bleddin was noticeably absent. Natalya hadn't seen him all day, which at least gave her body a chance to repair.

With Hansel and Gretl discussing work, she turned her attention to the pictures on the walls. They were a strange mix, their painted strokes subtly lit by the shimmer from the candles. There was a sunset, a bowl of fruit, an industrial landscape, and one of a man, wearing a flat cap, with a shepherd's crook and a black and white sheep dog. But the one that drew her attention the most was the landscape of the forest. It had fairy-tale spruce trees, snowy-capped mountains: it looked like the *Russian taiga* itself, the home of the bear, the fox and *the wolf*. She'd been reading up on the subject in the library. The place her ancestors used to call home.

Could this be where Bleddin had meant? Did he expect her to travel half way across the world? She'd probably get lost and be eaten by the buzzards, her remains buried in a coffin of snow.

Soames began to serve up the soup, ladies first, as usual. But whilst Gretl's dish had a silky brown texture, Natalya's bowl contained a leafy green mush with a subtle hue of pink. She looked at it in wide-eyed disgust. It didn't smell good, either.

'Soames?' said Gretl, equally surprised. 'What have you served Natalya?'

'General Bleddin's orders, Ma'am. He prepared the dish himself.'

Natalya almost giggled at the thought of Bleddin slaving away with a ladle, but any merriment was equally quashed by the sight of the green now sat before her. She could have sworn it was alive.

'I'm not sure I can eat this,' she said.

'Soames, please fetch Natalya some soup.'

'No, she eats what's in front of her. Or she doesn't eat at all.'

All eyes turned to Bleddin in the doorway. He took his usual seat at the table. Natalya eyed him, awaiting explanation, but he didn't say a word.

'Well at least tell me what it is that's going to kill me.'

He gave her that usual Bleddin stare. She poked her fork into the mush and turned it, scooping up a mouthful. The mere sight of it made her stomach churn. Surely he wasn't serious?

'When I served in the Franco-Prussian War,' said Hansel, 'food such as that was the norm.'

'Good,' said Natalya. She pushed the plate towards him. 'You can have it if you like.'

Bleddin's glare took on a whole new depth.

'Don't make me force it down you, girl.'

'Obadiah,' said Gretl, 'surely you're not...'

'She can eat it now, or warmed up later. It's entirely up to her.'

Warmed up? That sounded even worse. Natalya dragged the plate back towards her. She took a deep breath, closed her eyes, and forced a forkful of the mush into her mouth. It was chewy, oily, and gag-inducing. She snatched up her water to help swill it down. It took all she had not to be sick. She couldn't wait for dessert.

***

Dinner over, they withdrew to the lounge where they often spent their evenings. It was probably the cosiest room in the house, although it did smell of coal from the fire. At least it was preferable to the mustiness of paper that clung to the library's walls.

'Are you all right, Natalya?' asked Gretl, looking up from her book.

Natalya nodded, even though she wasn't. In fact, she didn't feel very well at all.

Somehow, she'd managed to make it through dinner, but there was now a war taking place in her stomach. The experience had put her off food for life, and the inflections of pink had been something else.

She tried to distract her mind with her book, another

early nineteenth century romance. But her eyes ached and her head was throbbing. After several attempts, she gave up on reading and turned her gaze to the room.

Her first port of call was Hansel, who was busy at the table cleaning out his rifles. He had three; they usually lived above the fireplace, *trophies* from his days in the *Franco-Prussian War*.

'This one here is a *Chassepot*,' he'd told her one day. 'Used by the French under Napoleon III. It was quite a revelation for its time. But the paper cartridges used to clog up the chamber, which is why they later switched to using metal. They're relics now; they belong in a museum, although they're still quite capable of firing a round.'

Such knowledge was a pleasure to behold, but he never spoke of the war itself. She'd had to read up about it in the library; over a hundred and fifty thousand dead. She couldn't even start to comprehend.

Next on her gaze around the room was Gretl. Her current novel was a comedic satire. She wasn't unknown for her *haha's* and *hmm's*, but this time she gave a proper snort. Natalya would have smiled herself if she didn't feel so ill.

Bleddin glanced across from his chair, annoyed by the intrusion. He was engaged in a game of chess with himself, his face in a continuous state of contemplation.

It brought back memories of her playing with her

father. She'd never beaten him; not even once. He was a master tactician, not unlike Bleddin. Now there was a chess game she'd like to have watched.

Her stomach churned and she swallowed back some vomit, but she already knew she was fighting a lost cause. Her fingers were tingling and her skin felt clammy. She couldn't hide it anymore.

'I don't feel... very well,' she said. Her stomach heaved again. 'In fact,' she said, 'I think.., I, oh...I think I'm going to be...'

'Not on the...'

She threw up on the carpet, a vomitus green that soaked into the pile. Hansel shook his head in despair. Gretl rushed to her side.

'Obadiah, what on earth did you give her for dinner?'

'A mixture of herbs and foxglove.'

'Foxglove?' cried Hansel, springing from his chair. 'For goodness sakes, man! The plant is toxic.'

He helped Natalya onto the settee.

'Obadiah,' said Gretl, 'how could you?'

'I shouldn't worry. The plant's emetic.'

'We know,' said Hansel. 'Just look at my carpet. It still doesn't mean she hasn't been poisoned.'

Natalya felt the world start to spin, as more green vomit leaked from her mouth. Their faces grew fuzzy; their voices louder. It was as though they were speaking inside a vast cave.

'Do you think she'll be all right, brother?'

'It's hard to tell. She's not exactly human.'

'She's a *wolfcaine*,' said Bleddin. 'She'll be absolutely fine.'

'No, you fool. She absolutely won't.'

Yes, Bleddin and Hansel didn't like each other much. Blackness claimed Natalya's mind.

***

A shrill screech, a brilliant light, and Natalya's mind flickered back into life. She sat up sharply, the softness of the bed doing little to ease her aching limbs.

To say she felt unwell was an understatement. At least the discomfort proved she wasn't dead. Her stomach heaved, she tossed back the bedclothes and made a dash for the washbowl. She just about made it as she threw up again, spattering the porcelain with green. The next time Bleddin cooked her dinner, she wasn't eating a forkful.

With vomit still dripping from her mouth, her ears tuned in to the rest of the world. People snoring. Sleepless footsteps. Patients' anxious cries. She tried to block them out, as she did with the bats, but for some reason this time it didn't work. An owl hooting. A gust of wind. The swaying thrash of the leaves on the trees.

She winced. What was going on? Was this down to

the foxglove, or something else? The air in the room felt suddenly ethereal, which had nothing to do with the glow of the moon.

The *veil of grey* that had plagued her before began to seep through the walls. Horrified, Natalya made a dash for the door. The *grey* cut her off, rising up through the floor. She fell back, not knowing where to go. She felt like an animal cornered in a cage. Her only escape seemed to be the window, and yet, she was up on the second floor.

With the *beast* making her braver than she ought, she ran towards the window. She leapt through its glass and plummeted earthwards, accompanied by a thousand shards of crystal. She rolled with the impact and landed back on her feet. Above, the *grey* followed her out.

The *veil of grey*. Another enigma. Another mystery to be solved. Was it friend or foe? Was it even an *it*. Was it sentient? Alive? Or did it merely exist?

She fled across the grass towards the wood, gargoyles from the battlements taking to the air. She stumbled, fell; carried on her way. But despite the *beast's* courage, her heart was filled with dread.

She reached the wood and ploughed into its undergrowth, leaping over roots and weaving between trees. She could sense the *grey*, chasing her down, causing the freckles to burn on her face.

She turned, tripped, recovered, slipped; she fell into

the mud, gasping, anxious. She scrambled to her feet and found herself surrounded. Everywhere she looked the *grey* was present. It smothered the trees, it ate up the leaves, it bled through the cracks in the earth. Natalya swallowed, closed her eyes and crossed herself.

The *grey* swam in and consumed her.

***

Natalya opened her eyes, the landscape vibrant with colour. From the fluorescent purples of the parasitic fungi to the multi-coloured leaves that fluttered on the trees. She blinked, her mind on the verge of tripping out. It was like she'd stepped into a painting.

She edged forward, the *beast* on alert, the feathery grass tickling at her feet. Her shadow stretched before her and behind. It stretched to her left; it stretched to her right. She gazed up through the canopy of trees and counted at least three suns in the sky. Was this heaven? Had she died? Was she now in the afterlife?

She licked at her lips and tasted their sweetness, coated by the sugary air. Her ears pricked at the sound of running water and she followed its lure to a stream. It reminded her of the one back home, the colours of the wood mirrored in its current. She crouched beside it; ran her fingers through its wetness. She drew them out to find them covered in… *paint?*

Fragments of images flashed through her mind: a

tree, a squirrel, a cluster of mushrooms. The *paint* felt warm, yet also cold, each band of colour a different heat. She watched as the dye drained back into the water, the images draining with it.

Once more she felt her freckles burn. She glanced about her surroundings. The trees were starting to melt into paint, the pigment swelling the stream into a river.

The next she knew the embankment was gone and she was being swallowed up by the current. But the water was thick with coloured sludge. She reached out blindly, snatching at the weeds. They only served to nettle her skin, and the more she struggled, the more she sank.

Think the problem. Work it through. How many times had Bleddin told her? But there was nothing of substance to grab a hold of, and the water was rising fast.

A rabbit came hopping out of the bushes, leaving paw prints of colour in its wake. He hopped nearby, stopped and stared, then started to melt like the trees. His fur became paint, his brownness turned blue, and then a *darkness* ate its way through his face.

Natalya gasped in horror.

The *darkness:* she could feel it drawing on the air, gorging on the landscape, eating up its life. More random images flashed through her mind. What was this place? Why did it exist? She swallowed some water and choked on its denseness. She found herself praying to the *Leshy* for help.

The next she knew the river was bubbling, roots breaking free from the riverbed below. The water grew wild, its flow obstructed, as the *Leshy* rose up from beneath the painted surface.

Coloured droplets rained about her, draining from the *tree spirit's* every branch. The *Leshy* twisted his hulk of a body, reached down with his hand and dragged her from the sludge. He raised her high, up into the air, wrapped in his fingers of twigs.

'Thank you,' she cried.

She thought he smiled; it was hard to tell through his beard of tangled sticks. He had a wise old face and whittled eyes, just as she'd always imagined he would look.

Suddenly, a groan, a splintering of grain, and the *Leshy* looked at her in anguish. The *darkness* ate its way through the bark of his flesh and the *Leshy* fell to his knees.

In his final moments, he flung her to safety, onto the far side of the river. She watched, distraught, as he crumpled to the ground and was eaten from the inside out.

The waters began to haze now, forming twin rainbows that arched through the sky. They absorbed the pigment up into their bows, brightening the world with their colourful glow.

But what world? The landscape was fading. Everything west of the embankment was dying. The colours of the rainbows bled between themselves and dissipated into *grey*.

Natalya stared at the empty blackness that had once been a world of colour. She quickly turned to view the wood behind her; at least the trees weren't melting here. Darkened clouds swept in across the sky, threatening the onset of rain.

A sound of thunder drew her attention. But no, not thunder: horse hooves. The closer they came, the more her heart raced. A stallion came charging out of the trees. Natalya gasped and leapt from its path. She managed to catch sight of its black-garbed rider.

'Obadiah!'

He rode off into the trees; Natalya gave pursuit. She was fast, but already the horse was out of sight. She sniffed at the air and breathed a wisp of smoke. It brought back haunted memories.

Full of dread, she followed her nose to the location of a small, pretty stone cottage. Beside it, someone had set fire to a woodpile, and tied to a pole at is midst was....

'Gretl!'

She now saw Bleddin trying to fight through the flames. It reminded her of Gretl's tale. Natalya ran forward, anxious to help, but then she felt her stomach churn. She dropped to her knees and vomited foxglove. The *veil of grey* returned to drag her home.

***

Natalya stood on the precipice of the roof, gazing out at London in the distance. The sunrise airbrushed the clouds in tangerine, basking the earth in its heavenly glow.

The night's events were a mystery. They'd left her both intrigued and afraid. A dying landscape. A recreated memory. A creature from folklore that shouldn't exist.

Footsteps crunched the gravel behind her; she could tell from their weight it was Bleddin. She took a deep breath, filling her lungs, keeping her face turned from him.

'Dr Schneider thinks you tried to kill me last night. I think you wanted to show me something else.'

'Your ancestors used foxglove for medicinal purposes. It helped to open your eyes.'

'What do they call it? The world beyond our own?'

'The wolfcaines called it the *Shadow Realm.*'

'But what is its purpose? Why does it exist?'

'No wolfcaine may be told what they must learn for themselves.'

She turned and stepped down from the wall.

'But you know?'

'Enough to guide you, nothing more.'

'You've been there?'

'That privilege is reserved for the few.'

She twirled a lock of her hair around her finger and gazed at its strands of interwoven blue.

'My hair's changed colour.'

'I'd noticed.'

'It won't wash out. I've tried.'

'Don't worry. Gretl can conceal it with a spell.'

'I never said I didn't like it.'

He glared at her and grunted. She tried to hide a smile. But she hadn't said it just to annoy him; she'd always liked being different.

'So now that I've been *there*, why all the training?'

'There's more than foxglove with its roots sown in the *Shadow Realm*.'

'The *Glass Slipper* orchid?'

'It's a plant of two worlds, but to exist in ours, it needs a human host. We've suspected Ella Cinders for some time.'

'Ella? You think it's bonded with Ella? But why does it keep on trying to kill me?'

'It senses what you are.'

'It doesn't like wolfcaines? Since when did a plant harbour a grudge?'

He took a moment to choose his words.

'Glass Slipper orchids are born in pairs. They remain together throughout their lives. But as you say, they have no self-awareness. Instead, they channel the nature of their host.'

'But it had no host when it attacked me.'

'There may be an echo from a previous master.'

'An echo?'

'A memory. An imprint. A mission. One that the orchid's trying to play out. They are not unknown to bind themselves to witches; just like the *witch* that murdered your kind. She, too, was host to such a pairing. One died with her; the other escaped.'

'What? You think it's the same plant?'

'The men that attacked your village were a sign.'

She looked at him; he diverted his gaze, which wasn't like Bleddin, at all.

'Thomas *Craven* was a colleague of mine. We fought together in many a battle. But he was killed by the very same witch that we hunted. What murdered your parents was an avatar of him. Glass Slipper orchids have the power to create. His image was a message. A warning from the past.'

'A message? But how would I know that?'

'The message was meant for *me*. There's a reason those riders were dressed like they were. To represent those who hunted the witch.'

Once more her brain felt overwhelmed. She took her

time to digest what he'd said. She felt the *beast* rise up inside; it forced the words from her lips.

'Then you're the reason my parents are dead.'

Kill him. Rip out his heart, screamed the *beast*. It took all she had to hold it back. She gazed down at her lengthening nails.

'The world is full of unexpected ripples.'

'Ripples!' she cried. 'You stole my life!'

Go on, urged the beast. *Tear out his throat.*

She took a step forward, her blood boiling up. Bleddin firmly stood his ground. She rose to her tiptoes, getting in his face.

'And what happens when I throw you off this roof?'

'Besides making Gretl a widow? You'd still be a wolfcaine. You'd still be wanted dead. And all you'd have done is help the orchid win. You're not the only one it's hunting, wolfcaine. It wants me dead, as well. Lest you forget, I'm the one who slew its previous mistress.'

She flexed her claws, her blood surging. Bleddin was trusting her not to kill him. But Gerard Dogman had made the same mistake, and look what she'd done to him.

No, we can't, she told the beast.

Kill him, it raged. *Honour our parents.*

But how could she hold Bleddin accountable for something that happened before she was even born?

Stand down, she told it. It chose to ignore her. She told it firmer. It protested its cause. She made her argument perfectly clear. The *beast* sloped off back to its lair.

'You say Ella Cinders is the orchid's host?'

'We believe. Suspect. We cannot be sure. Only a wolfcaine can see through such illusion. I've reserved you tickets for their Masquerade ball.'

'Then I guess I'm going to London, after all.'

She would see Nathan again.

Chapter 15
A Study in Crimson

Bustles were out. Ruffles were in. But Natalya's dress was neither. With London only a few days away, her outfit was still a roll of silk on the bed.

She eyed herself in the mirror, dressed in nothing but a chemise and pantalettes. Behind her, Gretl had a mouthful of pins, as she tried to fasten up Natalya's hair.

London was finally happening. Natalya should have been elated. But after weeks of thinking about nothing else, it now filled her with dread.

What if Nathan was holding a grudge? What if she bumped into Ella and Shah Ming? What if the Glass Slipper sensed her presence and tried to kill her again?

'There,' said Gretl. 'We're ready for the dress.'

There wasn't a needle and thread in sight.

'What about the corset?'

'It's sewn into the dress.'

Natalya eyed Gretl in the mirror.

'I know, it's unconventional,' said Gretl. 'But Obadiah's instructions were clear. The dress needs to give you the freedom to move. I've added in a few little tricks.' She moved around in front of her. 'Now, raise your arms to the sides and keep your head up straight. I don't want the *glue* sticking to your skin…'

'Glue?'

'Don't worry. It's just a term of reference.'

Raising her arms, as if about to conduct, Gretl began to sketch in the air. She moved around Natalya, uttering *nonsense*; there was certainly a scent of magic in the room. It was the strangest thing Natalya had ever seen, except for maybe that cactus in the bathtub.

Gretl came full circle.

'There,' she said. 'Time to get you fitted.'

She crossed to the bed and unrolled the silk. She tossed the fabric into the air. The silk spiralled up and around Natalya's body, hovering just short of her skin.

Natalya observed with nervous wonder, her heart thumping hard against her chest. The silk shrank inwards, embracing her torso, its thickness creating a corseted bodice. A slither of ribbon tied both front and back, the silk flowing down into a pleated skirt. It was soft and cool and clung to every curve. Natalya slid her hands down its satin. She felt like someone from out of her novels, and alas, she was going to her very own ball.

'Well, Natalya, what do you think?'

'I think I'll never want to take it off.'

She gazed at her bosom and bit on her lip. At least it would distract from her blue strands of hair.

'Don't worry,' said Gretl. 'I've got something for that.'

She took out a matchbox and slid back its lid. Inside was a big, furry caterpillar. She placed it across the bustline of the dress and softly blew on its hair. Natalya watched with a modicum of horror as its fur grew out at a ridiculous rate.

Soon her bosom was concealed by black fur, with more fur circling the cuffs of her sleeves. Gretl returned the caterpillar to its box. The poor little thing was now naked.

The front of the corset darkened to black.

'Any better?'

'I think I'm lost for words.'

'I also have you a new pair of boots. The heels on these are a little bit higher, but I'm sure you'll soon get the hang of them.'

Exhausted, Gretl sat down on the bed.

'Gretl? Are you all right? Do you want me to fetch your brother?'

'No, my dear, just give me a moment. Magic takes its toll, is all. In that box, over there on the dresser. Obadiah has sent you a gift.'

Now Natalya really was lost for words. A gift from grumpy old Bleddin? She opened the box and peered inside. He really shouldn't have bothered. Really. It was nothing more than a stuffed, square pouch, hung on a cheap string necklace.

'Oh. I must remember to thank him.'

At least her string bracelet served a purpose. She removed the *necklace* and felt her nose twitch. Was that a scent of...?

'Foxglove? He's filled it with foxglove pollen?'

'He thought it might be of some use. You know Obadiah: pragmatism rules. For my fortieth birthday he bought me a broomstick.'

'He never did?'

The witch burst out laughing. Natalya felt such a fool.

'No, dear.'

Natalya frowned, then ended up laughing, too.

Gretl got up slowly.

'Now then, time I was off to bed.'

'Here,' said Natalya. 'Let me help.'

They left the room, arm in arm, and headed along

the landing.

'Gretl?'

'Hmm?'

'You know I love the dress; but how am I supposed to get it off?'

'Untie the front ribbon and the dress will outgrow you.'

'Outgrow me?'

'It's made of magic, no less.'

'And to put it back on?'

'Just step back inside, re-tie the ribbon and the fabric will shrink.'

Lord, how Natalya loved magic. They reached Gretl's bedroom door.

'Goodnight then, Natalya.'

'*Guten abend, Frau Schneider.*'

Gretl laughed. 'And who's been teaching you?'

'Your brother.'

'Hansel? Really? I doubt it.'

'Well, I do pick up certain words.'

Gretl gave her a parting smile and entered into the bedroom. Alone, Natalya turned back the way she'd come. The world responded at a slower pace.

'Oh!'

She felt quite dizzy. She steadied herself with a hand against the wall. Not that the dress was too tight; on the contrary. She put it down to excitement.

She took a step forward and wobbled. She blinked her eyes, the world seemed strange. There was a grey, second outline to everything she saw. She itched at the agitated freckles on her face.

Suddenly, she saw a shape in the dark, making its way towards her. Its footsteps were silent, its movement laboured. She sought out the oil lamp and turned up the light.

'Hansel?'

It was, and yet, it wasn't. He was disfigured, with drool dripping from his mouth. His gaze was distant, he was dragging his foot, a scalpel clasped in his hand. She gasped.

She stood back against the wall and let him pass. He didn't even seem to know she was there. She watched him vanish back into the dark. What was going on?

A wise person might have turned and run. Natalya picked up the oil lamp and followed. She descended the staircase, her dizziness settling, but not her shadowed vision.

She caught sight of him near the front door. The door was shut; he merged through its wood. Her eyes widened. What was he, some ghost? But why should she be surprised? She lived in a world of witches, evil plants, Witch Finder Generals and centuries-old men. Not to mention that she was a wolfcaine. She even had a bestial self.

She unbolted the door and stepped outside.

She ducked in a panic as a gargoyle swooped past her. She gasped, anxious; it wasn't alone. There were other *phantoms* wandering the courtyard, each in some sort of comatose state. Their skin was grey, their clothes were grey, and none of them seemed aware of her presence. She touched at a *ghoul* and her hand passed straight through it. She swallowed and gave a shudder.

What was she seeing? The afterlife? Or maybe this was the Shadow Realm, again? She looked back at *Hansel*. His image seemed familiar. And then, it suddenly dawned. He looked like that drawing on the sanatorium wall, as if it had come to life.

She glanced back at the manor. Half of it was smothered in black. It was the same with the landscape that stretched beyond the courtyard, but this wasn't down to any lack of light. She could feel *it* watching, waiting. Ready to feast on anything that breathed. The *darkness*. And yet, it didn't seem to sense her. It was like she was observing through a mirror, from the *real-*world, looking in.

She returned to the manor and her bedroom. She gazed through the window and its newly magicked glass. She could still see the *ghosts*. She could still sense the *darkness*. She could still smell the scent of foxglove up her nose.

She crossed to the washbowl and doused her face in water, cleansing it of pollen. Bleddin had given her the necklace for a reason. She returned to the window; the *ghosts* were gone. The pollen had opened her eyes to the Shadow Realm. She could now glimpse its world from the safety of her own.

Untying the ribbon that fastened her bodice, she watched as the dress outgrew her to the floor. She picked it up and hung it in the wardrobe. She spent the next half hour trying to get to sleep.

Two more days and she'd be in London, but she couldn't shake that feeling of dread. She tried to convince herself all would be fine, but her own self wasn't listening.

Chapter 16

Masquerade

14th September, 1891

The horse-drawn carriage hurried down the road, heading for the outskirts of London. The waning day now streaked the sky in crimson, matching the silk of Natalya's dress.

She glanced at Gretl, sat beside her, wearing a gown of subtle lime. She looked elegant; beautiful, and very much at ease, whereas Natalya couldn't stop fidgeting.

Her stomach felt like a pit of despair, her previous worries now trebled. If only the night could be over already; she started to play with her hair. She turned her gaze to London in the distance, the impatient moon already in the sky.

'Now remember what Obadiah told us,' said Gretl. 'We're there to observe, not interfere.'

Natalya nodded, fingering her ringlets. Gretl gave a smile.

'Don't worry, dear, you'll be fine. Just do as we said and don't draw attention.'

Don't draw attention? What? In this dress? She could look like an ogre and still garner looks.

Soon they were approaching the city outskirts, cobble rising up to replace the dirt-track road. Despite the sprung wheels, the carriage still wobbled, making Natalya feel even more ill. She swallowed, her throat as dry as the day. By the time they arrived, she was going to be a wreck.

Houses of brick now rose to form the landscape, their neatly lined rows creating whole streets. Smoke from pot chimneys clouded the air, whilst the streetlamps emitted an otherworldly glow. The pavements were busy with the overworked poor; many hours laboured, and many more to go.

Her ringlets over-curled, she started playing with her necklace, sending pollen drifting up her nose. Like a drug to the brain, it intoxicated her senses, turning the world a monochrome grey.

The outline of the Shadow Realm now drew into sight, but to her disappointment, its contours flowed no different. It mirrored the real world in every possible way, except for those undefined areas of black.

She felt an iciness grip at her heart. She could feel *its* presence. Watching. Waiting. The *darkness*. It lurked everywhere she looked. Hidden in the shadows; seeking out decay.

A teenage girl stepped out into the road and straight in front of the carriage.

'No! Look out!'

The driver didn't slow. Had the girl been trampled? Injured? Killed? Distraught, Natalya looked to the rear. The girl was alive, and staring back her way. She was coloured grey, a phantom of the Shadow Realm, and yet, she was also the girl with white hair. Natalya thumped at the ceiling of the coach, calling on the driver to stop.

'Natalya, what is it? What's wrong?' said Gretl.

'It's *her*.'

The driver brought the horses to a standstill. Natalya leapt out and ran back along the road, but the girl was gone; vanished into nowhere. Natalya returned to the carriage frustrated, and blew her nose to clear away the pollen. Her wolfcaine vision petered out and she settled back for the rest of the ride.

By the time they reached Soho the day had yielded, the premature moon now kidnapped by the clouds. A slither of mist rode the frosty air, its colour changing as it twined between the streetlamps. They pulled onto the road outside CINDERS.

The street was busy; remarkably so, with carriages clung to every curb. They came to a stop in the middle of the road and the driver urged them out. Natalya tugged her shawl around her shoulders. The air was cold. The driver left them stood there.

'Natalya, quick, or you're going to get trampled.'

She joined Gretl up on the pavement. She decided to try her *wolfcaine vision* again. She watched as the world grew a second outline.

Again, she felt disappointed, and chilled by the dominant presence of the *darkness*. She raised her gaze, expecting more brickwork, and was treated to a sight that stole her breath away.

Rising from the brick were three circular towers, their turrets pointing high into the sky. They were hugged by vines that papered their stone, a balcony extending from the highest of the three. Natalya observed with a sudden excitement. In the Shadow Realm, CINDERS was a fairy-tale palace.

'Don't forget your eye mask,' said Gretl.

Natalya looked at her blankly.

'Your eye mask, dear.'

'Oh, of course. Sorry, Gretl. My mind was elsewhere.'

She positioned her eye-mask across her nose. It was large enough to cover half her face. She tied it in place and followed after Gretl; not even Nathan would recognise her now. They entered the cabaret bar and presented their invites. They proceeded into the hallway.

Once full of damp and threadbare carpets, the hallway was now transformed. It had flocked wallpaper and an inch-high piled carpet. She was careful not to stumble into the table. She could feel her heart racing ever faster. They stepped into the lounge.

The décor was much as she remembered, although parts had been refurbished. The stage had new curtains, the walls had new panelling, but the biggest change was in the clientele.

No longer was the floor just a sea of black suits, but a lake of glorious colour. Everywhere she looked there were ladies in gowns, the stink of cigar smoke overpowered by perfume. The sound of chit-chat cluttered the air; even the waitresses were wearing some clothes. Natalya had to wonder if the first-floor *entertainment* was now a thing of the past?

'Anything?' said Gretl.

Natalya applied her wolfcaine vision. Or rather, she tried, but failed.

'Don't worry,' said Gretl. 'We have all evening. Let's go for some refreshments. It might help calm your nerves.'

The witch led her down into the crowd. It was more

congested than Covent Garden market. Everywhere she looked there were heaving bosoms; she needn't have felt so exposed. She squeezed through a gap; a man eyed her up and down. She pulled her shawl firmly around her.

A flicker, a glimpse, a draining of colour, and her wolfcaine vision stuttered back to life. She gazed around the room in search of any changes; all seemed the same, then she looked to the guests. She came to a sudden halt.

Every inch of their skin was painted with something that looked like a weaving of vines. But more than a painting; these images were breathing. Natalya gasped and clutched at her arm.

They resembled the vines of the Glass Slipper orchid; the infection that had almost ended her life. They were wrapped around arms and coiled about throats, imbedding their fibres deep beneath the skin. But unlike with Natalya, the guests seemed healthy, as if the vines served some other purpose.

'Gretl?'

She looked around for the witch. She anxiously pushed her way forward. Laughter, merriment: they overwhelmed her ears, people blurring past, making her feel dizzy. She gulped down oxygen to feed her starving brain. She finally cleared the crowd.

'There you are.'

She spun to see Gretl.

'Don't stray now. I'll just be at the bar.'

'But Gretl...'

Already the witch was gone. Natalya returned her gaze to the lounge.

It was then she saw her, stood across the room. The girl with white hair, staring back. Natalya quickly fought her way towards her, only to arrive and find that she was gone. She saw her heading towards the balcony stairway, glancing over her shoulder as she went.

There was a sudden hush of expectation, and Natalya followed everyone's gaze towards the stage. The MC had found his way between the curtains. But more than the MC...

Her butterflies took flight.

'Nathan?'

It was undeniably him, despite his trimmed hair and his tailored suit. She couldn't explain how good it felt to see him. To see for herself that he was still alive.

'Ladies and Gentlemen,' he began. 'Welcome to *Masquerade Night* at *CINDERS*. If ya'd like to take yer seats, the show's about to begin. Allow me to introduce you to *les filles de danse de pantoufles de verre*.'

One moment she was squashed between a sea of bodies, the next she was practically stood on her own. The gents and their ladies now settled at their tables, whilst Nathan made his way off stage. The musical conductor raised his baton and the orchestra began to play.

A trumpet, a drum, a collection of strings, and music filled the air. The curtains flew out into the fly space above, and the showgirls took centre stage. They were both in time with each other and the music. They weren't the showgirls of four months earlier. They showed less flesh but gave more tease. You could still catch a glimpse of a pretty girl's thigh.

Natalya quickly scanned the room, but the girl with white hair was gone. She gave a sigh and, with her wolfcaine vision fading, started back towards the bar.

Where are you going?

Who was talking now? The butterflies in her stomach?

You're here because of him.

'But Gretl said I mustn't…'

Stop hiding behind their words. Don't be such a coward.

Of course, the butterflies couldn't talk, but if she ever got caught, she could blame it on them. She diverted backstage. The butterflies rejoiced. It was the same usual chaos as when she used to work there.

She caught a juggler's arm and he dropped all his balls. She mouthed the word *sorry* and hurried on her way. It was fair to say she was feeling warm, and it had nothing to do with the temperature of the room. She found him stood by the side of the stage, messing around in a prop box. How apt.

She removed her shawl and tidied up her hair; her bosom was positively heaving. She'd played out this scene a hundred times in her head, but now she was here, she felt so unprepared.

She took a deep breath and approached him. *Don't you coward out now.* She reached out to touch him, froze, withdrew her hand, half turned away, then turned back and tapped him quickly. He looked around. His eyes undressed her in a second.

'Hello, Nathan.'

'Can I help ya, Miss? I'm not sure I know…?'

He indicated her mask.

'Oh, sorry.'

She removed it with a giggle.

'I'm still not sure I know ya, though.'

'It's me. Natalya. Look. Freckles.'

'Yeah, I can see. Nice hair, by the way.'

'The ringlets, you mean?'

'I was thinking the blue.'

'Well you know how I like to be different.'

He furrowed his brow. 'Do I? I'm not sure we've met before, have we?'

She tried to laugh it off. 'Nathan, stop messing.'

'No, seriously, I don't know who ya are.'

A showgirl joined them, fresh from onstage. Her

cheeks were flushed from all that dancing. She was slim, sexy, and annoyingly pretty. Natalya found herself sharpening her claws.

'Who's the damsel in red, Nathe? Should the guests even be back 'ere?'

The girl rubbed her body against his. To Natalya's dismay, he didn't object. She shot the girl a glare.

'Natalya's a *friend...,* or so she tells me.'

'Really? Looks like a stranger to me. Please to meet ya, Natalya, luv. I'm the girl of his dreams.'

'What? You mean you're... together?'

'Yeah. Ya got a problem with that?'

'No. I mean... No, I'm sorry. You're right. I shouldn't be back here.'

She turned to leave.

'No. Wait!'

That was Nathan. She fled nonetheless. She still felt warm, but now with embarrassment, the butterflies in her stomach dead.

You idiot! she scolded herself. *Gretl is going to kill you. And all because of some stupid boy who's sharing his bed with some girl from a burlesque show.*

She returned out front to the roar of laughter. At first she thought they were laughing at her. Yes, CINDERS had certainly changed; even the comedian was funny.

In her haste to get back to the bar, she half knocked someone over. She turned to apologise and wished that she hadn't. Shah Ming shot her a charismatic smile. He placed his palms together and bowed in greeting. Natalya did her best to copy back.

'A thousand apologies, my dear,' he said.

'No. It was me who bumped into you.'

'Nonsense. Nothing as lovely as yourself could ever cause such disturbance.'

She smiled, squirmed, and quickly turned to leave. It was impolite, but she had to get away. Shah Ming moved to block her path, curiosity on his face.

'I think we've met before, have we not?'

'I'm sorry. I need to find my chaperone.'

'I'm sure she won't mind if you're here with me. Now then, where is my princess?'

He raised a hand and beckoned someone over. Natalya could have cried. She wanted to run, but her legs wouldn't let her. Ella swayed towards them. She was hugged inside a dress of fine, blue silk, and looking lovelier than ever. Even the cut to her cheek had healed. She came to a startled halt.

'*Natasha,* is that you? Yes, I recognise the freckles. They told me you'd taken a fall in the Thames and broken your lovely neck.'

She gave her a quick glance up and down.

'Well, you have scrubbed up well. I like the dress. Crimson suits you. And ringlets – I said you had the face to pull it off. I'm not too sure about the strands of blue, though.'

Natalya responded with an awkward smile. Her voice had got lost somewhere down her throat.

'Shah, you remember *Natasha*, don't you? The girl who *rudely* interrupted our engagement.'

'Ah, of course. I knew we'd met before. Didn't she cut your face?'

'Yes. But shall we let bygones be bygones?'

'Maybe she'd like her old job back?'

'I doubt she'll be climbing the rigging in that dress. Will you, *Natasha* dear?'

Natalya glanced around in desperation. Where was Gretl? And then she saw Nathan. She could only assume he'd followed her out. He was certainly looking her way.

'Ah,' said Ella, 'so you've been reacquainted? Don't tell me; he doesn't remember you. Well you did throw him pretty hard against that carriage. A bout of amnesia is a pretty good result.'

'Amnesia!' said Natalya. 'Nathan has amnesia?'

'Yes. Why, didn't you know? Aw, did you think he was just playing games? Truth is, he doesn't remember you at all.'

'My dear,' said Shah Ming. 'I can see the French Ambassador.'

'Then we must make our introductions. Natalya, I'm sure our paths will cross again. Oops, slip of the tongue.

I meant to say, *Natasha.'*

The prince and his princess set off across the room.

Natalya took a deep breath and swallowed. She could feel her whole body shaking. She felt a hand touch her on the arm. She spun around, hoping it was…

'Oh, Gretl. It's you.'

'You were expecting someone else? Did I just see you with Ella and Shah Ming?'

'I didn't say a word, I promise.'

'Oh, Natalya, that's not the point. I distinctly told you… Obadiah will be furious.'

'I'm sorry. I didn't intend for it to happen.'

'Come on. We're leaving. Now!'

Chapter 17
Those Eyes...

The journey from CINDERS was a silent one, with only the echo of hooves on cobble to announce their presence to the world. Natalya sat there, looking out the carriage window, wishing she was somewhere, anywhere, but here. What she wouldn't give to wake up in bed and find it had all been a dream.

They turned into a residential square, its communal park smothered by the dark. With the moon still lost, the only light came from the streetlamps, flickering shadow across the cobbled road.

The driver pulled up outside the hotel, pre-booked in the assumption they'd be out till late. Natalya and Gretl stepped down onto the pavement and were greeted by the cold. It was then Natalya realised that she'd left behind her shawl.

Gretl bustled her up the hotel steps.

The lobby was a sight to be savoured, with a floor and columns of grey-swirled marble. The curtains were velour, just like those at CINDERS, and Natalya observed with wondrous awe. Gretl signed them in at reception; they followed the porter up to their room. It overlooked the central square, and soon Natalya was sat, looking out.

A slither of fog crept its way across the cobbles, sneaking up on the flowers that hid in the park. The leaves of the trees shivered in the shadow, whitened by a forming coat of ice. Natalya watched with a troubled mind, and then she could bear it no longer.

'I'm sorry,' she said.

'Well, it's done now,' said Gretl, glancing up from turning down the bedcovers. 'I think we forget you're only sixteen. Besides, I'm as much to blame as you are.'

'No, you're not.'

'Aren't I, Natalya? I was supposed to be your chaperone.'

Now Natalya felt even more guilty. She frowned and returned her gaze outside. The moon attacked the blackness of the night as it escaped its cover of cloud.

'Did you know that Nathan has amnesia?'

Gretl looked at her in horror.

'Please don't tell me you spoke to him, as well? Oh, Natalya, what else should I know? The sooner we're home in the morning, the better. Lord knows what Obadiah's going to say.'

Natalya bit her lip and closed her eyes. Even the moon was laughing. Still, why not? Everyone else was. If only she could turn back the hour.

By the time *that bell* struck midnight, Gretl was fast asleep. She'd told Natalya to turn in, too, but Natalya had other thoughts on her mind. She gazed down at the pencilled portrait of herself, the one she'd *stolen* from the witch's bedroom.

Gretl having this made no sense. How and when did she get it? Of course, to find out, Natalya only had to ask, but that meant admitting she'd been snooping through her things.

The alternative was asking Nathan, but he was suffering from amnesia. And yet, she convinced herself it didn't matter. Any excuse to see him again. She'd long been regretting running out on him earlier. Now was her chance to try again.

She re-folded the sketch and shoved it down her bosom. Ease of access and all. Besides, it meant it was closer to her heart, which made *him* closer, too. She stole across the room, collected Gretl's shawl, and quietly made her exit through the door.

Her plan had been to flag down a Hansom cab; CINDERS was hardly a few streets away. But she'd forgotten that she actually needed money. It meant she'd have to walk, and she didn't know the way. She'd never ventured this far into the city, although perhaps if she could find her way to the Thames?

By luck or by chance she did just that, the homeless clinging to its banks en masse. It wasn't that long ago she'd been one of them. She felt rather awkward in her silken dress. She tugged her shawl closer around her and quickened up her pace.

But despite her resolve, it soon became clear that walking would get her nowhere. The Thames stretched on and on without end, and she was getting all sorts of unwanted attention. Not just from the drunks, but the *ladies of the night,* and she'd rather avoid confrontation.

And so, she flagged down a Hansom Cab. She fingered the fare from the driver's own pocket. She felt guilty at first, but what choice did she have? Then he groped her backside whilst helping her up. She pretty much called that even.

For the next half hour they trailed the Thames. She was right, the river went on forever. Then, as they passed by some half-constructed bridge, they turned off into the city's depths.

Street led to street and they all looked the same; she wasn't sure how the driver knew his way. It wasn't until they reached the theatre district that she gained some sense of place.

By now it was two in the morning, and even the *swan-slingers* had gone home to bed. Another ten minutes and she was stood outside CINDERS. The driver trundled off to collect his next fare.

With the bar shut, she snook down the alley, her heels resounding off its cobbles. She came to a stop at the foot of the drainpipe that ran past the third-floor window.

It would be just her luck if he'd now changed rooms, but it was a chance she was willing to take. She ditched Gretl's shawl - she'd collect it later – and grabbed a hold of the drainpipe. She started to climb, got her feet caught in her skirt, and dropped back onto the cobbles in frustration.

Suddenly, there was a scent of magic. She looked around in horror. Had Gretl followed? Worse, was it Ella? Thankfully, it was neither. Instead, she felt a chill to her legs. She gazed down at her skirt as the front shrunk upwards. This wasn't just a dress made from magic; the dress was magic itself.

Once again, she started to climb, and this time with consummate ease. Her boots gave her grip and the *beast* gave her strength, not to mention her added claws. She used the latter to strip out the window frame, loosening a pane of glass. She pushed it through onto the carpet beyond and, lifting the catch, started climbing in.

The window was smaller than it looked, and she got herself caught on the catch. There was a sound of ripping silk, she lost her balance, and toppled inside, head over heels. She landed in a heap on the third-floor carpet, a large rip along her outer thigh.

Oh, well done, Natalya. Try hiding that one from Gretl.

There was always a chance that Gretl wouldn't notice. There was also a chance that the sun wouldn't rise.

She clambered to her feet, tried to smarten her appearance, and found her nose twitching once more. She looked down as her dress regrew to the floor, whilst the tear miraculously re-stitched itself. She raised her eyes and gave thanks to God, although he wasn't the one responsible.

Collecting herself, she made her way towards *his* room. What if she found him in bed with the showgirl? She flexed her claws. *No,* she told herself. She eased the door open and peered around its edge.

'Nathan?' she whispered.

He was lying on the bed, still in his suit and fast asleep. To her relief, there wasn't any showgirl. It meant she could put away her claws.

Beside him on the bed was his sketchbook. She picked it up to observe his latest work. To her surprise, and great delight, the image that stared back at her was... *her*. She couldn't keep the smile from her face, although he would insist on drawing her with freckles. That aside, amnesia or not, she'd obviously made an impression.

Her heart encouraged, she sat down at the dresser and began unpinning her hair. She preferred it down, prostitute or not. Her curls flocked down around her shoulders. Then, she saw him stood behind her in the mirror. He was as light on his feet as ever.

'Nathan,' she gasped. 'You startled me.'

'I'm not the one who shouldn't be in here. How did ya even get into the place?'

She pointed at the door; full hand, of course. It was rude to point with a finger.

'Ya know what I mean. We're on the third floor.'

She stood and lifted her skirt to the knees. Her pantalettes were covered in grime, courtesy of the climb.

'Drainpipe,' she said.

'You climbed up in that dress?'

'Ah, but this dress is magic.'

'Magic, eh? So why didn't ya fly?'

He had a pretty good point.

'So what do ya want?'

'I've brought you something. Something to help you remember.'

'Remember what?'

'Me, silly.'

'I don't know who you are.'

'Precisely.'

She tried to recover the sketch from her bodice, but it had managed to work its way down. She turned from him, trying to loosen her corset without inviting the dress to fall off. She caught him watching her through the mirror, her bosom enhanced by her hand between her breasts.

'Do you mind?'

'What?'

'Staring. It's rude.'

The irony wasn't lost on her. She fingered the sketch and plucked it out. She readjusted herself and turned back to face him.

'Here.'

He took the sketch from her.

'It's warm.'

She frowned. 'Just look at the drawing.'

She thought she saw some recognition in his eyes. Her optimism grew.

'Where did ya get this?'

'Your sketchbook. I should know, I was there when you drew it. Look - *freckles*.'

'Yeah, ya told me. That still doesn't mean that I know ya.'

Her heart sank. Just what would it take?

'Although something tells me I ought.'

He dropped down onto the bed. She felt a pang of excitement. Hiding a smile, she sat back on the stool; at least, that was her intention. But in haste she misjudged its position and ended up on the floor. He sprang to his feet, trying not to laugh. Talk about embarrassing.

'You all right? Here, give me yer hand.'

'Are you sure your *showgirl* won't mind?'

'She's not my showgirl.'

'That's not what *she* said.'

'Precisely. They were her words, not mine.'

She begrudgingly accepted the offer of his hand and he pulled her back onto her feet. She overbalanced and fell against him. She looked up into his eyes; her anger fell away.

She swallowed, almost forgetting how to breathe, her heart pounding in audible betrayal. It was like they were back on the rigging that day, but this time he didn't turn awa…

He pulled back, drawing a gun. She found herself staring down its barrel.

'Nathan?'

'What are ya?'

'Don't say it like that.'

'Those eyes. Those eyes, they haunt my dreams.'

She glanced aside at herself in the mirror. Her eyes

were bloodshot. Damn the *beast*.

'No,' she cried. 'I'd never intentionally hurt you.'

He removed the safety catch from the gun. She sprang forward at lightning speed and snatched the weapon from his grasp. Now she was the one pointing the gun, albeit with a trembling hand.

'I'm sorry,' she said. 'This wasn't meant to happen. Nathan, we're friends. Why can't you remember?'

'Give me the gun.'

'I can't. Forgive me.'

She quickly turned and fled the room.

Slamming the door behind her, she kept hold of the doorknob, lest he try to follow. He didn't. Her heart sank even more. Was she that unimportant?

With tears in her eyes, she ran off down the hallway, discarding the gun in a flowerpot. She should never have come here. Gretl was right. What on earth was she thinking?

The freckles began to burn on her face.

'No,' she cried. 'Not now. Go away.'

She glanced behind to see the *veil of grey*. She stumbled and fell. No, she wasn't ready.

It flooded over her form.

Chapter 18
Confrontation

Natalya opened her eyes, her cheeks moist with tears. Wherever she was, it wasn't the hallway, the softness of the carpet replaced by stone.

She slowly gazed around. She appeared to be at the foot of a stairway. She licked at her lips; they tasted sweet. It confirmed she was back in the Shadow Realm.

With no way out except the stairs, she started to mount their spiralled stone. The steps were narrow, worn and triangular, a challenge for even her dainty feet. Burning torches lit her way, casting her shadow first before her, then behind.

The evening's events continued to plague her: the look on Nathan's face when he said, *those eyes.* But what did she expect after what she'd done? And yet, she'd never scared him in the past.

Round and round, she continued to climb. The steps seemed to go on forever. She quickened her pace, her anxiousness growing, her breathing becoming reduced to short rasps. She was starting to panic. She felt claustrophobic. What if there wasn't any way out?

She turned a corner and came to a door. She couldn't have been more relieved. It was arched; made of wood, like the one from the village church. She curled her fingers around its ringed handle. The latch clicked back and she entered through, the hinges creaking with years of disuse.

The room beyond was large and impressive, a fire crackling in a central hearth. It lit the walls with minimal shadow, aided by the daylight from a balcony terrace.

She must have been in that fairy-tale tower; the one with the stone balustrade. Her excitement stirred, she began to explore, smiling as she noted the cacti on the dresser. But her new-found enthusiasm soon began to wane, as she started to realise the nature of the room.

The floor was covered in animal skins, their fur still stained with the blood of their slaughter. The bureau was home to an unfortunate fox. Stuffed and displayed as a gruesome trophy. A stag's head stared out from its plinth on the wall, a series of tapestries portraying its demise. The terrifying hunt, its capture and murder. It sickened her to the core.

'So what do you think of my fairy-tale palace? You always did say I looked like a princess.'

Natalya spun, startled by a voice she only knew too well.

'My, you have grown jumpy,' said Ella. 'You looked uncomfortable earlier, too. Whatever happened to that feisty young girl? You know how I like a challenge.'

'I know what you are.'

'Oh, so you do speak.'

'You're the host of the Glass Slipper orchid.'

'Am I now? How's the arm, by the way? I thought you were dead for sure when it cut you.'

Ella's skin began to darken, the Glass Slipper's roots revealing themselves. They were like a network of veins beneath her skin, writhing and twining their way through her flesh. Natalya eyed them with stark horror. Ella gave a smile.

'Don't worry, it answers to me now, and I'd much rather play with my food than eat it. I give it life in return for its *craft*. You could say we were made for each other.'

'Careful, dear, or I might get jealous.'

Natalya spun to see Shah Ming. Like Ella, he'd just appeared out of nowhere. He gave his usual, magnanimous smile.

'As if I would stray from my prince's side? You know how you're never far from my mind.'

'I know I'm not. What say you, wolfcaine? Ella, why don't you show her the view?'

Ella led Natalya outside; Natalya kept the *beast* close by. A soft, warm glow seeped across her face, and just for a moment, she forgot her situation.

The view across London was a wonder to behold, the sky a mix of night and day. There were two crescent moons, a half dozen suns, and an exhibition of rainbows. The air was full of sugary sweetness and almost palpable to touch.

'It's beautiful,' said Natalya.

It mesmerised her mind. The Thames was pure blue; the smog a fluff of cloud. The bridge she'd passed earlier, under construction, now complete with angular towers. A large ship was sailing between them, the central road raised to allow for its sails.

There was a greenery of gardens – she recognised Hyde Park – monuments, steam trains, horses and carriages. Natalya observed in wondrous awe, the city coated in a dreaminess of haze.

'Glorious, isn't it,' said Ella, the vines rising up from the skin of her arms to bask in the warmth of the air. 'But do you know what the Shadow Realm is? Or why it even exists?'

'I know you're infecting the people of London.'

'But do you know the reason why?'

A rainbow fluoresced in brilliant colour, then drained away to grey. A hollow blackness burrowed through its bow. Natalya gasped. The *darkness*.

She could suddenly see it everywhere she looked, just as she could from the street. It mimicked the shadow, it lurked beneath water. It sat in the darkest clouds of the sky. Natalya shuddered, feeling its coldness; its disrespect for life.

'Does it scare you, *Sweetheart*? It should do. If you fear the Glass Slipper, you should well fear the dark. Nothing exists within it or beyond.'

'Are you saying that it's *death*?'

Shah Ming joined them on the terrace.

'War is coming. Boundaries are being drawn. The armies of the Shadow Realm rise. Join our cause or face the consequences. We could do with a warrior such as yourself.'

'I'm not a warrior.'

'Aren't you? It's in your blood. It's the reason you were born.'

'Remember,' said Ella, 'if you're not our friend, then you're not our friend at all.'

She made a sudden movement with her hand. A vine lashed out and slit Natalya's cheek. She clasped at her face, blood bubbling through her fingers. The last time the orchid cut her, she almost lost her life.

'There, that makes us equal, I think. Oh, Shah, look, the poor girl's scared. What, did you think I wouldn't bear a grudge for what you did to my face?'

Mortified, Natalya fled inside, heading towards the stairway door. It faded away, into the wall. She spun to see Shah Ming lift a rifle from the wall.

'In India, we hunt all types of things. But I've never shot myself a wolfcaine before.'

Natalya swallowed, panic in her brain. The *beast* begged for release and she let it have control.

In seconds she was brandishing a pair of claws. She raged at Shah Ming like some mindless animal. The prince raised the rifle, took careful aim, and blew a hole through her shoulder.

The impact threw Natalya off her feet. She landed on the floor, a numbness in her arm. At least the gun-wound didn't hurt, then a blistering heat surged through her flesh. Blood darkened the redness of her dress. She groaned through gritted teeth.

'You're slipping, my prince.'

'Not at all, Ella, dear. I merely wish to preserve her face. It's been a while since I've had myself a trophy, and her head would look so good on the wall.'

Natalya struggled onto her knees. She tried to stand, but the world just spun. Her stomach churned; there was vomit in her throat. What would Bleddin say if he could see her now? *Never give the beast control. It's there to do your bidding, not the other way around.*

She eyed Shah Ming through her peripheral vision. He was approaching from behind, rifle still in hand. *Use your brain, not your rage.* The prince was smug, which made him overconfident. She waited until he was directly behind her, then lashed out with her arm and sliced her nails through his leg.

The prince cried out and dropped the rifle. She sprang up behind him, her claws at his throat. The world spun again, threatening oblivion, but the *beast* returned to ease her dizzied mind.

Shah Ming gave a disconcerting laugh.

'Not quite the novice we thought her to be. But I think she forgets the realm in which we stand.'

She wasn't quite sure exactly what he meant, but the next she knew he'd vanished from her arms.

'Not your day, is it, *Sweetheart*? How's the cut? Feeling infected?'

Natalya nervously touched at her cheek. Ella gave a smirk.

'Oh, you always were naïve. I'd rather play with my food, remember? It's not infected; not this time, anyway. **Better to torture, maim and torment, than carry out the kill.**'

Natalya looked at Ella in confusion. The words were hers, but not the voice. Not that she'd time to think about it now. She had to find a way out.

She made a dash for the balcony terrace. Vines stole her legs and she fell against the dresser. The resident cacti tumbled all around. Ella held up a bottled potion.

'Nathaniel used to steal these from me. Add a cactus and you get an instant bath. I bet you felt special, soaking in that tub? I hate to tell you, *Sweetheart*, you weren't the only one. He played the same trick with every girl he met. Think you were special? Think again. Of course, he was only after one thing. I believe you're the only one he didn't bed.'

Natalya gave her an angry glare. How dare she? Nathan wasn't like that.

'You're only jealous because he didn't want you.'

'Wrong again, *Sweetheart*. I've already had him. Now then, time you had another scrub.'

She hurled the bottle of potion at the dresser. It broke, soaking the cacti with its content. They began to swell, outstretching their skins. Natalya scrambled to her feet and ran.

The cacti exploded, one after the other, creating a torrent of water. The resultant wave swept Natalya off her feet, smashing her through the balcony balustrade.

She reached out in a panic, water raining all about her. She desperately dug her claws into the stone. As the water drained away, she found herself dangling from the balcony's edge by nothing but her fingers. And it would be her wounded arm.

Shah Ming knelt above her.

'Can you feel the pull of gravity, *wolfcaine*? Can you feel it dragging you down?' He began to trace her arm with his dagger, the tip of its blade scratching at her skin. 'Heavier, heavier, dragging you downwards, forcing you to...'

He drove the blade into her shoulder, antagonising the existing gunshot. Natalya cried out, her hold weakening, fresh blood painting her skin. She frantically eyed the tower below, and then she was falling towards it.

She landed hard on its turreted roof and grasped at the vines that smothered its tiles. The vines broke away; she grabbed out again, a five-storey drop awaiting her below. She slid over the edge, gave an anguished cry, and shuddered to a halt. The vine in her grasp vibrated with her weight; she dare not even breathe.

Carefully, she began to climb back up, until she was safe back on the roof. A tapping of claw on tile drew her attention, and she looked to the gargoyle crawling her way.

The creature looked at her - did it smile? - and began to rip at the vines. Anxiously, Natalya tried to scramble up the slope. Her vine gave way; she made a final lunge.

The next she knew she was falling, the air sweeping past, drying out her clothes. She should have felt panicked; she should have felt scared. But she was more distracted by the speed of her descent. She wasn't falling like a rock to the ground. She was heading earthwards at less rapid pace. Perhaps her dress could fly after all? She turned her gaze above.

She found herself hanging from the leg of the gargoyle, the creature flapping to keep them from the ground. She must have grabbed it in that last, frantic lunge. And then, the gargoyle broke free.

She fell the final fifty feet at speed. She hit the cobbles and heard her ribs crunch. She remembered crying out, pain flooding her brain, and then she must have blacked out.

***

'Here. Fer you? Don't worry, I bought it.'
'With some of the money you stole, no doubt.'
'I never did get yer principles on stealing.'
'If it's needed to survive, then it doesn't count.'

Natalya raised her head from the cobbles. She groaned and winced with the pain. Across the alley was Nathan and herself. She remembered the conversation fondly.

'Oh, Nathan. Nathan. It's a chocolate cream bar. How on earth did you know?'
'How did I know? Ya mention the things every time yer stomach groans.'

She watched herself sit down beside him and bite off a piece of the bar.

'A dunt spze ud luk a peeze?'

'Ya might as well have said that in Russian.'

Her past-self laughed; Natalya laughed. Her ribs screamed out in protest at the movement. Her lips tasted sweet; she was still in the Shadow Realm. But she didn't understand this.

Was it a memory? But it wasn't in her head. It was being played out before her very eyes. Plus, she'd been unconscious, which meant the only person who might be recalling it was Nathan. But Nathan had amnesia. She felt so confused.

Unconsciousness claimed her again.

Chapter 19
The Journey Home

Wetness splashed Natalya's skin. She slowly opened her eyes. She found herself lying face down in the alley, rain spattering off its cobbles.

She gritted her teeth and managed to sit, her ribs and her shoulder competing for most pain. Her lungs felt like they were being squeezed of all life; no wonder Nathan had been incapacitated for weeks.

It was dark, and yet she could sense the nearing dawn. She gazed to the sky; the towers were gone. It seemed she was no longer trapped in the Shadow Realm, the sugary air replaced by London's soot.

Eying Gretl's shawl near the drainpipe, she began to crawl towards it. Each movement pummelled her brain with pain; she called on the *beast* to lend its support. She somehow managed to make it across the cobbles, her chest on fire and blackness threatening a return.

Pulling the shawl best she could around her shoulders, she part crawled, part hobbled, towards the main street. She couldn't afford to be found by Ella. Another encounter and she wouldn't survive. But where would she go? Who could she call on? And then, she gave a smile.

Dimitri Igorevitch Gusev. She was sure the old man would help. What's more, his shop was only several streets away. She gathered her strength and struggled to her feet.

As she walked, the rain became torrential. The downpour was short, but it soaked her to the skin. She must have looked like some half-drowned rat, but her looks were the last thing on her mind.

She reached the shop in agony, the clay Russian toys observing through the window. She banged against the door. No sign of life. She banged again, even louder. She slunk into the doorway.

At least, for now, she was safe. She could feel her eyelids growing heavy. She tried to fight it, but the pain was too much. Her mind drifted back to black.

***

Natalya opened her eyes. It was day, and yet, the

curtains were drawn to keep the sun from the house. She tried to move and wished she hadn't. She observed the room with just her eyes.

It was small, quaint and cosy. The sideboard graced with a familiar photo. She'd been here before, on this very settee, reciting prayers for her parents.

She carefully eased herself up. Her hair was still damp, as were her clothes. She peeled back her sleeve to inspect her shoulder. The wound was raw, and plugged by congealed blood.

She slowly lowered her feet to the carpet. She crossed to the sideboard, hugging her ribs. She observed the elderly lady in the photo; she could only assume she was Gusev's wife. And yet, he appeared to live here alone. Perhaps the old woman had died?

Someone entered the shop below; there were footsteps on the stairs. She looked to the doorway and saw Gusev enter. His face betrayed his surprise.

'What? You are better? Already?'

She made a slight movement and winced.

'No, of course not. I'm just an old fool.'

'I can't thank you enough for taking me in.'

He helped her back onto the settee.

'I'm not used to young ladies knocking at my door at such an early hour. Lilian would have said I was dreaming.'

'Lilian?'

He glanced at the photo. 'My wife.'

'Is she...?'

'Dead? Yes. These past two years. Consumption. She put up a fight, though. Your Mr Croft did help her so, what with all his potions.'

'Potions?'

'Lillian liked her baths. They seemed to somehow ease her pain.'

Natalya swallowed. She could have kicked herself. She'd almost fallen for Ella's lies. This was why Nathan was stealing the potions, not to charm some stupid girls.

She heard the shop door open again. There were hurried footsteps on the stairs.

'In here,' cried Gusev.

Nathan rushed in. Natalya's heart forgot to beat. Nathan quickly noted her state; horror crossed his face.

'Good Lord, Natalya. What happened to ya?'

'It looks far worse than it is.'

'I suspect she's broken several ribs,' said Gusev.

'Yeah, I know how that feels.'

Nathan took a closer look at her shoulder.

'I've seen wounds like this before. Natalya, have ya been shot?'

'Shot, stabbed, and thrown off a building. And those were just the bits I remember.'

'The sooner we get ya to the manor, the better.'

'The manor?'

'The one ya've been hiding out in.'

'You know about the manor?'

'Yeah. Long story. I've a carriage outside. Gusev, I owe ya.'

He helped Natalya to her feet.

'Thank you, Gusev Igorevitch,' she said.

She held out her hand. He shook it.

'The pleasure was all mine, Natalya Ivanovna. And if anyone asks, you were never here.'

***

Natalya gazed out of the carriage window. The park in the square looked so pleasant in the day. No blanket of shadows; no creeping fog. Even the leaves had lost their layer of frost. They'd made a detour to pick up Gretl. She glanced back across at the hotel steps.

Nathan came hurrying out of the entrance. He descended the steps, two at a time. He spoke to the driver and re-joined her in the carriage. She looked at him in question.

'Where's Gretl?'

'She signed out early this morning. Left a message; she's gone back to the manor.'

The carriage jerked as the horses pulled forward. Natalya winced, muffling a groan.

Soon they were back amongst the rush of the city,

people cluttering up the pavements, horses cluttering up the roads. She glanced at Nathan and caught him watching. He looked away. She looked away, too. She looked back and caught him watching. She gave an inner smile.

'What?' she said. 'Is there something in my hair?'

'Apart from the blue that matches yer eyes?'

'My eyes are green.'

'Yeah, I'd noticed.'

'Then why say blue?'

'To match yer hair.'

Was he purposely trying to confuse her?

'Anyway, I thought my eyes haunted your dreams?

'They do, but only in a good way now.'

'That wasn't what you said last night?'

'Yeah, well, I've started to remember. Yer not quite the stranger I thought ya to be.'

She could have cheered. She could have cried. She tried her best to do neither. But she also felt a sense of dread. What if he remembered her trying to kill him?

'So who was it that did this to ya?'

'Shah Ming; with a little help from Ella.'

'I always said I didn't trust the woman. What exactly happened?'

Her story occupied their journey out of London. As she narrated it, it seemed absurd. Fairy-tale palaces, princes and princesses, not to mention blood-thirsty plants. He listened intently, just as always, accepting each fact as if everyday life.

'Sounds like ya've had a bit of a night.'

'I'm not quite sure how it is I'm still alive.'

'Well I'm glad that ya are.'

Her heart danced a beat.

'Otherwise, I'd be talking to me-self.'

Did he honestly say such things on purpose?

The coach began to slow. She looked at Nathan, worried. He pulled down the window and stuck out his head.

'There's someone approaching up the road.'

Natalya *pricked* her ears, then heard a gravelled voice. She swallowed. She knew exactly who it was. The horseman dismounted and opened the door. Bleddin gave Natalya a stare.

'Does it hurt?'

She nodded.

'Good. Maybe next time you'll do as you're told. I was hoping for at least a degree of restraint.' He glanced at Nathan. 'But obviously not. Driver, on your way.'

He returned to his horse and joined them as escort. It made her feel like a prisoner. It certainly killed the mood with Nathan, and they spent the rest of the journey in silence.

By the time they arrived at the manor, she'd

prepared herself for a serious dressing down. Nathan helped her out of the carriage. Gretl came running out of the house.

'Natalya. Good Heavens. What happened?' She sounded more concerned than mad. 'Soames, will you fetch my brother, please. We'll take her into the lounge.'

The butler nodded and returned inside. It seemed her dressing down could wait. She glanced back over her shoulder at Bleddin. He was guiding his horse towards the stables.

'I don't think he's very happy with me.'

'I'm sure he's glad you're alive,' said Gretl.

'In case I forget, this dress is *amazing*.'

'I did say it was a bit special.'

Soon she was soon laid out on the settee. She felt fatigued; exhausted. She saw Gretl motion Nathan aside. She extended her wolfcaine hearing.

'I take it your memory's returned then?' said Gretl. 'So much for the *forgetfulness* spell.'

'*Forgetfulness* spell?!' said Natalya, sitting sharply. Her ribs screamed out with pain.

'Now that's what you get for eavesdropping.'

'But I thought that Nathan had amnesia?'

Gretl frowned and crossed to the settee. Nathan took himself off to the window, leaving the witch to explain.

'That day you thought you'd killed him. He was

with Obadiah when you fell off that pier. They brought you back here. Nathan told us what had happened. As soon as he mentioned the *Glass Slipper,* we knew. But your life wasn't just at risk from the infection; chances were, they'd still want to hunt you down. Nathan was concerned he would give you away, so he agreed to me using a *forgetfulness* spell. It erased all memory of you from his mind. It was as if he had amnesia. But *forgetfulness* spells are delicate things, which is why we tried to keep you apart.'

'Nathan gave up his memories... for me?'

'Hey, it was the chance of a lifetime,' he quipped.

She stuck out her tongue. He stuck his out back. She tried not to laugh, but still her ribs pulled.

'Anyway,' she said. 'I forgot about you, too, and I didn't need any spell.'

'I think you might want to check that with Gretl.'

Natalya looked at the witch; she looked away.

'You put a spell on me, as well? Is that why I couldn't remember?'

'I might have done.'

'You made me forget?'

'Well it didn't do much good, did it?'

Hansel rushed in with his medical bag. Gretl moved out of the way.

'Hmm, someone's been caught in the crossfire. Let's have a look, shall we, Fräulein?'

He examined her injuries, *hmm*-ing and *ahh*-ing, but without any actual words.

'Well, brother. How is she?'

'Lucky. The bullet passed straight through. The dagger has done some damage to the tissue, but it's already started to heal.'

'And her ribs?'

'She's broken three or four. Healing time, normally four to six weeks.'

'She'll be up in no time,' said Bleddin from the doorway.

Hansel gave him an incredulous look.

'Damn it, man. She's sixteen years old. I don't care if she's human or *beast*. When you face the enemy, circumstances change. She was quite clearly out of her depth.'

'She's alive, isn't she?'

'Barely, man. And we're still none the wiser as to what's going on. All this preparation. All this training. For what?'

'I think they're planning an attack.'

Four pairs of eyes turned Natalya's way. It made her want to squirm.

'*War is coming. Boundaries are being drawn. The armies of the Shadow Realm rise.* Those were Shah Ming's very words. He wanted me to join their ranks.'

'An army?' said Bleddin. 'Have you seen this

army?'

Natalya shook her head. 'But everyone at CINDERS had been infected by what looked like Glass Slipper spores.'

'Spores?' said Gretl. 'And you didn't think to tell me?'

She sounded like Natalya's mother when cross. No raised voice. No angry movement. Just the vexed tone of her speech.

'I tried to tell you, Gretl. Honest. But you couldn't hear me for the crowd.'

'And later? When we were back at the hotel? Oh, but of course, your thoughts were on *him*.'

Natalya tried not to look across at Nathan.

Bleddin cleared his throat. 'Politicians. Ambassadors of State. CINDERS has recently played host to them all. If they're using the guests as carriers of spores, who knows how many people are infected by now.'

'Then surely the solution is simple,' said Hansel. 'Kill the source and you kill the infection.'

'Except this isn't an outbreak of cholera. And Ella Cinders is not your source. The source you seek is the *Glass Slipper* orchid, and its roots are sown in the Shadow Realm. There's only one person can enter that world, and she's the one you say's *out of her depth.*'

A clicking sound, a scuttling of feet. Natalya's ears pricked. No one else seemed to hear it, but then no one else was a wolfcaine.

'Gretl,' she said. 'I can hear… *something*.'

Gretl sniffed at the air.

'Yes, and I can smell magic at work. Something's about to take place.'

Bleddin stepped forward and drew his sword. Hansel grabbed a *chassepot* from the fireplace. He loaded it with a paper cartridge, locking it into place.

'Gretl, get her into the basement. You, *boy*, help my wife.'

By *boy,* he was meaning Nathan, which must have gone down well. Nevertheless, Nathan helped Gretl assist Natalya to her feet.

'No, I can't,' said Natalya.

'Can't what?'

'Leave. They'll need my help.'

'Didn't last night teach you anything?' said Gretl. 'You're in no condition to fight.'

Clawed feet began to click against the window. Feet that should have been stone. There was a screeching sound, a shadow in the glass, and a gargoyle smashed straight through the window.

Like a swarm of locusts, the gargoyles invaded, snarling and spitting saliva through their teeth. Hansel took aim and fired his rifle. Bleddin swung his sword, slicing off a gargoyle's leg.

Gretl and Nathan helped Natalya to the door, but she

still felt like she should be helping. A gargoyle swooped to block their path, digging its claws into the plaster of the wall.

Without thinking, Natalya lunged forward. She grabbed the gargoyle by the wing and slung it across the room. The pain in her ribs almost tripped out her brain; she could barely find the air to breathe.

'You silly girl. I told you,' snapped Gretl.

'Come on,' said Nathan, supporting her once more.

They bundled Natalya through the doorway. She felt like the biggest burden in the world.

Another gunshot. Another gargoyle fell. The innards of another sprayed the papered wall. But for every gargoyle the two men killed, another crawled into its place.

Nathan slammed the doors shut behind them.

'Now where?' he said.

'Down there,' said Gretl.

They started down the hallway. The doorknob to Hansel's study rattled; there was someone – or *thing* – trying to get out. They came to a halt as the door finally opened and a ghoulish figure stepped through.

'What on earth..?' gasped Gretl.

The parody of *Hansel* turned to face them. It was the same twisted abhorrence from the other night, but now existing in their world. More ghoulish figures joined it in the hallway, wielding scalpels, needles and knives.

'What are they?' said Gretl.

'The nightmares of your patients. The horrors of a fragile mind. Gretl, I can't smell magic, can you? I think these were summoned by something else.'

'Something else?'

'The Glass Slipper orchid. Obadiah said they have the power to create.'

'Ladies,' said Nathan, 'I hate to interrupt, but what are we gunna do about them?'

The ghouls were almost upon them now, despite their laboured movement. Nathan drew a gun from his pocket and aimed it at the creatures.

'Didn't I throw that…?'

'Into a flowerpot? Yeah. Let's hope it doesn't shoot dirt. Are they real?'

'Why?'

'I'm not a murderer.'

'No. At least, I don't think they are.'

He looked at her. She shrugged her shoulders. He frowned, rolled his eyes, and fired just the same. *Hansel* fell, not a cry to mark his passing. Nathan shot down another.

'This is far too easy.'

The *Hansel* ghoul shuddered, opened its eyes and began to get back up.

'How come? I shot 'im straight through the heart.'

'I have a theory. If I'm right, they can't be killed.'

'Can't be killed? Now she tells me.' He looked at Gretl. 'Any ideas?'

'Throw your gun amongst them.'

'Throw it?'

'Quickly. Trust me, Nathan, I'm a witch.'

He did as instructed, Gretl uttered a spell, and the gunpowder inside the bullets exploded. The force sent the ghouls sprawling to the floor. They laid there a moment, then started to revive.

'Come on.'

They hurried between the figures. At the end of the hallway, Gretl turned left.

'No,' said Natalya, turning right.

'The basement is this way.'

'I've a theory to prove.'

Gretl gave a frown. 'But Obadiah…'

'..won't know if we're quick. Gretl, please. I'll crawl if I have to.'

'You'll get me divorced, you know that?'

'If she doesn't get us killed, first.'

They set off towards the sanatorium, Natalya grimacing with every stride. But she had to know if what she thought was true. This was where she proved herself.

They entered the sanatorium.

'My Lord, what's happened?' gasped Gretl.

The staff were laid out, unconscious on the floor.

Natalya called on her wolfcaine vision. It stuttered. She sniffed more pollen up her nose.

'They're infected,' she said, her vision kicking in.

'What? Like the guests at CINDERS?'

Natalya crossed to the nearest cell and peered in at its patient. She checked out the cell next door, then the next. The story was the same.

'They're all asleep. Infected.'

'I don't understand?' said Nathan.

'Their slumber's unnatural. This is down to the Glass Slipper. It's stealing their nightmares and using them against us. I think I know what the Shadow Realm is. It's the place we go to dream.'

'Well done, *Natasha!* Now say goodbye.'

An invisible force threw Natalya off her feet. She landed on the floor and cried out in pain. She called on the *beast* and struggled to her knees. She gazed across at Ella.

'You followed me here?'

'Of course I did. I wondered where it was you'd been hiding out. So good of you to oblige me. And now your friends are going to die.'

'What have you done with Natalya?' cried Gretl.

'I swear, if ya've harmed her,' snapped Nathan.

But Natalya wasn't sure what they meant. She was knelt right here in front of them.

'Oh, Nathan, stop your fawning,' said Ella. 'It's

pathetic. I think I preferred you with amnesia.'

'Bring her back.'

'I'm here,' said Natalya.

'And yet they can neither hear nor see you. I've trapped you in a dream, *Natasha* dear. They think I've made you vanish.'

Natalya anxiously looked around her. If this was a dream, then it looked no different. She licked at her lips; they tasted sweet. She applied her wolfcaine vision and saw the outline between worlds. Ella's image reflected in both.

'Now, *Natasha,* observe as your friends die.'

Ella pointed at the wall of sketches, feeding their scribbled lines with life. The lines began to spiral, creating a vortex that grew from the page into a raging maelstrom.

The vortex tore the wall apart in seconds, sucking its mortar high into the air. It grew with such force that it ripped apart the ceiling, its funnel widening to suck up the floor.

'Run!' cried Natalya. 'Run!!'

But Gretl and Nathan couldn't hear her.

'If you harm them, Ella…'

'You'll do what? Spank me? Accept it, *Natasha.* Bad girls do bad things. ***You're going to suffer for what you've put me through. Just like the rest of your kind.***'

'What?' said Natalya.

Ella looked at her blankly. 'I told you. Bad girls do bad things.'

'Natalya!'

'Nathan, we have to go. Now!'

Gretl and Nathan fled the sanatorium.

The maelstrom changed direction after them, and all Natalya could do was watch. She turned to Ella, her fingernails growing, a pricking in her eyes.

'End this now, or you die with them.'

'I'd be more concerned with saving yourself. You think I'd put you out of harm's way? This dream is dying, and you'll die with it. As for me, I know the way out. Pity that you don't.'

Natalya sprang forward, grasping at the witch. Ella calmly stepped back into the real world. Natalya landed on the floor with a crunch, another rib snapping like a twig.

Ella wandered off into the ruins.

A blur of colour skirted Natalya's vision. The walls of the dream were starting to melt. The world was breaking down into pigment, just like that first time she entered the Shadow Realm. Reds. Blues. Greens. Yellows. Natalya glanced around in desperation. Nathan. Gretl. Hansel. Bleddin. How could she save them if she couldn't save herself? She tried to stand and collapsed back to the floor, pigment lapping against her skin.

A feeling of hopelessness consumed her. She swallowed; she could feel *its* menacing presence. She turned to face the dying dream, and the *darkness* that nourished on its carcass.

Chapter 20
The Girl with White Hair

A breeze swept across Natalya's face. One moment she was trapped, the next she was here. Water lapped against the suede of her boots, a grittiness of sand eating up her heels.

It reminded her of the seaside, those trips to the coast with her parents. It stirred up memories she cherished beyond all others. Memories of happier times.

But she couldn't be here, remembering this now. Nathan and the others needed her help. She had to save them. She had to get back. Every second lost brought them closer to death.

'Hello, *wolfcaine.*'

Natalya turned sharply. The beach was small;

cocooned by rock. An old, rotting ladder led to steps in the stone, which in turn led to a grassy embankment. Stood at its edge was the girl with white hair, a fringe shielding the pinkness of her eyes.

'I need to get back to my friends,' said Natalya.

'Their fates are already decided.'

'Decided? No, I won't accept they're dead.'

'I just meant whatever might happen has happened. Even a wolfcaine cannot change the past.'

Natalya opened her mouth to protest, but something told her it wouldn't make no difference. The girl seemed wiser than her visible age, but if Natalya played along, she might find a way back.

'Where are we?'

'The Shadow Realm.'

'But here? This place?'

The girl gazed around. 'Some would call it home.'

'You live here?'

'I visit. As often as I can. This place is not my prison.'

Her voice was soft; therapeutic. Natalya blinked and the teenage girl was gone. She found her stood beside her on the beach, the sea lapping at her feet.

'What? Are you a witch of some sort?'

The girl shook her head. 'Witches aren't allowed here.'

'But Ella...?'

'Was invited by the Glass Slipper orchid. It breaks her direct contact with the world. This landscape - this *dreamscape* - is the source of all magic. Never must the *source* and its *outlet* meet.'

'Dreams create magic?'

'Is magic not a dream? The subconscious mind is a powerful thing.'

'Who are you?'

'A friend. You're *ugly,* like me. *He* says I should hide away from the world.'

'He?'

'A tale too long to tell. That's not why I've brought you here.'

Natalya ran a hand through her hair. Strangely, her ribs didn't pain.

'So why am I here?'

'I need you to learn. Learn how the Shadow Realm works. Do you like rainbows? I like rainbows.'

A rainbow suddenly formed in the sky.

'Yes. Yes, I always have.'

'They embody the circle of life. You are familiar with the *veil of grey,* are you not?'

'I know it all too well.'

'The *grey* forms the dream; the dream then thrives. It exists as though it was part of the world. Then the dream starts to fade. Its substance turns to pigment. The pigment forms a rainbow. The rainbow fades to grey.

And so the cycle repeats.'

'And the *darkness*?'

The girl looked at her sharply. 'The *darkness* is not a place you should go. Nothing ever dreamt may escape it forever. It pursues all life, its only gift, *death*. Here, I thought you might like these.'

She held out her hand; there was nothing in it. The air around it melted. The pigment poured into her palm like melted wax and formed a posy of foxglove flowers.

'How did you do that?'

'This world can be shaped by those with the talent to do so. The *grey* is like a clay to be moulded. The material foundation of every dream.'

Natalya took the flowers from her. They felt so real that they might have been.

'Thank you. They're lovely. Obadiah always said that foxglove has a medicinal purpose.'

'In your world, yes, but they're not needed here. This realm is a medicine all in itself. How do you feel? Do your ribs still hurt?'

'No. No, they hardly hurt at all.'

'Your skin absorbs the moisture in the air. It heals your body. Makes you strong.' The girl was silent a moment. 'Would you like to learn how to pass between worlds?'

It was foremost on Natalya's mind. Despite what the girl had said about fate, Natalya needed to know what was happening to her friends.

'Everything you touch. Everything you see. All is a gateway between worlds. But some doors are easier to open than others. Master the simple, and you'll conquer the hard. The weakest points are where there's decay, but beware, for that's where the *darkness* lurks most. It feeds on the dying pigment of the dream. It turns all it touches to death.'

One moment Natalya was stood on the beach, the next she was back in the asylum. The sky, the sea, were all disappeared. She felt the life drain from the air.

Horror and panic returned to her mind. She span in search of the girl. She found her stood on the steps to the catwalk. Natalya ran to the foot of the stairs.

'Why bring us back?'

'We never left. I simply remoulded the *clay*.'

'We're trapped?'

'You need to find a way out. Tell me, do your freckles ever burn?'

'Yes.' In fact, they were burning now. Those damnable freckles she hated so much. 'Why? What does it mean if they burn?'

'Why don't you follow their guidance?'

Natalya turned, feeling confused. She waded forward through the pigment. Her freckles grew hot, and then they grew cold, depending on her direction. Her father had once shown her how to dowse for water.

Now the dowser was her.

She followed the warmth of her face across the dream, but she still wasn't sure what she was looking for. Suddenly, the *darkness* lurched out of the pigment; she gave a gasp and dove from its path. She landed in the coloured paint of the dream, her *wolfcaine vision* flickering in her sight. The outline between the two worlds widened, revealing a divide in the symmetry of their structure.

She glanced back at the girl.

'Is this it? Is this what I'm looking for?'

'Imagine it's a doorway. Take a step through.'

'What about you? Aren't you coming?'

'I can't. But we will meet again, I promise. All you have to do is survive.'

'No. Wait!'

The girl melted from sight.

'I don't even know your name.'

Alone, Natalya felt her confidence ebb. What if this wasn't the way out at all? The pigment was rising. The dream was almost dead. The tendrils of the *darkness* were closing in around. She gazed back at the faltering outline and launched herself towards it.

***

Natalya landed amongst a pile of stone. Above, a wall toppled down towards her. She quickly rolled clear, brick deafening her ears as it smashed into the ground, clouding her in dust.

She sat, coughing the dirt from her lungs. A rainbow glowed brightly overhead. She observed its beauty, its farewell performance, and then the dream and the rainbow were gone.

Somehow, she'd managed to escape. She licked at her lips, just to make sure. She pricked her ears, but she couldn't hear the maelstrom. All she could hear was the deafening quiet. She ran her gaze across the landscape. Ruin met her eyes.

Distraught, she clambered to her feet, dust clinging to the air. Even the woodland had not escaped unscathed, its trees ripped out and strewn across the land.

'Nathan! Gretl! Obadiah! Doctor Schneider!'

Her only reply was the echo of her voice. She saw an arm sticking out from the rubble. She ran across and started lifting stone.

Her ribs protested at the effort, but with the *beast* in tow, they were nothing but an ache. Like the girl had said, the Shadow Realm had healed them. She moved a slab of concrete and horror met her eyes. She stared at the contorted mess of flesh and bone. It was one of the patients. She vomited her guts.

Dread now spiralled within her. How could anyone survive such a thing? But she had to be strong; push the notion from her mind. She had to believe that *they* could still be alive.

A noise. A stirring. Someone groaned. She hurried and stumbled her way across the rubble.

'Hello?'

There was movement from beneath a piece of wood. She prised back what was left of the old grandfather clock.

'Mr Soames? Oh, my. Thank the Lord, you're alive. Careful now. Let me help you up.'

She sat him down on what used to be a dresser. By some miracle of fate, he'd only suffered cuts. He looked at her, his body trembling. She dabbed at the blood running down his face.

'It's all right,' she said. 'Just take your time.'

He nodded. He looked tired. Or maybe it was shock?

'Does it hurt anywhere?'

He shook his head. He clasped her hand in his.

'You must find the others, Miss Natalya. We were heading for the basement when the wall fell in on me. There's a tunnel that leads through the hill to the temple. If they made it underground, they could still be alive.'

'The temple?' Since when did they have a temple?

'Just follow the river upstream. There's a grille…'

He took a moment to catch his breath. She didn't want to push him, but she really had to ask.

'What about Nathan? Was Nathan with you?'

He nodded. 'But a gargoyle swept him up into the maelstrom.'

'He's... dead?'

The world broke away beneath her feet. She'd just got him back; now she'd lost him again?

'I'm sorry, Miss. I couldn't say. Go find them, Miss Natalya. Go save the others.'

She set off across the rubble again, but the haste was gone from her stride. Her life felt over; she no longer cared. It was selfish, she knew, but she couldn't bear the heartache. Rather the agony of a dozen broken ribs than the anguish of knowing he was dead.

But the truth was, she *did* care. Life was precious, and she'd always believed that. Besides, he wasn't dead until she found his body. She picked up her pace, searching for the living. More bloodied bodies graced her trodden path.

She finally reached the brow of the hill. Below, the stream flowed freely through the grassland. She began her descent, her direction upstream. She was two thirds down when she saw someone walking along the embankment, jacket in hand. Her heart became frozen in time.

'Nathan?' *Oh, please, let it be Nathan.*

She quickened her pace; she began to run.

'Nathan.'

He seemed distracted elsewhere. She ran even faster.

'Nathan!' she cried.

He looked her way and came to a standstill. His bloodied face lit up in shocked surprise.

Twenty feet. Ten feet. Five feet. Two. She sprang into his arms and knocked him flying off his feet. They hit the water with a grandiose splash. Its coldness shocked any tiredness from their limbs.

'Gah! What ya trying to do? Drown us?'

'Sorry,' she laughed. 'But I thought you'd been killed.'

He stood upright in the foot-deep water. She looked at him, still flapping like a duck. She stopped. She must have looked ridiculous. At least it brought a smile to his face. He returned to the embankment and picked up his jacket. She stood, water draining from everywhere.

'The magic dress aint waterproof, then?'

She yelped and plucked a fish from down her bosom. His grin widened. She waded from the river, her skirt rising up to allow her legs to dry.

'Are you staring, again?'

'Yer dress just shrunk.'

'I told you before. It's crafted with magic.'

He gave a groan and hugged at his ribs.

'Nathan?'

'It's fine. I just had an awkward landing. It's not every day ya fall outta the sky.' He looked at her and gave a grin. 'It's good to see ya, too, by the way.'

She smiled. 'I'm looking for a temple.'

They set off along the embankment. She hated herself for being so happy. People were dead; all those innocent lives, and here she was acting like a lovesick child.

'There. Is that what yer looking for?'

It was a square-shaped building with a spired, domed roof. Impaled on that spire was a lifeless gargoyle, its blood having spattered the panelling with green.

'Is that the gargoyle…?'

'That grabbed me? Yeah. Luckily, I landed in that tree. What do ya want with this place, anyway? It's just an empty building.'

She entered into the temple, its ceiling depicting some story from the Bible. A good churchgoer would have known its chapter and verse. Natalya didn't even know which testament.

Like Nathan had said, the room was empty. She looked to the iron grille in the floor. She dropped to her knees and curled her fingers through its bars. She called on the strength of the *beast* and pulled.

'Careful,' said Nathan, rushing to help. 'I thought ya'd broken yer ribs?'

'They're better now.'

He looked at her, astonished. 'Better? I was in agony fer weeks.'

Together they heaved the grille aside. She stuck her head down into the darkness. It stank of damp earth and stagnant air. She pricked her ears and heard distant voices. One was definitely Gretl's.

'What is it?' said Nathan.

She sat back and smiled.

'I can hear them,' she said. 'They're alive.'

***

With Gretl, Bleddin and Hansel rescued, they returned to the hill and the manor. They stood there, staring at the total devastation, hardly able to comprehend the truth. Natalya's cheer was now forgotten. They spent the whole afternoon sifting through the rubble.

Occasionally, they'd find a survivor, and Hansel would patch them up best he could. But there was no denying the number of dead, and every stone turned added more to their total.

It took its toll on all of them, especially Hansel; these were his friends. Or, at least, his colleagues and patients, and his frustration turned to angry words. Words seemed aimed at Natalya.

'Had Ella Cinders not been led here... someone should be held accountable for this. There's no excuse. Actions have consequences... Some people here just need to grow up.'

He was right. The blame was hers to bear. And all

because she couldn't do as she was told. She'd followed her heart and run after Nathan, and in the process got everyone killed.

She felt sick to the pit of her stomach. She deserved to be swallowed by the *darkness* alive. How could she ever live with herself? How could she even go on?

'*Casualties of War,*' Bleddin had called them.

Hansel's response had been explosive. The tension between them had been building all day, ever since Bleddin had prioritised the search for survivors in favour of the horses.

'Horses? What about the people, man?'

'My duty is to **our** survival, not theirs.'

'You heartless bastard.'

'We're at war, Doctor Schneider. You of all people should know what that means.'

He did. In fact, both men did. But their experiences of battle came from different perspectives. As a physician, Hansel had been there to save lives. As an officer, Bleddin had been there to take them, strategy being part of his psyche. Perhaps that was why the two men clashed? And yet, Natalya felt there was more.

As night drew in, they retired to a fire just short of the temple steps. The building had become a make-shift hospital, not that it had many patients. The atmosphere remained as sombre as the day, with only the sound of fire eating wood to occupy their ears.

As Bleddin marched off to check on the horses, Natalya moved closer to Hansel.

'There are far worse monsters than those with claws. What did you mean when you said that?'

He looked at her, his eyes glazed over. She gave an uncomfortable shudder.

'That war is fought in the interest of the *Cause*, and not the welfare of the men fighting in it. Men sacrificed by people like Bleddin.'

'You don't like his methods?'

'I don't like his *Cause.*'

'Which is what?'

'His loyalty to the *wolfcaines*. You!'

His comment caught her by surprise. So that's what he had against her.

'I'm not really that important, you know.'

'He'd sacrifice his own wife to save you.'

'No, he'd never allow Gretl harm.'

'Excuse me. I have patients to attend.'

He left her sitting there, lost in her own thoughts. She could feel the tears welling inside. She glanced at Nathan, longing to be with him, but knowing that now was not the right time. Beside him, Gretl looked exhausted. She'd been using her magic to help with the search.

Inhaling deep, Natalya stood and took herself off to the river. She watched as the moon shimmered in its current; a glimmer of light on an omnipresent dark that hid the world from view. There were footsteps in the grass behind her.

'We set off early in the morning,' said Bleddin. 'You'd do well to get some sleep.'

'I can't get today out of my mind.'

'I told you before, they're *Casualties of War.*'

She found his words insensitive. She turned to gaze him in the eye.

'Those people are dead; because of me.'

'This falls on Ella Cinders and the Glass Slipper orchid.'

'But I led her here, everybody says so.'

'And why should you listen to them? You think Hansel Schneider was born a good surgeon? That he never lost a patient who should have survived? You think I've always been worthy in battle? That people didn't die whilst I nurtured my skill? We make mistakes and we learn from them. That is the path that great men walk. You have my faith, now earn theirs. Prove to them I was right.'

'But how can we beat an army of dreams?'

'We can't. The doctor was right about one thing. Our only chance is to take out the source. We need to destroy that Glass Slipper.'

By *we,* of course, he was meaning *her.* And recent events had hardly held her in esteem. She'd been careless. Irresponsible. Seriously so. She was lucky to be alive.

'I'm not ready. Even Ella and Shah Ming said I was a novice.'

'Then use their ignorance to your advantage. Employ it as a weakness.'

She fingered her bracelet, but prayers wouldn't help. There was a difference between having faith and being prepared. Somewhere out there was a Glass Slipper orchid, and at its command, an army of dreams. An army only restricted in size by the number of people within its reach.

'Now sleep. We have a long journey ahead.'

'Why? Where are we going?'

'That's up to you.'

'Who? Me?'

'A place you know well enough to dictate the fight.'

'But there's only one place I've known all my life.'

'Then that is where it must be.'

She never thought she'd be saying this.

'Then it's time that I went *home*.'

Chapter 21
A Dogged Tale

Natalya wearily opened her eyes, the smell of smoke pungent up her nose. Embers from the fire flitted through the air, performing a dance in the midnight sky.

She sat up slowly and gazed around. Everyone was sleeping, apart, that was, for Nathan. His bed of grass was strangely vacant. She glanced around, searching through the dark.

'Nathan?' she called in a whisper, which kind of defeated the point.

She got up slowly and stepped between the others, wandering off into the night.

'Nathan?'

A shiver squirmed down her spine. She couldn't

even hear the running of the river. She looked to the putrid blackness of the hill, its shape almost lost beneath the darkness of the night. She felt drawn to climb its grassy embankment, and reached the top far quicker than she ought.

The ruins of the manor sat before her, its rubble lit by a luminescent fog. The vapour added a disturbing aura, caressing the graves of all the many dead.

She felt the need to turn and run, but her body pulled her forwards. She began to climb over plaster, brick and stone, occasionally stumbling on the uneven surface.

'Natalya.'

She span about sharply. The voice was low; only meant for wolfcaine ears.

'Nathan?'

She followed the voice's direction, the mist drawing goose bumps up from her skin.

An ear-wrenching shriek came tearing through the silence, followed by a frenzied flapping of wings. Her immediate reaction was to think it was gargoyles. Tiny, clawed feet started tearing at her hair.

Natalya screamed and dropped to her knees. More clawed feet. She swiped out blindly. One of the creatures landed on her arm. She looked at the large, black bat in horror.

Grabbing its wing, she tore it from her skin, flinging it back into the night. Suddenly, the air was silent again.

The bats were gone, as if never there.

'*Now what's the poor bat ever done to you?*'

Nathan's silhouette shifted in the mist.

'Nathan? What it is? What's going on? What on earth are you doing up here?'

'*The bats, they come for the foxglove...*'

'What?'

'*..and they, in turn for the bats.*'

It mimicked what Bleddin had said that day when stood outside the cave in the wood.

Something was wrong. Something wasn't right. Nathan. The ruins. The bats. Everything. She called on the *beast*, but it didn't respond. It was as if it had abandoned its lair.

Nathan set off across the rubble. She followed after him, dread in her heart. A piece of stone gave way beneath her feet. She half fell, half stumbled. She looked up; he was gone.

'Nathan.' Louder. 'Nathan!'

'*Over 'ere.*'

Again, she followed the direction of his voice. She tripped over something soft on the ground. There was a sickly-sweet smell and a disturbance of flies. She felt her stomach churn.

'*Sorry about the stench,*' he said. '*But ya get used to it after a while. Besides, ya can hardly complain, can ya? If it weren't fer you, I'd still be alive.*'

The mist revealed him laid at her feet, his body a stinking, rotting corpse. He grinned at her from his decomposing face, his eyes wide and bulging from his skull.

She screamed.

He grabbed her leg. She fell to her knees. More skeletal hands grasped at her body. She scrambled to her feet, driven by fear. She started to run, and found him stood before her. He grabbed her arm with his skeletal hand and pulled her close enough to smell his rancid breath.

'But now we can be together,' he said. *'Just like ya always wanted us to be.'*

'No!' she cried. She tried to break free. His grip was like a vice.

'Don't be like that.'

'Let me go.'

The remains of his face turned into a frown.

'Yeah, yer right. Yer far too alive and yer certainly far too pretty.'

He let her go. She fell back to the ground. The corpses grabbed at her body once more. She screamed again; they screamed in mimic, their cries so intense that she couldn't block them out. They groped at her flesh and they licked at her skin, like a million leeches trying to suck her dry. More of the dead rose up to devour her, the emaciated cook staring her in the eye.

'You murdered us.'

'You stole our lives.'

'I'm sorry,' cried Natalya. 'I never meant to hurt you.'

'You took away our future.'

'You don't deserve to live.'

'It's time you came and joined us.'

'We're dragging you to Hell'.

The blackness flared white and Natalya blinked, the foulness of the air choking up her throat. She tried to lash out, but her limbs were unresponsive; she found herself strapped to a bed in a cell. A shadow grew up against the far end wall.

'Hello, Natasha.'

'Ella? Is that you?'

Shadowed vines reached out across the walls. Anxious, Natalya struggled with her bonds, but without the *beast's* strength, she was helpless.

'You did well to escape that dream I trapped you in. How did you survive? Did you have help? You call me Ella, **but is that who I am? Or am I someone else?'**

A cloaked figure drew out from the shadow, its robes a patchwork of animal skins. Natalya fought even harder with her bonds. The figure glared at her with muddied, yellow eyes. It raised a hand and pointed a finger, its nail like a serrated claw.

'Tell him I'm coming. Coming for her. Tell him

she's going to burn.'

***

Natalya sat up sharply, swallowing on the air. The embers of the fire glowed amongst the ashes, the sunrise adding colour to the day.

Her nerves wrought, she glanced about. She was the only person present. She tried to get up, became lightheaded, and landed back on her derriere. She took a moment to allow the blood to flow back to her brain.

She couldn't shake the nightmare from her mind. Nathan. The dead. That shadowy figure. Her fears had been stolen and used to scare her senseless. Had it really been a dream, or was it something else?

She caught sight of Gretl approaching. She was pinning up her hair, having washed it in the river. It reminded Natalya of the girls in Hyde Park. It seemed so long ago now.

'Natalya, you're awake. How do you feel? You look a bit pale.'

'Bad dream. At least, I hope it was a dream. I need to find Obadiah?'

'He's saddling up the horses, down by the river. Another half hour and we'll be on our way.'

'But we can't just leave. What about the injured? What about the dead?'

'Soames is going to fetch help from the city. Don't

worry, we haven't forgotten them. Are you sure you're all right?'

Natalya nodded. 'I just need to see Obadiah.'

She set off towards the river, seeking out the oak tree where the horses were reined. Nathan was helping Bleddin with the saddles. He gave her a smile; she managed one back. But the dream had renewed her previous worries. What if he was holding a grudge? What if all this was some sort of ruse? Payback for trying to kill him?

Bleddin narrowed his gaze.

'Wolfcaine?'

'I need to speak with you.'

She wandered away, forcing him to follow.

'What is it?' he said.

'The witch that killed the wolfcaines. What was the colour of her eyes?'

'Her eyes? Brown.'

'Not yellow?'

He faltered. 'Not till the *darkness* burnt out her soul.'

'I've seen her.'

'Seen her?'

'She appeared in my dream.'

'She's dead. What you've seen is an *imprint,* at best.'

'*Tell him I'm coming. Coming for her. Tell him she's*

going to burn.'

'What?'

'She sent you a message. She's coming for Gretl. Why would she want to kill your wife?'

Bleddin turned, avoiding her gaze. What was he trying to hide?

'No. It's just the Glass Slipper playing games. Channelling the emotions of its previous host.'

'But we must warn Gretl.'

'What? About some dream?'

'Except the Shadow Realm isn't a dream. It's a world…'

'I know very well what it is. You think I'd risk my own wife's life?'

'No.' But she knew a man who thought otherwise.

'Come on,' he said. 'We need to be going.'

***

They set off shortly afterwards, leaving behind a scene of devastation Natalya would never forget. All those bodies laid out in the sun like an army of broken soldiers.

With Bleddin upfront, they made good progress, Hansel and Gretl on the horse just behind. Next followed Soames, riding alone, then Nathan, paired with Natalya.

She sat there, her arms wrapped about his waist. She

should have felt elated. But despite Bleddin's speech the night before, her guilt remained a burden.

As they neared London, they detoured south to avoid unwelcome attention. Soames, meanwhile, carried on into the city, seeking help for the wounded and the dead.

By midday, the city was behind them, its industrial landscape replaced by green foliage and fields of yellow rapeseed. Bees and butterflies speckled the sky, enjoying the freshness of the smog-free air. Birds sang in trees, rabbits twitched their noses, squirrels gathered nuts for their winter hibernation. It helped to distract Natalya's mind, easing the passing of the day.

'I know ya don't want to fall off,' said Nathan, 'but a little less tight around the ribs, if ya please.'

'Sorry.'

'What, no witty reply? Blimey, I must be losing me touch.'

She managed a smile, not that he could see.

'You know that your being here's a *death knell* from Ella?'

'I've lived with that *death knell* most of me life.'

'But it's different now, Nathan. She's host to the orchid.'

He gave her his usual, nonchalant shrug. 'Well I know where I'd rather be, right now, and it certainly aint at CINDERS.'

Again, she should have felt overjoyed, but the *dream* continued to disturb her mind. He'd never once mentioned her leaving him for dead. Never once mentioned her trying to kill him. She had to know. She had to find out. And yet, she dreaded the answer.

'Is your memory fully recovered now?'

'I guess. If not, how would I know?'

Normally, she would have laughed, but she wasn't in the mood.

'So you remember what I did that day?'

'I don't know what ya mean?'

'That I threw you across the street, into that carriage. That I nearly ended your life.'

There. She'd said it. He made no reply. She swallowed. Ignorance would have been better. If only she'd kept quiet. The silence seemed to last forever.

'Ya know, I once had a dog,' he said. 'Was a stray, he was, and we became best pals. I disturbed him one night, whilst he was sleeping. He woke with a start and bit me. Not that he meant to, he was just confused. I still have the scar on me arm. We remained best pals till the day he died. If I thought ya'd meant me harm, I wouldn't be here now.'

A smile puffed out the flesh of her cheeks, the butterflies in her stomach rejoicing. She should have known. It was all in her head. Never would she doubt him again.

She laid her head against his back and hugged him all the tighter.

Chapter 22
A Drunken Tale

It was afternoon before they stopped for a break, and even then, it was mainly for the horses. Natalya felt stiff, her back aching from the journey, and she took herself off into the wood beside the stream.

It reminded her of being back home; soon enough, she'd be there for real. She chose a seat on a rock by the stream and used the time to pray for the dead. In the scope of things, it was the least she could do. She'd been there ten minutes when she heard a twig snap.

'Sorry, Natalya. I didn't mean to disturb.'

'No, it's fine. I could do with the disruption.'

Gretl smiled and sat down beside her. The witch gazed around at the silent trees.

'Peaceful, isn't it. How do you feel, dear?'

'All right.'

'That didn't sound too convincing.'

'At least I know Nathan doesn't bear me a grudge now.'

'Why would Nathan bear you a grudge?'

'I did try to kill him, Gretl.'

'No, you didn't. You thought he was Craven. Nathan has always understood that, you know. For someone so bright…'

'..I can sometimes be stupid?'

Gretl gave her a laugh and a hug. Yes, she loved Gretl dearly.

'Have you ever seen the Shadow Realm, Gretl?'

'It's not a place any witch should go. It's written that even the *Warlocks of Scholomance* refused to enter its realm.'

'*Warlocks of Scholomance?*'

'A mythical cult. A gathering of the most dangerous wizards alive.'

'But what about the witch that hunted the wolfcaines?'

'Even a *Shroud Witch* knows she has limits.'

'Shroud Witch?'

'That's what she eventually became. They live inside the rotting skins of their victims.'

'How dangerous was she?'

'As dangerous as they come. But to harness such power comes at a price.'

Tell him I'm coming. Coming for her. Tell him she's going to burn.

She had to warn Gretl. How could she not? She didn't care what Obadiah had said.

'Gretl…'

'I can make it go away, you know.'

Natalya looked at her. 'Make what go away?'

'I know you feel guilty about what happened at the manor. I can make all that sense of guilt disappear.'

'What? You mean like a *forgetfulness spell*?'

'It's a little bit more discreet than that. It will leave the events intact in your mind, but remove their emotional tie.'

Natalya looked to the stream and its flow. Just one little spell, and all would be healed. Her sense of blame, her feeling of guilt. She turned her eyes to the canvas of the wood, its spectacle and beauty.

'Earlier, I used my wolfcaine vision to see what the countryside looked like in the Shadow Realm. All it revealed was a landscape of black. All that beauty, undreamt by any person. That's what awaits us should we fail to stop the orchid. A world consumed by the *darkness*. I don't want the guilt; I don't want the torment, but I need it to know what's at stake if I fail.'

'I'll take that as a *no* then, shall I? Natalya, your

parents would be proud.'

'Don't, Gretl. You'll start me off crying.'

'Just pretend there's a fly in your eye.'

'Sister,' called Hansel from down the embankment. 'It's time that we were going.'

Gretl stood. 'It seems we've been summoned.'

'I wonder what's for dinner? I'm starving.'

***

As the sun rolled towards the horizon, they came across a countryside tavern. It was either good fortune or deliberately planned, and knowing Bleddin, probably the latter. Natalya stared at the sign above the door. Maybe he had a sense of humour, after all?

For a tavern on a road in the middle of nowhere, *The Witches Brew* was anything but quiet. They'd heard its rowdiness from the open road, an ill-tuned piano strangulating the air.

Gretl led the way inside, whilst Bleddin and Nathan took the horses to the stables. The bar reeked of men, sweat and spilt beer, the waitresses overworked and equally groped.

'It's bedlam,' said Natalya.

'Isn't it,' said Gretl. 'Let's see if there's room at the inn.'

They squeezed through the chaos, the presence of both drawing unwelcome attention. Many an eye was quick to turn their way, leering grins brightening up faces. A man grabbed Natalya by the arm. She turned and winced at the stink of his breath.

'Come over 'ere and sit with me, love.'

Hansel shoved him back into the crowd. Who'd have thought? Hansel Schneider rising to defend her honour.

'Thank you,' she said.

'You're welcome.'

Another man tried to make a move on Gretl. She uttered a spell and his forearm shot backwards, soaking himself in his beer. He was still trying to work out exactly what had happened by the time they reached the bar.

'A room? You must be joking, luv,' said the large-breasted woman with a nose like a pelican.

'Nothing?' said Gretl.

'Aint ya seen it in 'ere?'

She was right, it was brimming over.

Natalya yelped as someone slapped her bum. Once more, Hansel came to her defence. But this time the man shoved him back; Natalya readied her claws to strike. A hush swept over the tavern.

Bleddin forged a path through the crowd, eyes narrow and foreboding. The mob parted like a rift in the sea, scarpering back to their tables and chairs and their half-drank jugs of ale. It didn't matter who they thought he was; he projected an image of menace. The landlady fought to see why the silence. Bleddin joined them at the bar.

'I'd like you to meet my husband,' said Gretl.

The landlady's face drained of colour.

'First round of drinks is on the 'ouse,' she said. 'I'll bring the keys for yer rooms to yer table.'

Gretl turned and winked at Natalya. 'Seems like a very nice woman.'

'Where are we sat?' said Bleddin.

'We're aren't.'

He grunted. 'Leave it to me.'

He trudged his way towards a table by the fire. It emptied as soon as he neared. Soon the four of them were sat around its edges, the flames in the hearth heating up the air.

Food followed drinks washed down by more drinks; it should have been an enjoyable evening. But the mood of the day still hovered like a cloud, and Hansel's despondency only deepened with each passing round of ale.

The more he drank, the more sullen he became, dwelling on the loss of the people in his care. His accent thickened, his temper shortened, and Gretl seemed to squirm every time he talked.

Natalya, meanwhile, kept herself to herself, the sky growing dark through the window behind her. The sun had retired and the moon was late rising, allowing the world to be hidden from sight.

'Another drink, anyone?' said Nathan.

He'd kept his head down, too. He'd initially tried to lighten the mood, but had long since given up hope.

'I vill,' said Hansel.

'I think you've had enough.'

'Don't tell me, Bleddin, vhat I can and cannot do. You might think of them as *Casualties of War*, but some of us have a conscience, you know.'

Natalya lowered her gaze to the bubbles that floated up through her drink. They fizzed to the surface then popped in the air before being reborn at the bottom of the glass.

She heard Bleddin respond with a grunt.

'Vhat? You think I'm being unreasonable? Vhy don't you tell them of the witch that you killed?'

'Hansel!' snapped Gretl. 'This isn't the time.'

'Vhy not? Don't you think it's time the *wolfcaine* knew?'

Natalya kept her eyes on her bubbles. It wasn't an argument she cared to join.

'Well, *wolfcaine*? Vhat do you say? Wouldn't you like to know?'

'Know what?'

'About the witch that cursed your bloodline? The one your mentor killed.'

'I know all about the *Shroud Witch*,' she said.

'So you know who she actually vas? You know her name? Vhy Bleddin killed her? That the very same woman was Bleddin's *wife?*'

Natalya felt her eyes widen. She looked at Gretl in question. But Gretl's gaze was firmly on the table. She could have sworn Bleddin was grinding his teeth.

'That doesn't make sense. Gretl's his wife?'

'My zister was not his first.'

Gretl stood sharply, scraping back her chair, as though trying to drown out his words.

'I think it's time we retired to bed. We have a long journey ahead of us tomorrow.'

'Agreed,' said Bleddin, standing beside her.

Gretl looked to Natalya.

'I'll be up shortly,' said Natalya, trying her best not to look Nathan's way.

'You're not staying here on your own, Natalya.'

'It's all right,' said Nathan. 'I'll see she gets up safe.'

Natalya cheered – in silence. Gretl frowned, but said no more. She was far too concerned with quietening her brother. She took him by the arm; Bleddin took his other, and they supported him towards the steps and upstairs.

Nathan glanced at Natalya.

'Did you know he'd been married before?'

Natalya shook her head. 'But it does explain the

friction between them. I can see why Hansel wouldn't trust him now? If he was willing to sacrifice one wife for the wolfcaines, why not sacrifice two?'

'So you think it's true?'

'Well no one denied it. And what happened to my parents... The witch hunters... Craven. Obadiah said it was a message sent for him. I think his wife is actually still alive. I don't think that she's an imprint, at all.'

The thought of it sent a shiver down her spine. The stakes had suddenly risen. She took a deep breath; this was worse than any orchid. This witch – this *creature* – had murdered all her kind.

She gazed around the tavern. It suddenly dawned that this might be the last night of her life? She looked back at Nathan. If that was the case, she was going to make the most of it.

'What did you call your dog?' she said.

The change of subject caught him off guard.

'Call it? Err? *Dog,* I suppose.'

'Dog?'

'Yeah, well the dog didn't mind. Here. I've got a sketch of him somewhere.'

He began to root through his jacket pockets, pulling out a notebook or three. He flicked through their pages, found the one he wanted, and slid it across the table. It was open at a sketch of a furry-faced mutt, with long floppy ears and a whiskered, short snout.

'Aw, he's adorable. What was his type?'

'A *boy*, I think.'

'I meant his *breed?*'

'How should I know? He wasn't a *wolfcaine.*'

'Go careful, Mr Croft, or I might just bite.'

He burst out laughing, which made her laugh, too, but the worries of the world remained close at hand. He returned the sketchbook to the safety of his pocket and rose up from his chair.

'Would you like another drink?'

'Ooh, yes, please. But not lemonade. I'm all fizzed up.'

'Ya want something stronger? Yer sure about that?'

She nodded. She watched him cross to the bar.

Despite everything, her butterflies were flying. If only this night could last forever. She felt like their friendship had turned another corner; she no longer wanted to be just friends.

A man joined her at the table. She looked at him with uncertain eyes. He was three times her age, dirty and unshaven. He desperately needed a bath. He leered at her with a toothless grin; she fidgeted in her chair.

'Now what's a priddy thing like you doing 'ere? Feeling cold? I could warm ya up.'

His breath wasn't overly pleasant, either. She found herself looking for Nathan.

'I'm warm enough, thank you.'

'But I could make ya warmer. Ya know what they say about bodily heat. Don't be fooled by me age, me darling. There's plenty o' life in the ol' tool yet.'

That was it, she readied her claws. He gawked at her with a filthy expression.

'You're in my chair.'

She looked at Nathan. She almost could have cheered.

'Think ya'll find it's my chair now, chum.'

'I won't ask again,' said Nathan, firmly.

'I've got me a knife,' said the man with menace.

'Funny you should say that. Does it look like this?'

Nathan stabbed a blade into the table. The man stared at it, then felt at his waist. Natalya gave an inner smile. She wouldn't be needing her claws, after all.

The man hastily made a retreat, scuttling back to wherever he'd come from. Nathan yanked the knife from the table and sat back down. He hid the blade away.

'Thank you,' she said.

'Yer welcome.'

'I see you haven't lost your light-fingered touch.'

'Yeah, well I didn't want ya bloodying up yer claws.'

'Oh.' She hid her hands beneath the table.

'Don't feel the need to hide 'em fer me.'

'Where are our drinks?'

'The waitress is bringing 'em.'

'Oh, so you're in with the waitress now? I bet she doesn't have a *wild* side, like me.'

She winced. What on earth was she saying? Gretl would be appalled.

'Nor does she have blue hair,' he grinned. 'But I bet I can pronounce her name.'

The waitress arrived, carrying their drinks; she was a buxom young thing with blonde, dishevelled hair. She served Nathan with a smile and heaving bosom; she served Natalya with a look of disdain. She turned and winked at Nathan as she left. He pretended not to notice.

'What is it with you and these women?' said Natalya.

He shrugged. 'Ya'd have to ask them, not me.'

'Every man I meet only wants to grope my bum.'

'Well ya do have a grope-able... *everything*, really.'

She looked at him in mock outrage. 'Nathan Coft! Wash your mouth out.'

He turned bright red. 'I blame it on the ale. I apologise. I should get ya up to bed.'

'Really?'

'What? To Gretl, I mean. Yeah, upstairs to Gretl.'

But Natalya wasn't going anywhere. She'd only just got him alone to herself. And there was no way she was leaving him alone with a waitress who didn't need a corset to flaunt her ample chest.

'Well we can't go yet. I haven't finished my drink.'

'Ya haven't even started.'

'Well just you be careful where it is you've put that knife. We don't want any accidents, do we?'

***

Natalya raised her head from the table; the tavern seemed noisier than ever. She looked to her left, the room span to the right. She looked the other way, the opposite happened. It made her feel just a little bit queasy. Lord, she hoped she wasn't going to be sick.

At the end of the table, Nathan looked blurry, each movement of his body ghosting like an echo. *Not another nightmare, please,* she thought. *Not another evening spent with the dead.*

'Nathan?'

'Yeah?'

'The room. It's spinning.'

'Well try closing yer eyes.'

'Nathan?'

'Hmm?'

'The blackness is spinning.'

'And ya've only had half a pint.'

She forced her eyes back open, the room performing a waltz around her head. So much for enjoying the perfect evening, even her dinner was threatening a return.

'Can ya stand?'

She tried; pathetically so.

'Looks like I'll have to carry ya.'

There was a wisp of a breeze and the next she knew she was in his arms, being carried. She wrapped her arms about his shoulders, trying to snuggle in against his chest.

'Nathan, I can't feel my legs anymore.'

'Ya really should have stuck to drinking lemonade.'

'All those bubbles, going *pop, pop, pop*.'

Her head seesawed as he dodged a couple of chairs.

'It's the *beast's* fault. It can't handle its drink.'

'Nothing to do with the teenage girl, then?'

'Don't sound so worried. Gretl won't notice.'

'Course not. Provided she's deaf and she's blind.'

He started climbing the stairs. A hint of nausea threatened her throat. She swallowed it back and gazed into his eyes, her own like a child's, large and wide. She could feel the blood puffing out her cheeks, her inhibitions stolen by the alcohol. She tried her best not to hiccup. She gave a mischievous smile.

'Nathan?'

'Hmm?'

'My lips are tingling. In Russia that means they're about to be kissed.'

'In England it means yer about to pass out. Careful

now, I'm putting ya down.'

He stood her down at the top of the stairs. She clung to the banister for dear life. He knocked at one of the many doors; the sound exploded through her mind. He returned to guide her. She gagged a little more. Now her hands were tingling.

'Nathan, I...'

'Shh!'

'But Nathan...'

'Quiet.'

'But Nathan, I think I'm going to be...'

Her stomach heaved and she threw up down his trousers: a whole bowl of soup and a wedge of bread. The door opened and she gazed up at Gretl, regurgitated broth dripping from her mouth.

'Natalya? What on earth...?'

She was never going to live this down.

Chapter 23

The Foreshadowing

Natalya opened her eyes, dark clouds forming overhead. She vaguely remembered being tucked up in bed, so what had happened to the ceiling?

She slowly sat and gazed around, her mattress a crib of emaciated grass. Nearby, a squirrel was burying some nuts, its bushy tail swishing in the air.

She licked at the sugary coating on her lips; she was back in the Shadow Realm again. But she hadn't eaten foxglove and she hadn't seen the *grey*. How had she even got here?

She struggled to her feet and almost wobbled over. It was as though her mind wasn't quite in her body. She edged her way forward, into the trees, her heart pounding as to what she might see.

There, in the middle of a clearing was a bed, and sat on the bed was Nathan. He was sketching away in one of his notebooks, oblivious to the wood and everything around him.

'Nathan?'

He glanced towards her, but despite his gaze, he didn't seem to see her. He shook his head and returned to his drawing. She dared to venture closer, her footing still unsure. The Shadow Realm remained a mystery to her brain. Was she actually here, or was she merely dreaming?

The ground beneath her feet began to quiver; at first she thought it was moles. Then twisted roots broke their way through the earth, snaking their way around the legs of the bed.

'Nathan, look out.'

He remained oblivious. The bedcovers shifted; there was someone underneath. Ella rose up and pressed her naked flesh against him. She glanced Natalya's way.

'He's mine. He belongs to me now. You had your chance, *Sweetheart*, and you let him get away.'

'I think you'll find he doesn't know you're there.'

'You're still too late. He's branded with my mark.'

She prised back his shirt to reveal his *tattooed* skin, home to an infection of Glass Slipper spores.

'What have you done to him?'

'I told you, he's mine.'

'I'll never believe that.'

'Then let's see who wins.'

The clouds above flashed suddenly white, followed by a roll of thunder. Out of the foliage came a galloping horse. Natalya quickly leapt out of its way. She caught sight of its black-garbed rider. Bleddin steered the horse back into the trees.

'Obadiah?'

She'd seen this dream before, the first time she'd entered the realm. It was as though it was interweaved with Nathan's, and yet, neither dream infringed on the other.

'Admit it, *Natasha*. You're out of your depth. How can you ever hope to stop me?'

'I'll find a way.'

'Such brave little words. Now, excuse me, **there's a witch to be burned.**'

Natalya felt a sudden dread as Ella's eyes turned a muddied yellow. A cloak of flayed skin crept across the witch's body and she melted into the air.

Her stomach knotting up, Natalya took off through the trees. This may have been a dream, but she couldn't take the chance. What if events here affected the real world? If someone died here, would they die in real life?

She followed her nose and the stench of thick

smoke. She entered another clearing. Beside a pretty cottage was a fire-ravaged woodpile, and tied to a stake at its midst was Gretl. Bleddin was trying to fight towards her through the flames. A shadowy figure emerged from the trees.

'I warned you, husband. I told you she'd burn. Observe, wolfcaine. Witness my wrath.'

'Leave her alone. Ella, I'm warning you…'

'The name is Rosalinda Lovell.'

The landscape behind the witch began to melt, breaking down into pigment. It flowed into her body, feeding her with power. She lunged forward and thrust out her arms. A wall of liquid flame surged forward like a tidal wave, obliterating everything lying in its path.

Gretl screamed, her skeleton stripped bare; the firewall hit Bleddin and erased him from the earth. Natalya watched in mortified horror, the landscape turning to hell.

Panicking, she turned and ran. She could feel the heat baking at her skin. She weaved through the trees as they burst into flame, the ground at her feet melting into pigment. The hairs on her skin began to shrivel, wisps of smoke rising from her hair.

She came across Nathan still sat on his bed, drawing away in his sketchbook. With no time to waste, she ran towards him, her crimson dress melting to black. She leapt onto the mattress, entering his dream. The question was, would the two dreams interact?

The flames surged around them like a maelstrom, ripping up the landscape, turning dream to death. The *darkness* moved in and gorged on its colour, eating up the rainbow that formed from its haze.

Natalya observed in terrified silence, but at least on the bed, she seemed to be safe. And then the landscape was gone. Devoured. They were floating in an empty sea of black.

She gazed out into the hollow void. Vast. Cold. Silent. She crawled across the bed and draped her arms around Nathan, pressing her body up against his back. She stole a peek of what he was drawing. Suddenly the darkness was forgotten. It was a sketch of *her*. He was dreaming of *her*. A joyful tear wept from her eye.

***

Natalya gasped and sat up sharply, water draining from her hair and down her face. She blinked, her vision a blur of swishy colour. She focused in on Gretl with the empty washbowl.

'Wha..? What was that for?'

'I've been trying to wake you for the past half hour. We should have been downstairs by dawn. Obadiah will be waiting.'

'But it's still night.'

Gretl crossed to the window and opened up the

shutters. Warm sunlight caressed Natalya's face.

'Oh!' So much for her throbbing head.

'Right,' said Gretl. 'I'll be downstairs. At least you won't have to wash now. You'll find your dress hung up in the wardrobe. And Natalya, please don't take all day.'

Natalya watched her leave the room. It was good to see her alive. At least, this time, the dream had stayed a dream, but its events still made Natalya want to vomit.

She threw back the covers and climbed out of bed, her wet chemise clinging to her skin. She steadied herself with a hand against the wall, her legs as shaky as they had been in the dream. The previous night's events remained a little fuzzy, and the last thing she remembered was Hansel's revelation.

Rescuing her dress from the mothballs in the wardrobe, she slid into its silk. She tied the front ribbon and the dress shrunk back, fitting snug against her body. She glanced in the mirror and frowned at her hair. It looked like the bats had been at it, again. She picked up her boots and pulled them on. She hurried from the room. In her haste, she bumped into Nathan, standing on his foot.

'Oh, no.'

'What?'

'Stand on me back.'

'What?'

'Stand on my foot in return.'

He looked at her blankly; anyone would think she'd spoken the sentence in Russian.

'I'm serious, Nathan. Stand on me back, or it means we'll both fall out.'

'Are you sure?'

'Just stamp on my foot, will you.'

'But…?'

'Nathan, just do as I say! Ow!!'

She began to hop around in a circle. Nathan watched her, amused.

'I didn't say stamp on it that hard.'

'Ya didn't say *softly*, either.'

She came to a stop, placed her hands on her hips and stared him in the eye.

'Nathan Croft, if you don't mind…' She wrinkled her nose and pulled a face.

'What?'

'Nothing. I was just saying…' She wrinkled her nose again. 'Can you smell that?'

'What? Damp hair?'

She scowled. 'Do you want to see another birthday? No, it smells like... I don't know. It smells like... someone's been sick.'

He raised his eyes and shook his head.

'Hmm, I can't imagine why. By the way, yer late.'

'As are you.'

'We better get downstairs, then. I take it ya don't need carrying this morning?'

'Carrying? Why would I need carrying?'

He started off down the stairs.

'Nathan, why would I need carrying? Nathan, what are you talking about?'

By the time they stepped out into the day, she was still in want of an answer. A welcome breeze eased across her face, promising to dry the dampness from her hair.

As expected, everyone was waiting, with Bleddin already mounted on his horse. Gretl was trying her best to distract him, and he looked just a little bit anxious for her silence.

Natalya smiled. Poor Obadiah. That would teach him for rising early. Nathan collected their horse from Hansel. Natalya swallowed and approached the doctor, too.

'Doctor Schneider?'

He turned, perfectly sober, and also very stern.

'I... I'm sorry about your colleagues at the manor.'

'Really? I thought they were *Casualties of War?*'

'That's not what I said. I didn't say that.'

'No. But we're both aware of who did.'

'I'm not his *puppet*, you know. I'm not.'

'Hmm. That remains to be seen.' He turned his back on her and mounted his steed. 'Gretl, are you ready?'

Natalya frowned and gave a sigh. Nathan brought their own horse to bear. It nestled its nose into her person, not a single hoof raised in defiance. She gave its mane a stroke.

'Let's go,' said Bleddin.

He turned his horse onto the road. Hansel and Gretl followed. Nathan offered Natalya his hand; she took it and swung up behind him.

'Oh, and if yer still feeling sick, turn yer head to the flank.'

'Sick?' she laughed.

'Ya really don't remember?'

'Nathan, what are you talking about?'

***

The day moved forward slowly, which suited Natalya fine. She was in no rush to return to the village; besides, once there, what did she do? They were relying on her to destroy the Glass Slipper. She was more likely to get them all killed. The thought preyed heavily on her mind, until the point she felt overwhelmed.

When they stopped for a break, she took off again, this time across an empty field. She could sense Gretl, following after her. She quickened her pace, hoping not to be caught.

'Natalya, wait. What is it? What's wrong? Natalya, please, will you just slow down?'

'I'm in a hurry.'

'A hurry to where? We're walking through the middle of a field.'

Natalya came to a halt and turned.

'I can't do this, Gretl.'

'Can't do what?'

'You're all going to die. Because of me.'

'Natalya, your only duty's to yourself. The rest of us are here of our own free will.'

'Hansel's not. He's here to save you. He thinks you're in danger, because of me and Obadiah.'

'That's still his choice.'

'You don't understand. I saw *her* last night. I can never defeat that.'

'Her?'

'The Shroud Witch. Your husband's dead wife. Gretl, she means you harm.'

'I know she does. Obadiah told me. It seems you convinced him to tell me the truth.'

'Oh. Then what are you doing here? You shouldn't be anywhere near.'

'If the Shroud Witch lives, it doesn't matter where I am. She'll find me, one way or the other.'

Natalya noted Bleddin approaching. So much for being alone.

'Did he really kill her, Gretl?'

'You'd have to ask him. He rarely speaks of *her*.'

'What's going on?' said Bleddin, drawing near.

'We were just discussing your *wife*.'

He gave Natalya that usual glare. She was getting used to it by now.

'I saw her last night.'

'The *Shroud Witch*?' he said.

'I was there when she destroyed your dream.'

'Gretl, if you could give us a moment?'

Gretl nodded and returned the way she came. Natalya stared him in the eye.

'What Hansel said…?'

'Was true,' said Bleddin.

She couldn't believe the speed of his confession.

'You killed your wife?'

'I killed a witch. One possessed by chaos and magic.'

'She was still your wife?'

'There are many things you've yet to understand. There's a reason *Dark Witches* are more powerful than *White*. Why Gretl uses magic both infrequently and slight. Pure magic corrupts; it nourishes on the soul and destroys the living mind. Ella Cinders is protected by the Slipper; it insulates her mind from the chaos of the *source*. But my wife had no such barrier. It took who she was and ravaged it away. When she lost her child, she lost her mind. Her only hope of peace was death. I did what I did because I had to, but don't ever think I did it lightly.'

There was a tremor in his voice that showed remorse, and a resolve that told her he'd do it all again. For a man who spoke so very few words, it was all she needed to hear.

'I'm... sorry', she said.

'Then let's not speak of it again. We've wasted enough time here. We need to make the village by sunfall, and we've still a long journey ahead.'

Chapter 24

In the Name of the Cause

17th September 1891

WOODLAND VILLAGE - ¼ mile; it was a sign she'd hoped she'd never see again. She closed her eyes and wished herself away. Anywhere, but here.

All around sat the darkness of the wood, her nose poisoned by its presence. The smell of damp earth, the stink of moist fungi, the perfume of the bark that clung to the trees.

She tightened her hold around Nathan; he could probably feel the pounding of her heart. Her mouth felt dry, her skin felt wet, its hairs half-drowned by tangible fear. She gave a cold shiver. Was that a scent of smoke? Was that the sound of crackling flame? Her senses were playing tricks on her mind, plaguing her with the past.

'What am I doing here, Nathan?'

'What needs to be done, whether ya want to or not.'

'I can hardly stop shaking.'

'And yet yer still here. I think that says something, don't you?'

She smiled; he was trying to make her feel better, but nothing could save her wretched nerves. And what of the village? Was it still a burnt out shell? Had the townsfolk abandoned its ruins to nature? What if her parents remained on the ground, their skeletons stripped bare by the nourishing maggots?

They rode the final bend into the village.

The shadows of the trees drew forward to greet them, like a nest of vipers across the trodden earth. The sun fled the sky to perform a distant sunrise. Bleddin brought the party to a halt. Natalya nervously dismounted.

She stepped forward onto the earth, fingering the knots of her bracelet. The village looked snug, quaint and tranquil; it was as though the attack had never taken place. Another step forward. Dare she take another? She looked to the place where *they* fell.

She sniffed, trying to hold back the tears, but she still felt their warmth curve down her cheeks. She looked to the sky, her vision all blurry; she blinked several times, but it only made things worse.

It had been five months, and yet it felt like five minutes. The village on fire; the trees choked with smoke. That sight of Craven charging towards them; their bodies bleeding into the earth. Her life had changed so much since that day, and yet, she still felt like some helpless child.

'See if there's room at the tavern,' spoke Bleddin.

Two pairs of feet strode off to her right. His heavier tread approached her from behind. She tried to discreetly wipe back the tears.

'Memories,' he said. 'They haunt us all.'

She nodded, trying to clear her choked throat.

'We start making plans first thing in the morning.'

She looked at him. 'That might be too late.'

'What do you mean?'

'Nathan's infected. I caught Ella spying on his dreams last night.'

'What? And you never thought to tell me of this?'

She frowned. 'It's not his fault. He doesn't know.'

A scream emanated from the tavern.

'Gretl!'

They turned and ran towards the inn, Nathan joining them from tending the horses. Natalya's speed got her there first. She burst in through the door and everyone turned. She anxiously looked for Hansel and Gretl. They were stood at the bar, unharmed.

'Natalya, what is it?'

'That cry wasn't you?'

Bleddin and Nathan followed her in. The waitress looked at Bleddin and froze. She dropped her tray of drinks and screamed.

'Witch hunters!'

Mass hysteria followed, as the residents knocked aside tables and chairs in their panicked rush for the rear door. Friends were forgotten, it was everyone for themselves, viewing Bleddin as the Witchfinder General.

But as they ran, they started to fall, drawn into a state of comatose slumber. Within moments the room had turned to silence, the villagers trapped in their own personal nightmares. Natalya applied her wolfcaine vision and quickly scanned the room. Dread welled up inside her.

'They're infected,' she said. 'They're all infected.' She looked at Bleddin. 'She's already here.'

'And them seeing me was exactly what she wanted. She's drawn us into a trap.'

'A trap?' said Hansel.

'She'll use their dreams against. Dreams we cannot possibly defeat.'

'Then we have to wake them up.'

'We can't,' said Gretl. 'This is old magic. We'd need to kill the source.'

There was a moment of uneasy silence.

Suddenly, Bleddin moved behind the bar. He grabbed a bottle of Whisky from the shelf. He began to pour its contents on the counter, the excess spilling to the floor.

Nathan touched Natalya on the shoulder.

'Is he thinking what I think he's thinking?'

'Of course not. Even Obadiah's not that heartless.'

There are far worse monsters than those with claws.

Horror lit her face.

'No!' she cried. 'Obadiah, you can't.'

'We have no choice. As long as they live…'

'I know, but we're talking about innocent people.'

Hansel grabbed Bleddin's arm across the bar.

'Don't be a fool, man.'

'Let go of me, doctor.'

'Or what? Are you going to murder me, too?'

Bleddin's response was a fist in Hansel's face. The doctor crumpled to the floor.

'Obadiah!' cried Gretl, rushing to her brother's side.

Bleddin removed a box of matches.

'No!' cried Natalya. 'I won't let you do this.'

There was a pricking in her eyes and a lengthening of her nails.

'Stand down, wolfcaine. You're making a mistake.'

'Am I? Well, it wouldn't be the first time.'

'Obadiah, please, this is madness,' cried Gretl.

'A few lives today could save millions tomorrow.'

He took out a match and attempted to strike it.

Natalya raged forward and seized him by the throat, shoving him back into the shelving. Bottles came crashing down all around them, turning the floor into an icefield of glass.

He lashed out with the hilt of his dagger. She foresaw the move and rolled with the blow. But she slid on the glass and lost her footing. He grabbed her by the hair and slammed her head into the bar. For a moment, her world blacked out.

She'd never beaten him in combat before, but this time she had a cause to defend. A moment's confusion and her mind was back alert. She eyed his reflection in the spill of the whisky.

Urging her dress to free up her legs, she spun and kicked him square in the chest. He landed on the floor amidst the many broken bottles, a look of stunned surprise on his face.

'You wanted a *wolfcaine*? You've got one,' she cried. 'You want my help? We do it my way.'

Go on. Take him. He's ours, cried the *beast*.

She straightened her stance and told *it* to heel. A sound of *thunder* intruded on her ears. She offered Bleddin her hand.

'They're coming,' she said. 'I can hear them. I need you, Obadiah. Your skill in a fight.'

He glared at her; Natalya glared back. He accepted

her hand and she helped pull him up. He straightened his attire.

'How do you intend to stop them?' he said.

'I don't intend to stop them at all.'

'That doesn't sound like a plan to me.'

'Who said anything about a plan?'

She led the way outside, Nathan providing a reassuring wink. If only she had such faith in herself. She stepped out onto the clearing.

The pounding of *thunder* was audible now, even to those with human ears. The only thing louder was the beating of her heart, the hairs on the back of her neck standing erect. She knew what was coming. She knew *who* was coming. She knew **he'd** be amongst them.

Seven witch hunters rode into the village, their faces a mosaic of misremembered dreams. They had splintered eyes and skull-like features; some of them didn't even have a mouth. Their leader's face remained unseen, his hat tilted low across his brow. Natalya's heart raced even faster. The man who'd murdered her parents was back.

Bleddin drew his sword. Hansel pulled a gun; he tossed a spare to Nathan. Gretl readied herself for magic. Natalya stepped forward and dropped to her knees.

'We surrender!' she announced.

***

Craven dismounted from his horse. Natalya gazed up into his face. A cold shiver ran down her spine, turning her soul into ice.

Like his colleagues, his face was a mosaic, but there was no denying it was him. The tautness of his skin; the sign of the Pentacle. As a dream, he didn't seem to recognise her, but she remembered him.

A vengeful hatred surged through her body, the *beast* demanding that she rip out his throat. She did her best to keep it at bay; there was more at stake than her own revenge.

'We what?' said Hansel.

'Surrender,' said Natalya.

'Is she out of her wolfcaine mind?'

'No,' said Bleddin. 'She's using her mind.'

He threw down his sword and surrendered, too.

The witch hunters disarmed them, taking their weapons and binding their hands. They tethered them behind the horses, all except Hansel and Gretl, that was. Instead, they were marched in the opposite direction, much to Natalya's dismay.

'Where are you taking them?' she cried.

Craven gave her a silent look. By surrendering she'd hoped to avoid any bloodshed, but she'd never intended the group to be split. Craven and his men mounted their horses and hauled the remaining three of them towards the woodland path.

With the day now dead, the moon lit their way, silhouetting the trees against the colour-drained sky. Unblinking eyes stared out between the branches, searching the dark for some unsuspecting mouse. A subtle breeze disturbed the sleeping leaves; it was as if the wood was whispering to itself.

There was no going back now. The stone had been chiselled. *Fate* awaited them all. Natalya found herself wishing for the dawn; that's if she ever saw it.

They followed the snake of the path in silence, climbing the hill en route to the church. The horses were as mute as their soulless riders, the only sound being that of their hooves. The woodland path had never seemed lonelier, and then they reached the cemetery.

Dismounting, the witch hunters untied them, shoving them down onto their knees in the dirt. A creepiness of mist snuck between the gravestones, infused by the glow of a dozen burning torches. Natalya exchanged a glance with Nathan. He looked as anxious as she felt.

'Well, well, well…'

They looked to the church. Ella Cinders swayed her way towards them. She looked like some ghostly apparition, the mist parting as she stepped through its cloud.

'..your refusal to die is starting to annoy me. This ends tonight. I give you my word. None of you will see another sunrise. Except, for you, my loyal and trusted servant.'

She ran a hand through Nathan's hair. He looked at her in panic.

'I swear, I don't know what she's talking about.'

'Oh, honey, please. He's such a tease. I'm sure *Natasha* will understand. After all, childhood crushes never last.'

'You're such a piece of work,' said Natalya.

Ella smirked. 'Adorable, aren't I?'

'That wasn't the word I had in mind.'

The smirk became a scowl.

'Well, I guess I did *steal* your man. Sour grapes are bound to be expected.'

'Except you never had him in the first place. Didn't you see his sketch last night? It was a sketch of me. He was drawing **me**! You were the *monster* he drew in the trees.'

Ella approached and grabbed her by the hair, yanking back her head. Her *sweet* breath caressed Natalya's face, its fragrance as deceiving as the woman who breathed it.

'Quite the little *wolfcaine*, aren't we? Last chance, *Sweetheart*. Join us now, or die.'

'I'd rather die.'

'You dare defy your *princess*?'

'A princess serves her people, not the other way

around.'

Ella struck her hard across the face. It stung like hell, but she suffered it in silence. She gave the witch a defiant glare. Ella turned and walked away.

'Oh, and I'll be taking that, as well.'

She waved a hand and Natalya's necklace tore itself from her throat. It rose into the air and burst into flame, its pollen floating to the ground as embers. Ella turned to Craven.

'General, return to the village with your men. You know what you have to do.'

Craven bowed and the witch hunters departed. Natalya tensed; this was her chance.

Her heart racing, she leapt to her feet and raced at Ella, claws drawn to strike. She almost had her when some unseen force pummelled her face into the ground.

Nathan and Bleddin leapt to their feet.

'Ah ah, I wouldn't,' said Ella, a wisp of magic shimmering from her finger.

But it wasn't magic that had grounded Natalya. She looked up into her enemy's face.

'Good evening, Miss Yavorovskaya.'

Shah Ming looked as smug as ever. He grabbed her by the throat and dragged her to her feet. Her cheeks began to fatten with blood; his grip was stronger than Bleddin's.

'Leave her alone,' cried Nathan.

'What have I just told you?' said Ella.

He chose to ignore her and made a dart forward, ramming his shoulder into Shah Ming's back. The prince fell aside, dropping Natalya to the ground. Ella laughed out loud.

'Oh, Nathan. You're such a hero. Now, time to go to sleep.'

She waved a hand and he slumped into the dirt. Natalya hurried to his side.

'If you've harmed him.'

'On the contrary, *Natasha* dear. Nathan Croft will live a very long life. So long, in fact, that he'll wish he was dead; his years spent in a spiral of despair, blaming himself for your dying.'

She uttered a spell and the next Natalya knew her body was suspended in mid-air. She tried to move, but her limbs were unresponsive, her arms outstretched like Jesus on the cross. Ella approached with a confident stride and eyed her up and down.

'Nice dress.' She sniffed at the fabric. 'Do I detect a scent of magic?'

She grabbed a hold of the frontal ribbon and ripped the bodice apart. The dress instantly renewed itself. Ella looked impressed.

'My, it really is a magic dress. I could do with one of these myself.'

She uttered yet another spell and the fabric seemed

to drain of life. She ripped the bodice apart once more, and this time the dress stayed ripped. She tore a hole through the chemise underneath, exposing Natalya's stomach.

'Shah, my love.'

He passed her a bottle. Natalya observed with nervous eyes. She glanced at Bleddin, but he was still on his knees. Unlike Nathan, he was biding his time.

'You remember my potions, don't you, *Sweetheart.* Of course, cacti don't grow in these parts. Hmm, I wonder what else could I use? Oh, I know. I have just the thing.'

She held out her palm and a plant-like tendril grew from within its crease. It twined through the air towards Natalya's naval. Natalya squirmed, but the magic held her firm.

Suddenly, Bleddin made his move, lunging at Ella's hand and the vine. Shah Ming was quick to intercede, and sent Bleddin reeling back into a gravestone. Ella smiled smugly.

'I did wonder how long it would take you. ***How long you could bear to watch your wolfcaine writhe.***'

For a moment Ella's eyes flared yellow, and then they were blue again. Natalya quickly looked at Bleddin; there was horror in his eyes.

The vine tickled at Natalya's stomach, feeling its way across her skin. It then grew a thorn of bloated poison and tore a gash through her flesh.

'Argh!'

Blood oozed out onto her skirt. The vine withdrew, minus its thorn. Natalya could feel the barb inside her stomach, making her more than anxious.

'Oh, don't be such a baby, *Natasha*. It's only a little tear.'

She unstopped the bottle and peeled back the wound, causing Natalya to grind her teeth. The witch poured the liquid content onto the flesh-lodged thorn.

'Now, this is the bit I really like.'

At first, Natalya felt nothing, but it still didn't stop the panic in her mind. Was this how it ended? Was this how she died? The unknown awaited and it left her terrified.

Whatever was meant to happen happened, like an explosion of shrapnel throughout her insides. She gasped, swallowed air, struggled to breathe, shock and pain eating up her flesh. Ella released the *holding* spell and Natalya crumpled to the ground.

'Wolfcaine?'

Natalya gazed down at her midriff. Her skin was already turning green. She tried to stand, but her legs gave way beneath her. She touched at her neck and felt the tendrils squirming up it. She coughed, her lungs choked with mucus. Drool began to leak from her mouth.

'Oh dear,' said Ella, 'the poor little thing. I'm afraid, Obadiah, your wolfcaine's going to die.'

'Stop this now.'

'You want her to live?'

'You can save her,' said Shah Ming. 'But it comes at a price.'

'Observe,' said Ella, 'the foxglove in the wood, dripping pollen like a medical elixir.'

'Observe,' said Shah Ming, 'the burning stockpile in the village, with your wife and her brother tied at its midst.'

'But who are you going to let live?' said Ella.

'And who are you going to let die?'

'The choice is yours, but you don't have much time. Choose now, or all will die.'

No, Natalya couldn't let this happen. She wouldn't let Gretl be sacrificed for her. She'd become like a second mother to her; she was the closest thing she had left in the world.

'Go save Gretl,' she spluttered.

Bleddin looked at her, conflict in his eyes.

'I swore an oath. To you and the wolfcaines.'

'I absolve you of your oath. Now go save your wife.'

'I won't desert you.'

'I've seen your dreams, remember? It's Gretl you're scared of failing, not me.'

He still looked conflicted.

'Go, Obadiah. If you respect me at all, go save your wife.'

He turned and took off down the hill, choosing the most direct route to the village. Ella and Shah Ming looked taken aback, but it didn't surprise Natalya, at all. An entire village: *Casualties of War*. The woman he loved? He'd sacrifice it all.

'*No! How dare he choose her?*'

Ella's persona had changed again. But Natalya couldn't worry about that now. If she wanted to live, she had to save herself.

Poison coursing its way through her veins, she dragged herself through the mud. It took every ounce of strength that she had, and then required more. Her flesh was hot, her mind disorientated, there was pain in every limb. Her body spasmed, she vomited green, her heart struggling to pump her thickening blood.

She fought on, groaning as she went. The foxglove at the edge of the wood grew in sight. She reached out towards it and watched in horror as the plant shrivelled up and died.

Ella knelt down beside her.

'Maybe I didn't explain myself. The spell forbids you from saving yourself. So tell me, *Natasha*, how does it feel, to serve your people, not the other way around? Do you honestly think they'll remember you for this? Was it really worth you dying?'

'My name's *Natalya*.'

'Of course it is.'

'Ella, my love, we're missing all the fun.'

'Coming, my dear. Until we meet again. Oh, what am I saying? This is goodbye.'

She stroked a hand through Natalya's hair, stood, and left her to die.

Chapter 25
Foxglove and Hiccups

Silence. Infinite silence. A place without conscious existence. No life. No warmth. A place without hope. A place of eternal despair.

Natalya could feel its oppressiveness beckon, inviting her under its shroud. But her awareness of death meant she still graced the living. Somehow, she was still clinging on to life.

She tried to move, but the pain was unbearable, her body screaming in torment. Her stomach churned, acid burnt her throat; a thick bile drained from her mouth. A beaded tear leaked from her eye. It dripped to the earth as blood. She gazed at her arm, its skin crusted black, pulsating boils secreting stinking pus.

She'd always thought herself selfless, but at this moment in time, she felt anything but. She wanted to live. To grow old with Nathan. To get married; have children. She was sixteen years old. She didn't want to die, to be swallowed by the *darkness* and never again see the light. But the *darkness* was where she was heading, and she couldn't see any way out.

More pain. More hurt. Her consciousness started to fail. The crust on her skin began to sizzle, the boils vomiting putrid phlegm.

But this time the pain was different. Despite the stench, there was a scent of something else. An aroma Natalya had known all her life, and undeniably *foxglove*.

Her stomach heaved and she vomited mucus, the swelling of her brain drawing back from her skull. Her body was a warzone, and yet, the tide was turning, her hot and fevered flesh starting to cool. She touched at the crusted blackness on her skin and felt it crumble to dust.

#hiccup#

'That's what ya get fer swallowing air.'

She quickly turned and groaned with the pain.

'Careful. The pollen's still working its magic.'

She squinted, trying to clear her dizzied vision. It looked like him. It sounded like him. And yet, what if she was dreaming?

'I thought you were sleeping?'

'I must have woken up.'

'You can't have.'

He smudged a blob of pollen on her nose.

'Is that real enough? I can always go away. Ya know, and leave ya to die.'

She touched at her stomach and felt its sticky coating. She glanced at the leaf in Nathan's hand. It was smeared in liquid foxglove pollen. She sat up sharply and threw her arms around him; who cared if her ribs felt like they might explode.

'Oh, Nathan. Thank you. Thank you. *#hiccup#* I thought I was dead for sure. I should have known you'd come and save me. What about Hansel and Gretl?'

'Dunno. I was more concerned with you.'

'What? They're still in danger?'

She sprang to her feet and immediately fell.

'Careful now. Ya nearly just died.'

He was right. She felt so weak; so helpless. She called on the *beast*, but it was still recovering, too. What she wouldn't give for a dose of the elixir that coated the Shadow Realm's air.

'Help me. Please. I have to know.'

He supported her towards the lip of the hill. She steadied herself against the drystone wall and gazed down onto the village below.

The scene that met her eyes was one of nightmares,

with Hansel and Gretl tied to a stake at the centre of a burning woodpile. Its flames were monstrous, out of control, and only held back by a bubble of magic that was shrinking by the second.

Bleddin, meanwhile, was embroiled in a fight that he couldn't possibly win. For every witch hunter he fought to the slaughter, another one revived.

'Can't Gretl use her magic to free them?'

'I think it has to do with Ella's spell. It wouldn't allow me to save myself, either. Nathan, we have to #*hiccup*# help them.'

'What, in your condition?'

'You make it sound like I'm pregnant.'

He looked at her. 'Yer not, are ya?'

'Come on, I'll race you down.'

She flashed him a grin and took off down the hill, following the path of Bleddin's descent. The resident brambles clawed at her skin, ripping the hem of her dress into shreds.

She stumbled and fell head over heels, her body still slow to respond to her brain. She landed in a heap about a quarter way down. She regained her footing and set off again. All that mattered was Hansel and Gretl. She'd never forgive herself if anything happened.

She reached the bottom and fell flat on her face; too much momentum and not enough control. She reproached herself, mimicking Bleddin. At least the shock had got rid of her....

#hiccup#

There again, maybe not.

She clambered to her feet and started forward. She could feel the *beast* growing stronger inside. There was a pricking in her eyes and a lengthening of her nails, the promise of the fight like a drug to its mind.

The first of the witch hunters never saw her coming. She leapt onto his back and ripped out his throat. He fell, his blood spurting into the soil. Blood? A pang of dread stabbed her heart. Why was he bleeding? Were they not dreams? Had she been mistaken?

Someone struck her down from behind. She fell into the earth, swallowing dirt. She turned to see a witch hunter's sword swing towards her. Nathan tackled her assailant to the ground. The witch hunter elbowed Nathan in the face and raised a dagger to his throat.

'No!' she cried.

She scrambled forwards and drove her fangs into the witch hunter's arm. His blood was wet, but it had no human warmth. She grabbed hold of his dagger and drove it through his chest. He fell into the earth.

'Thank you,' said Nathan.

'Likewise.'

'I'm probably a bit more use with a gun. I'll see if I can find our weapons.'

He took off towards the tavern.

The first witch hunter jolted back to life. She grabbed up a sword and ran him through. Another witch hunter tried to take her head off. She barely dodged the blade with a gasp.

Stay alert, she warned herself.

She lashed out and spilled the horseman's innards. She felt an immediate need to be sick, but she didn't have the time.

'Obadiah!'

'Wolfcaine?'

He sounded surprised, so engaged with the fight he'd not noticed her presence. He might have even given a smile, but she could have just imagined it.

'Bleddin,' came Hansel's distressed cry. 'Gretl can't hold the flames back much longer.'

The fire was almost upon them now, the witch's magic nearly depleted.

'Go,' cried Natalya. 'I've #hiccup# got your back. Go, Obadiah. Save them.'

He took off without the need for further words, despatching another witch hunter en route. Natalya turned to face her next opponent, and found herself confronted by *Craven*.

Like a *Scourge of Nature* she tore towards him, hate swelling up inside. He wielded his sword; she read its path, leapt over its blade and sliced apart his face.

She gazed at the blood dripping from her claws. She

grinned with satisfaction. She lashed out again; his blood sprayed the air. He staggered backwards and crumpled to the ground. She drove the heel of her boot through his throat and twisted it, crushing his windpipe.

'That was for mama,' she said.

The witch hunter somehow was still alive. She grabbed up his sword and drove it through his skull.

'And that was for papa.'

A witch hunter grabbed her from behind. A gunshot went off and the witch hunter fell. She looked at Nathan, a gun in his hand, and gave a welcome smile.

Behind them, Bleddin attacked the burning woodpile, using his sword like an axe. With both hands on the hilt, he swung it like a pendulum, sending wood splintering in all directions. Natalya had never seen him so determined; flame caught his sleeve and he smothered it out. He soldiered on, grunting and gasping with every swipe of the blade.

Ahead, Gretl's magic failed. The flames surged in towards her and Hansel. Bleddin quickly sliced apart their bonds; Gretl collapsed into his arms. He carried her back to the safety of the clearing, Hansel following them out.

'Thank you,' said Hansel. 'I might have misjudged you.'

'You can save your thanks for when this is over. Now, Doctor, take care of my wife. I'm trusting you with her life.'

He returned to join the others in the fight. Natalya spun to face Craven again. She dodged his attack, countered with her own, and drove a dagger through his chin into his brain.

He fell. Three times she'd killed him now, but the pleasure was starting to wane. He was just a dream. A re-imagined nightmare. He wasn't the monster who'd butchered her parents. Bleddin slew the last of the witch hunters; at least, until they revived.

Natalya gazed around the village. Time to face her fate.

'Where are you?' she cried. 'Show yourselves, cowards. I'm sick of playing your stupid games.'

Shah Ming came running out of the air and snatched Bleddin back into the Shadow Realm. Natalya felt a sudden panic. They were supposed to take her, not Bleddin.

'Obadiah!' cried Gretl, struggling to her feet. 'Natalya...?'

'Don't worry. I'll get him back.'

But despite her words, she felt far less optimistic. To enter the Realm was to face them alone.

'Then go,' said Hansel. 'We'll play our part here.'

'Catch,' said Nathan, throwing him a gun.

'Natalya, what happened to your dress?' said Gretl.

'Ella took its magic.'

'Then let me give it back.'

She uttered a charm and the silk returned to life, the rips and the tears fading from sight. The blood and the dirt faded back to crimson. It looked brand new again.

'Now go save my husband.'

Natalya nodded and followed the burn of her freckles.

Chapter 26

The Devil's Bridge

Natalya hurriedly ran through the trees, her freckles practically scalding. But everywhere she looked, all she saw was haze. Not a single outline of a gateway, anywhere.

She came to a stop, feeling overwhelmed. As a wolfcaine, this should have been simple. But here she was, with Bleddin's life at stake, and not a single clue as to how to get through.

She ran a frustrated hand through her hair and felt a wetness on her palm. She gazed at her hand and furrowed her brow. Her skin was painted in pigment.

Once more, she touched at the strands of her hair. Its blueness was bleeding dye. She placed her painted hand against a tree and watched as the *veil of grey* formed around it. It swam up her arm and enveloped her person, leaving her tasting the sugary air. She gazed around, the landscape changed; remoulded to form a different plain.

She was now stood on the brow of a hill, overlooking a lake in the valley below. The moon luminesced against its frozen surface, whilst an ancient bridge curved across its breadth. Something told her she needed to be down there. She set off down the slope.

The thick undergrowth drew back before her, creating a guided path. The word *trap* kept screaming through her mind, but what choice did she really have? Soon she was entering the darkness of the wood. She shuddered, her heart rate increasing with each stride.

She found herself skirting a stream. It forged a path where the ground was most frail. She followed its flow, her freckles now cooling, implying she was heading towards the central dream. She slowed her pace, questioning her decision, and came to an abrupt halt.

The stream had ended without warning, becoming part of the frozen lake. She gazed across at the ancient bridge, its curve a perfect half-circle. It framed the forest behind it like a picture, as if a gateway to another realm.

'Welcome, *wolfcaine*.'

Natalya spun. Shah Ming had stepped out onto the

edge of the ice. She swallowed, watching him walk towards its centre. What she wouldn't give for another ounce of courage.

'Where's Obadiah?' It took all she had to keep the tremble from her voice.

'You think yourself in a position to dictate?'

'Well I didn't come all this way to lose?'

'Good Lord, Shah. The audacity of the girl. Reality check, *Sweetheart*, you're going to die.'

She spun again to see Ella Cinders, the Glass Slipper's vines writhing through her skin.

'I'll not ask again. Where's Obadiah?'

'I think she means to challenge us, my princess.'

'Ha! She can't even challenge herself. She's only alive because of some boy. How did you manage to wake Nathan, by the way?'

'What? You think I'd tell you my secrets?' If only she knew herself.

Ella joined Shah Ming beneath the bridge. The witch gazed up at its structure.

'They say that only the Devil can cross it, its width so slim, its path so curved. I find it enchanting. Can't you feel its mystique, inviting you to your doom?'

'The armies of the Shadow Realm rise. And you, wolfcaine, are the *key* to its gateway. The *key* to every dream across the realm. The *key* to an army of millions.'

'You think I'm a *key*?'

'We know you're the *key*.'

'And yet, you left me to die?'

'My husband was supposed to save you, not his wife. Just like he chose his wolfcaines over me.'

The voice sent a shudder down Natalya's spine. The Shroud Witch was in their presence. Shah Ming dropped down onto one knee and bowed his head in allegiance.

'My Queen,' he said.

Ella looked impressed.

'Not you, *false-princess*. I bow to the *Shroud Witch*.'

'Shroud Witch? What are you talking about, Shah?'

'I serve a higher mistress now.'

Ella creased her brow.

'Don't be ridiculous. I gave you life.'

'And yet, I'm no longer the dream in your head.'

'Life?' said Natalya. 'You gave him life. You mean, Shah Ming's your dream?'

No wonder she knew so little about him.

'Yes, delicious, isn't it,' he said. 'But that was then, now I exist. No longer the puppet of some self-absorbed *harlot* who thinks herself worthy of my service.'

'How dare you?' cried Ella. 'You exist, because of me. I can just as easily melt you back to pigment.'

'Except I'm no longer yours to destroy. Like I said, I serve a higher mistress now.'

Ella's body began to spasm, as the vines tore themselves up from her flesh. She gasped, her blood spattering the ice, her beautiful face twisting in agony.

'What's happening? What are you doing to me?'

'Not I, *false-princess*. The mistress rises.'

'You are mine, Ella Cinders. Your body a vessel to be used for my immortal soul.'

The vines wrapped together around her, forming a shrouded, second skin. Her eyes flared yellow, her stance became stooped, the vines concealing her face beneath a hood. The Shroud Witch cackled insanely.

'Ella?' gasped Natalya.

'The harlot is gone.'

Natalya faltered. What did she do now? She had a set of claws and a pair of fangs. They weren't any match for what she'd seen the previous night.

'Come here,' said Shah Ming.

Natalya backed away. If she was the *key*, then best they didn't have it. She turned to run. She felt like such a coward, but an army of millions risked every life on Earth.

'Yes, run, but then you won't save him. You do want to save your precious Obadiah?'

Natalya stopped before she'd even started. She turned back, fearing the worst.

The ice beside the witch began to break, a growth of wood rising from beneath. The wood sprouted branches, the branches formed a tree, its roots imbedded in the frozen tundra. Bleddin appeared, stood beside it, a noose from the tree roped around his neck.

The sun began to rise above the trees.

'Obadiah!'

'My husband lives, but heed the ice that melts beneath his feet. The thinner the layer, the tighter the noose, till he hangs as a deadweight, like our child, upon the tree.'

'No. Let him go. I'm warning you.' As if the big bad witch was going to heed her words.

'The wolfcaine thinks we should let him free. What say you, my servant?'

'I say *not*,' said Shah Ming smugly.

'So tell me, Dreamscaper, do you fight or flee?'

Dreamscaper? That was a new name. Her mind flashed back to the girl with white hair.

'This world can be shaped...'

Were those not her words?

'..by those with the talent to do so.'

Could it be Natalya had that talent? That the wolfcaines were more than simple tooth and claw?

No, what was she talking about? If that were true, Bleddin would have told her. Besides, she'd never experienced such a thing? Even the *Leshy* had had to save her twice.

Her brain froze on that one, single thought.

The *Leshy*. A creature of folktale and legend. Rarely seen, and no real friend of humans. So why had it always answered her call? And why did it always look as she imagined? Could it be it was moulded from pigment? A creation of her mind?

Again, what was she thinking? The thought alone was completely absurd. And yet, here she was, with her hand against a tree, willing the *Leshy* to life.

Nothing happened. Of course nothing happened. She attempted the same thought in Russian. *Try something smaller,* she told herself. She dropped to her knees and curled her fingers around a feeble weed.

She willed it to live. She begged it to live. She demanded it spring into life. But if anything, it just fell more limp, confirming her opinion.

'Have faith, Natalya.'

They always said that. She glanced at her parents' reflection in the stream. She fingered her bracelet, tears in her eyes. She missed them so much, and now they were... *here?*

She looked up sharply. There was no one there. She looked back to the flow of the stream. They smiled at her, holding hands, willing her to succeed.

A tear dripped from her chin to the earth. The limbs of the plant twitched into life. Natalya blinked; her mind was playing tricks. The plant upped its roots and started to march. She watched as it trudged out onto the ice and towards the Devil's bridge.

'Is that the best you can do?' mocked Shah Ming. 'I find the lack of effort insulting.'

Natalya looked to her parents once more, and yet, they were no longer there. The sense of loss grew within her like a chasm. She wiped away more tears.

The marching plant now started to grow, each fall of a teardrop fuelling its physique. Its stem became a stalk, its stalk became a twig, its twig became a trunk that sprouted leaves. Natalya watched in confused amazement, and then, it suddenly dawned. It wasn't about any conscious desire. The *dreamscape* was moulded through *emotion*.

Two feet, four feet, ten feet, twenty, and still the plant continued to grow. Natalya smiled; Shah Ming cowered, as the tree began to rage towards him.

Suddenly, the ice gave way, and the tree ploughed through into the depths of the lake. It caused the surface of the ice to crack open, dropping Bleddin waist high into the water. The noose tightened around his neck, threatening to choke the life from him.

'No!' cried Natalya.

She ran onto the ice, or rather, what remained of it. She slipped and went sprawling across its frosted surface, panic and dread spiralling inside. If she wanted to save him, she was going to have to swim. She scrambled to her knees and crawled towards the water.

As soon as she touched it, it started to freeze. She didn't need to swim, at all.

Channelling her fear into the lake, she began to freeze a path towards the tree. She leapt onto her feet and ran out across it. Her foot went through the surface and she fell back to her knees. It required more depth. She concentrated again, and thickened the mass of the ice.

This time, the path held beneath her weight. Bleddin was now in reach. She leapt into the air and sliced her claws through the rope. He plunged into the depths, his arms and legs tied.

Without hesitation, she dived in after him. The coldness sent shockwaves screaming through her body. She swam into the dark, clutching at the shadows, her desperation growing as all she grabbed was weeds.

Then, the threaded stiffness of a rope. She followed its lead to Bleddin. She grabbed him by the collar and kicked out with her legs. Her dress shrank back, allowing her to swim. She broke the water's surface and dragged him up onto the ice. She pulled the noose from around his neck and yet, he lay there still.

'Breathe, Obadiah, breathe.'

She tilted back his head and breathed into his mouth. He didn't stir; she did it again. She sat back and pumped away at his chest.

'Come on, Obadiah. Don't die on me now.'

She'd seen the technique performed as a child. A boy had fallen into the village pond. But unlike the boy, Bleddin wasn't responding.

Once again, she breathed into his mouth. He coughed. He spluttered. His body convulsed. He spat out water; she sat back in relief. And then he spewed up vegetable matter. His body liquesced before her very eyes, smothering the ice in a stagnated matter.

'What?'

A dizziness flooded her mind, her vision blurring and her mouth turning dry. She tried to stand but her legs felt unsteady, the cackle of the Shroud Witch echoing through her ears.

'A Mandragora spell: meant to deceive, formed from the root of the mandrake plant. By breathing him life, you've swallowed its poison. The baby rocking on the tree.'

Natalya fell backward, her mind in a spin, the edges of her vision fluorescing like a dream. And then she heard it, both calm and disturbing, the hum of a sweet *lullaby*.

Chapter 27
Lullaby

Natalya rubbed at her eyes, trying to focus their vision. The softly focused images took on new shape, revealing a woman knelt on the ground, rocking back and forth. Her eyes were red from a million tears, her gaze fixed somewhere beyond the world. She was humming a lullaby, over and over. It sent a shiver down Natalya's spine. There was something about it. Something haunting. It made her feel unsettled.

'Are you all right?'

The woman looked at her. She was early twenties, with long, auburn hair. She seemed so lost, beyond all comfort. There was an emptiness in her hazel eyes.

'Our baby's gone.'

'Gone?'

'Taken.'

A baby's cradle formed on the earth. It was tipped on one side, the basket broken, having fallen from the branch of a nearby tree.

'I waited all night. Hoping. Praying. Pleading for God to return our baby's soul.'

'Your baby's dead?'

'*They* took it from me.'

'They?'

'The wolfcaines. My husband's *monsters.*'

There was a sudden hatred in the woman's voice, a narrowing of the eyes that foretold unspoken menace. It made Natalya want to run, and then, she suddenly realised.

'You're *her*, aren't you? Rosa-'

'*-linda Lovell. I sense the beast. You belong to them.*'

'No! Yes. But I only want to help.'

'*That's what they said, and then they stole my child.*'

The ground beneath their feet began to tremor. Natalya spun, nervous; afraid.

'What's going on?'

'*This is what happens to those who cross my path.*'

Wooden poles broke up through the earth, carrying the slaughtered corpses of her victims. They had wolf-like faces and fur-clad skin, their blood like a sludge down the grain of the wood. They'd been tortured, mutilated, disembowelled. Natalya spun, mortified; disgusted. Whatever their crime, they didn't deserve this. This was beyond revenge.

'You murdered them.'

'They murdered me.'

'They only tried to help.'

'They stole my future. I stole theirs. And yet, they now live on, through you. I'm going to make you suffer, wolfcaine. I'm going to make you pay. All you possess; all you desire. I'm going to take it from you.'

The air around the witch began to blur, her hazel eyes turning yellow. She rose to her feet like a ghostly apparition, her grief becoming a personified shroud. The pigment of the dreamscape flowed into her body and she raised her arms to strike.

Horrified, Natalya turned and ran. An invisible force swept her off her feet. It tossed her like a rag doll across the broken earth. She landed on the embankment of a stream, its waters red.

She gazed across at the carcass of a wolfcaine, dead in the earth, its eyes plucked from its skull. Its fangs had been ripped from the depths of its gums, its innards exposed to a nest of swarming flies. She felt the nausea well within. She could hardly bear to look.

Struggling to her feet, she took off down the

embankment. She could feel herself trembling, her heart filled with fear. The earth gave way and she fell into the current. She looked to see a baby's basket bobbing down the stream.

Warily, she reached out and grabbed it, but dare she look inside? It was empty, apart from a small, embroidered blanket. The needlework read: *15th April 1692.*

15th April? Natalya swallowed. That was the date that her parents had been killed. Bleddin was right; their deaths had been a message. They'd been murdered for nothing but to prove a witch's point.

Someone grabbed her hair from behind and dragged her back across the frozen ice. Ice? Was back in dreamscape? She felt so confused, her mind in delirium. Her stomach heaved and she vomited mandrake. She gazed up into Shah Ming's face.

'What have you done with Obadiah?' she spat, trying her best to refocus her mind.

'He fights with your friends, back in the village.'

She furrowed her brow. That didn't make sense.

'But I saw you abduct him?'

'A ploy, nothing more.'

'A ploy?'

'To lure you here.'

Then why not snatch her? Why Obadiah? And then she remembered what the Shroud Witch had said: ***I'm*** *going to make you suffer.*

A sharp pain shot through her mind. She looked to her hand and the dagger driven through it. Shah Ming had impaled her hand to the ice. She watched as her blood flowed across its white.

Its redness began to break down into colour. The colours hazed to form a vibrant rainbow. The rainbow grew and stretched out across the lake, until it was one with the arc of the bridge. Shah Ming gave a smile.

'The *key* is turned, My Queen.'

The Shroud Witch flung her arms towards the sky. The sun grew hotter, turning ice to water, reforming the mirrored stillness of the lake.

'Observe,' said Shah Ming, 'the opening of the lock. The forming of the circle in the water. Soon the armies of the Shadow Realm shall rise. And the bloodshed will be glorious.'

He was right, the rainbow was reflecting in the lake, threatening to form a perfect sphere.

'No!' cried Natalya.

She closed her eyes and channelled her emotion into the ice. Its crystalline structure began to reform, masking the mirrored reflection. Shah Ming roughly grabbed her by the hair, yanked back her head and swung his sword at her throat.

'No! The dreamscaper must not be harmed.'

Shah Ming froze, confusion on his face.

'But My Queen...?'

'You will do as I say, Shah Ming.'

The prince grudgingly lowered his sword.

This was her chance, whilst Shah Ming was distracted. Natalya closed her eyes and thought of *him*. She could feel *him* forming, out of the water. Swimming upwards from the depths towards the surface.

'He's coming for you,' she said in Russian.

'What?'

'He's coming to take you home.'

'You think to scare me with another angry weed?'

'Oh, the *vodyanoy's* anything but a weed.'

The ice behind Shah Ming erupted upwards and the *vodyanoy* shot up into the air. One moment the prince was stood on the ice, the next he was being dragged deep into the lake. Natalya watched as he sank into the depths, a horrified look on his face. And then they were gone, their substance returned to the pigment from which they were dreamed.

Natalya grabbed hold of the daggers hilt, grimaced, and drew it from her hand.

'You learn to dreamscape well, wolfcaine. But nothing can prevent the opening of the gateway.'

Natalya turned and threw the dagger at her. The witch raised a hand. The dagger melted into paint.

'You'll have to try a lot harder than that if you

want to vanquish me.'

The heat of the sun now tripled, the ice melting faster than Natalya could reform it. She scrambled to her feet and made a dash for solid ground. She threw herself onto the steps of the bridge.

Now without hindrance, the rainbow grew full circle, the lake between its lines starting to drain. It was replaced by a kaleidoscope of splintered images, a billion peoples' dreams compacted into one. Their hopes, their fears, ambitions and regrets, the vastness of the Shadow Realm laid bare for all to see. Natalya observed it with both wondrous awe and fear. It was beautiful, beguiling, and a bridge to Armageddon.

She glanced around in search of the witch. She was stood on the uppermost arc of the bridge. Natalya swallowed and scrambled to her feet. She followed the curve of the narrowing steps. There was no way on earth she could ever outfight her. She was going to have to use her head.

'So now that I've been there, why all the training?'

'There's more than foxglove with its roots sown in the Shadow Realm.'

'The Glass Slipper orchid?'

'It's a plant of two worlds, but to exist in ours, it needs a human host...'

A human host? What if it didn't have one?

'Kill the source and you kill the infection.'

Of course, the source was the Glass Slipper orchid. It was the orchid she needed to stop, not the witch.

She carefully stepped out onto the bridge. It was three feet wide and slippy with moss. One ill-placed step and she'd be falling through the gateway, leaving the Shroud Witch to raise up her army.

Despite her caution, she slipped and nearly fell. She could feel her stomach turning into mush. The Shroud Witch gave her a nonchalant stare. She didn't even see her as a threat.

'Then use their ignorance to your advantage. Employ it as a weakness.'

The number of times she'd hated Bleddin's wisdom, but now she cherished every word.

'So tell me, Ella, how does it feel? To be the slave of some ancient old hag?'

'The harlot is gone.'

'Then you don't know Ella Cinders. I think you'll find she's tougher than you think. Isn't that right, *Eleanor Jane Henry?* Come on, speak to me, or are you just a fraud? It's me. *Natasha.* The girl who slashed your face. I thought **you** made the rules, not the other way around.'

The witch's eyes flickered blue. *Oh Lord,* thought Natalya. *It's actually working.*

'She can't hear you. She's gone. Buried.'

'I don't believe that any more than you. She's the

fairy-tale princess. You're the evil witch. Come on, Ella. Prove to her I'm right. I know you've murdered and done wicked things, but it's not your fault that your father was a whore.'

'Shut up, *Natasha*.'

'Ella?'

'Who else?'

'You need to reject the Glass Slipper orchid.'

'I can't.'

'You must.'

'No, I can't. Because of what you did.'

The *masking* spell across Ella's face faded, revealing the festered cut to her cheek. Its infection had eaten up half of her face, stealing her beauty, making her grotesque. A green, putrid mass was clung to her jaw, its tendrils imbedded deep in her throat. Natalya stared at the abomination in horror; it was the nucleus of the Glass Slipper.

She rushed forward; she forgot about the moss. She lost her footing and went flying off the bridge. She lashed out with her claws and dug them in the stone. She hung there, gasping, the gateway below.

Calling on the *beast*, she dragged herself back up, her heart pounding and her nerves a tangled mess. The Shroud Witch's eyes had now returned to yellow. She'd taken back control.

Springing to her feet, Natalya ran forward, taking the

gamble that she wouldn't slip twice. She sank her claws into the Glass Slipper's flesh, a stinking green matter spurting from within. The Glass Slipper squealed, lashing out with its vines. Natalya winced as they sliced at her skin.

'Oh, no. You're coming back with me.'

She tugged on its mass; it refused to let go. She pulled again. Still, it resisted. The Shroud Witch began to cackle at her plight. She had to act, and she had to act now.

Keeping her claws imbedded in the Slipper, Natalya leapt up high into the air. Her dress shrank back, freeing up her legs, and she kicked the Shroud Witch firmly in the chest.

They both fell backwards, in opposite directions. There was a squelching sound and an agonised scream. The orchid came free in Natalya's hands and they plummeted into the lake.

The orchid's vines now tightened around her, trying to squeeze the air from her lungs. She kicked down with her feet and broke the water's surface, the orchid trapped in the cage of her hands.

High above, the sun was melting, like runny egg across the canvassed sky. The ground was sinking, eating up the trees, the Devil's bridge crumbling as it started to collapse. It fell in lumps of rock into the lake, sealing the gateway shut.

With the orchid still fighting against her, Natalya tried to kick-swim to shore. The *darkness* ate its way onto the landscape, its cold, empty aura feeding on the paint.

She gasped; and then, the undercurrent caught her. It dragged her down, deep into the depths. The vines grew tighter; she struggled in vain. And then she felt the burn of her freckles. A blueness of pigment melted from her hair and swam around her person.

***

One moment Natalya was drowning, the next she was rolling around in the dirt. The sugary taste of the Shadow Realm was gone, her nose besieged by a scent of woodland damp.

She was back in the real world; the cemetery no less, the orchid's nucleus still caged in her hands. Its vines now started lashing at her wrists, trying to make her weaken her grasp.

She resisted the pain for as long as she could, but the nucleus was bloating out of control. She wasn't sure if the growth was intended, or as a result of it having lost its host. The orchid broke free and escaped to the earth. It began to transition back into the Shadow Realm.

'No!'

She lunged forward and impaled it with her claws. It lashed out with its roots, its vines around her throat.

'You're going nowhere.'

'You think that you've won?'

'You killed my parents, you *bitch*!'

She kicked out at the overlooking gravestone, using such force that she shattered its base. The headstone came crashing down on her arm, crushing both it and the Glass Slipper orchid.

Putrid green exploded forth, the orchid's dying shriek like a banshee's wail. Its vines fell limp; its roots became pigment. And then it existed no more. Natalya groaned and dragged her crushed arm out from beneath the stone.

She must have looked a bit of a sight, blood down her face, her arm a slab of meat. But she knew it would heal, she was a wolfcaine, after all, and even if it didn't, the price was worth the cause.

With the orchid dead, exhaustion kicked in, but then she remembered the others. She anxiously dragged herself up against the wall and gazed down onto the village.

She found them stood just outside the tavern, gazing around with a look of confusion. One moment they'd been fighting the witch hunters to the death, and the next their opponents had vanished.

But where was Nathan? She couldn't see him. Dread returned to her heart. He couldn't be dead. She couldn't lose him now. He wandered into view from just out of sight.

She slid back down behind the drystone wall, a joyous smile on her lips. A slither of green ran into her mouth. She spat it out with a *yuck*.

Chapter 28
The Departed

Natalya stepped through the early morning mist, the gravestones glistening hoarfrost. Her arm was tucked inside a makeshift sling, made from the remnants of a shredded cassock. She hadn't slept an hour all night, reliving the events of her encounter with the Shroud Witch.

She felt on edge. Alert to every movement. Expecting the sorceress to strike at any time. But the orchid was dead. The danger was over. So why did her mind remain unconvinced?

'You think that you've won?'

Those words weren't just defiance. They were a

threat, a promise, a call to the future, and the mere thought of it filled her with dread. She'd tried to relay her fears to Bleddin, but who knew what thoughts were going through his head.

The villagers, meanwhile, remembered nothing. They'd just assumed they'd had a drunken night. What they did remember was five months earlier, and the attack of the witch hunters on their village. Bleddin's appearance reminded them of that, and the group had been exiled to the church for the night. Even in summer, the church was cold, much to Hansel's irritation.

'So much for saving their lives,' he'd said.

A prayer mat for a pillow was not his ideal bed. Nor the chime of the clock on the hour, which had kept them all awake.

Natalya reached the edge of the cemetery, the leaves of the trees heavy with dew. According to the priest, this was where they were buried. She noticed a grave with a simple wooden cross.

Ivan Grigorevich Yavorovskij
15.04.1891
Annie Elizabeth Yavorovskaya
15.04.1891

'Hello, Mama. Hello, Papa.'

Water moistened her eyes. She crossed herself; traced their names in the wood. It must have taken forever to carve. She lowered her head and said a little prayer, her bracelet dyed green by the gunge from the orchid.

There were footsteps in the earth behind her and she spun sharply to see Gretl.

'I'm sorry, Natalya. You know Obadiah. Eager to be on his way.'

'It's fine. At least, I know where they are now. There's plenty of time to revisit.'

Gretl linked her arm in Natalya's and they headed back for the church.

'You're sure you won't return with us to London?'

'I just need some time to clear my head.'

'Well, it's peaceful here, and very picturesque. I'd have stayed myself if it wasn't for my husband scaring half the villagers to death.' Gretl glanced towards the drystone wall and Nathan leant against it. 'Of course, I'm sure that's not the only reason why.'

'I don't know what you mean?'

'I'm sure you don't.'

There was no point in arguing. The witch knew Natalya far too well.

They reached the path and its chalkings of hopscotch.

'Remember, Natalya, our home is always yours.

We'll be in touch once we've found somewhere to stay.'

'Which will no doubt be at the workhouse,' said Hansel, bringing his horse to bear.

He helped Gretl climb up behind him. He nodded at Natalya.

'Fräulein.'

'Doctor Schneider.'

She still wasn't sure if he liked her or not. But at least she seemed to have earned his respect, and that would do for now.

'Take care, Natalya.'

'You, too, Gretl.'

The siblings turned for the woodland path. Bleddin brought his own horse to bear. He tipped his large-brimmed hat.

'*Wolfcaine.*'

'Obadiah. Oh, and my parents say *thank you.*'

He brought his horse to a momentary stop, nodded, and carried on his way. Who else would have taken all that time to carve their names on the cross?

She watched them ride off into the trees, then made her way towards Nathan. He looked her way as she neared. She swallowed, her throat turning dry.

Below, the valley was as beautiful as ever, a distant train puffing white amongst the green. Natalya leant back against the drystone wall. *Be brave, Natalya. Be brave.*

Nathan placed his sketchbook aside. 'It's lovely up here.'

'I always thought so.'

'And now?'

'I love it still.'

'That green aint fading.'

She touched at her hair, its strands now graced with more than blue.

'I know. The orchid's parting gift.'

'At least it matches yer eyes.'

'Great. The girl with *blue* and *green* hair.'

'It helps to break up the brown.'

Across the valley, a glorious rainbow began to feed through the morning mist. Natalya observed it with a sense of sorrow. Another dream soon to be lost to the *dark.*

'I wonder what happened to Ella?' she said.

'Knowing 'er, she's haunting someone's dream.'

The church door creaked and the priest stepped out. He hurried off down the woodland path.

'So much fer yer new chaperone?'

'I can't believe Gretl asked him to watch me.'

'I guess she was thinking of yer reputation.'

'Where's the fun in that?'

She swallowed and took a step forward, trying to conceal the pounding of her heart. She had to ask him.

She had to know. She took a deep breath and turned. She found him stood directly behind her. He didn't turn away.

'Have I ever told ya, ya've got great freckles?'

'Now don't you go calling me *freckles*, again.'

'Ah, ah. Mind the toes.'

'Are you implying...?'

'Ya've got big feet?'

She thumped him in the arm. 'No. That we might fall out.'

He burst out laughing and she laughed right back. She ran a hand through her multi-coloured hair. She felt a burst of warmth to her cheeks and hoped he wouldn't notice.

'Are you all right? Ya look a little flushed.'

'I think my lips are tingling.'

'And what with you being Russian an' all, it must mean…'

'..that they're…'

'..about to…'

'..be…'

Their lips met, her heart swooned, and she melted into his arms.

ঌঌঌ

Author's Note

When I first created Natalya over ten years ago, her name was Louise and she wasn't even Russian. Since then, she's been on a bit of a journey, but the *soul* of her character has never changed. Even Nathan was two different characters, which were spliced together to create the one.

In other words, the story in your hands has been through a few twists and turns of its own. I hope you enjoyed the final product, and thank you for taking the time to read. But life never ends on a neatly written sentence, and Natalya's future is about to get much worse.

NATALYA is the first book in a planned trilogy, with another potential trilogy after that. Think you know what's going on? Think again. Nothing's what it seems.

But before we talk about that next book in the series, may I ask you a favour? If you enjoyed this book, could I ask you to leave a review on Amazon? Authors depend on valued readers like yourself, and especially new authors like me. Those reviews are vital to Natalya's future, and you'd be doing us both a great favour.

And don't forget my free story. It's available to

download at TERRYVERNON.COM. It's a prequel, set six months before this book, and details that first awakening of the *beast*.

So what dangers await Natalya next?

We're off to the fayre, the seaside, and Scotland. Would you like to know more about the girl with white hair? Did the *Warlocks of Scholomance* pique your interest? It's time to prepare for a turning of the tale, and ready yourself for **THE DARKENING.**

Once again, thank you for your time. We'd love for you to join us for the ride.

Terry & Natalya

Readers Club

If you'd like to be kept up-to-date with all things Natalya, simply subscribe to my Readers Club. It's free to join, and as a member, you'll not only receive updates on future books, but also have access to any free stories and downloads, such as WOODEN HEART.

Unsubscribing is easy, too, plus you get to keep any freebies.

To join my Readers Club, just visit
TERRYVERNON.COM

Printed in Great Britain
by Amazon